THE SIGN OF THE SYMEAN

A FANTASY ADVENTURE: BOOK 1

R.A. LINDO

For Kija

CONTENTS

WELCOME TO A MAGICAL UNIVERSE

Welcome to the secret, magical universe of **The S.P.M.A. (The Society for the Preservation of Magical Artefacts.)**

If you want to delve deeper into the magical universe of the S.P.M.A., <u>**sign up**</u> to become eligible for free books, private giveaways and early notification of new releases.

You can also join <u>**my private Facebook group**</u> where all things S.P.M.A. are discussed.

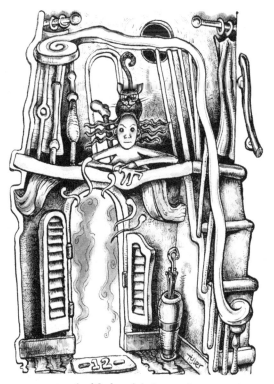

1. Kaira Listens In

KAIRA LISTENS IN

Kaira lay silently on the bedroom landing, out of sight, her eyes adjusting to the darkness as she tried to listen in on the conversation below.

Why had Aunt Phee just arrived with a strange glass object under her arm and who else was her dad talking to in the middle of the night?

Kaira was familiar with these evening meetings and the various adults who came home with her dad, always explained to her as 'work meetings' by Aunt Phee before she was promptly sent off to bed.

Tonight, however, was different: the adults were on edge and the little Kaira could pick up from their conversation suggested something was wrong...

"Searings, Casper. In *broad daylight*."

She recognised Farraday's voice immediately which reassured her a little. Farraday, her dad and Aunt Phee made up 'the trio', as Kaira liked to call them: the three adults who had been ever-present in her life, and although Farraday wasn't *actual* family, he was to Kaira. She always pictured him in his uniform of black trousers, black leather jacket and brown waistcoat, his thinning hair falling to his shoulders, partially hiding the gold, hoop earring in his left ear.

The next person to speak was the stranger sitting with his back to Kaira in the half-open kitchen doorway: a small, stocky, bald figure dressed in black:

"Melackin causing problems again," the bald figure uttered, more to himself than the others.

"We don't know that, Smyck." Her father's voice, typically calm and assertive.

The small, bald figure (who Kaira now knew to be Smyck) stood and stretched with a tired sigh, causing Kaira to momentarily panic as any sudden movements she made would wake her beloved cat who was currently curled up on her back. Knowing only too well Churchill's distaste for surprises, she lay still, hoping Smyck would sit back down on the kitchen chair which, thankfully, he did.

"The Parasil is ready, gentleman," came Aunt Phee's voice, and the clink of china followed.

Kaira had no idea what a Parasil, Searing or Melackin was; she had given up trying to figure out her dad's *real* job and the meaning of all the strange words long ago although she wasn't naïve enough to believe he really was just a 'curator'. She was *twelve* now, for goodness sake. She smiled at the memory of her younger self imagining the secret world her dad worked in with spies, missions and battles.

"Could do with a bit of Jysyn Juice in this," came Farraday's voice, breaking the temporary silence between the adults.

Kaira listened intently, wishing she knew what all these things were.

"You're already fearless, Farraday," complimented Aunt Phee.

"There's concern in The Cendryll," interjected Smyck. "People are getting nervous."

Kaira shuffled back a little, careful not to wake Churchill, as Smyck stood from the kitchen chair again.

She then saw something in his hands ... an unfolded piece of paper with a drawing on it. Kaira pushed her face up against the bannister, brushing her long, brown curls out of her face, desperate to get a closer look. The light from the kitchen allowed her to decipher a drawing in black ink. A face...? A creature...?

A creeping curiosity grew - a curiosity which turned to electricity at Aunt Phee's nervous utterance: "The Sign of the Symean" ... the final word (pronounced "S-I-I-M-E-E-U-N") sending a chill through her.

THE KITCHEN DOOR closed soon after to Kaira's great annoyance. Perhaps she had inadvertently shifted positions to get comfortable and Smyck, already on edge, closed the door as a precautionary measure. Whatever the reason, the adults' voices were now muffled, inaudible sounds so Kaira crept back to her bedroom.

She moved through the darkness and slipped into bed, pulling the white, cotton duvet up to her chin. Churchill jumped onto the bed and took up his favourite position on the pillow next to her.

Kaira's mind was flooded with the picture on the paper in Smyck's hands: The Sign of the Symean ... another thing she had never seen nor heard of, although it was clear from Aunt Phee's tone that this was *definitely bad*. But bad in what way? A banned sign that people weren't supposed to use...?

Some type of bad omen like seeing black cats in the street...?
Did the sign link to the Searings Farraday had mentioned...?

The more Kaira questioned, the clearer it became that she was no closer to understanding her dad's secretive world - or so she thought.

LITTLE DID SHE KNOW, as she finally gave in to sleep, that her life was about to drastically change...

2. A Place Like no Other

A PLACE LIKE NO OTHER

Kaira lay in bed, wrapped up in the white duvet, trying to gather enough energy to get up and have a bath. Although she had been asleep for ten hours, her fatigue and grumpy mood was a sure sign she had barely caught the wings of sleep. Thankfully, it was a school holiday so the normal rush and routine could be ignored, if only for a week. The intrigue surrounding last night's secret meeting continued to occupy her as she struggled to make sense of the handful of words she had heard:

Searings, Melackin, Parasil, Jysyn Juice, The Cendryll... Kaira turned the words over in her head a little longer before giving in to Churchill's scratching at the bedroom door, her cat's eagerness heightened by the smell of bacon emanating from the kitchen. She gathered her dressing gown and opened the curtains, pushing the long, brown curls away from her face. She briefly studied the muted, autumn light encompassing the small market town before averting her attention to the dark circles under her eyes and drained complexion: sure signs she had stayed up too late.

A sudden rush of anxiety crept over her as she turned

back towards her bedroom door, heading down to the kitchen. What if her dad or aunt had spotted her on the bedroom landing last night, listening in on the meeting? Is that why she could hear Aunt Phee's voice in the kitchen? Was her aunt still here to act as a 'supporting adult' in Kaira's punishment? Her dad was a gentle man yet Kaira knew the consequences of disobeying him.

Kaira listened outside the kitchen door before entering to assess the mood, but her dad and Aunt Phee were no longer talking. The adults' silence caused a flush of red to touch her face as she entered ...

Aunt Phee turned first and, much to Kaira's relief, smiled and nodded to the orange juice and toast at the table. "The toast should still be warm."

Kaira sat at the table, glimpsing the glass object Aunt Phee had in her possession last night: the strange, dome-shaped object filled with an odd green liquid...

Jysyn Juice? Kaira wondered.

This thought passed quickly, however, as her dad, who had been staring out of the window, sat down opposite her in silence: a silence Kaira knew meant trouble. She studied her dad's expression to try and guess how angry he was but the smooth, brown complexion and dark, brown eyes were unreadable. Casper Renn was a mixture of his father's Jamaican sternness and his mother's English reserve - the sternness being the part Kaira was currently worried about.

"Sleep okay?" her dad finally said, reaching for some toast.

Kaira, not wanting to fold straight away, merely nodded and bit into her toast.

"Your Aunt and I were talking last night..."

Another nod.

"About something important," her dad continued with

Aunt Phee now standing behind him, her expression softer than her brother's. Philomeena Renn (or Aunt Phee to Kaira) shared her brother's symmetrical features and smooth, brown skin.

"As your aunt keeps reminding me, you're not a little girl anymore. I was told when I was your age."

Kaira studied them both, sensing this may not be a trap after all. "Told about what?" she queried.

"About *our* world."

Kaira gulped down her orange juice in shock as the rush of excitement suddenly returned. Had they heard her last night? Or maybe this was a trick to get her to spill what she knew? Was she truly going to be allowed into her dad's secretive world?

"More toast?" offered Aunt Phee, holding a plate in front of them both. Kaira grabbed two slices, suddenly feeling light-headed.

Her dad got up from the kitchen table and moved over to the glass object Churchill was currently inspecting; he placed his empty mug at the base of it and turned the brass tap, releasing the warm, green liquid. Kaira watched, mesmerised, as the green liquid bubbled and refilled to the top of the glass object... as if by magic.

Her dad sipped the strange, green liquid and continued. "You've been asking more-and-more about my job - what I 'really do', as you like to put it."

Kaira, sensing this almost certainly *wasn't* a trap, gathered the courage to speak. "You're a curator. You look after old things: important things."

"Yes."

"So you *really are* a curator?" queried Kaira with a tinge of disappointment.

"Yes, but in a very special place. A unique place which very few people know exists..."

"Like a secret society?"

"Yes, of sorts."

"And I can finally see it!? You're going to show me?"

"Yes," interjected Aunt Phee with a warm smile.

"When?" asked Kaira, jumping up from the kitchen chair, hardly able to contain her excitement.

"Today," her dad replied with a smile, "so you'd better get washed and dressed."

12 SPYNDALL STREET was a typical street in a typical English market town and, up until this point, Kaira Renn had lived a typically mundane life there. A rather ramshackle house over three floors, it would most likely be described as 'quaint' or 'rustic' had it been for sale due to its ill-fitting windows and oddly-shaped rooms; however it was merely home to Kaira and had been all her life.

On the day that would change everything, Kaira got ready on the third floor in a state of frenetic excitement whilst her dad and aunt tidied up in the kitchen silently, Aunt Phee putting a reassuring hand on her brother's arm. The choice had been made for them, they had agreed last night. Searings meant trouble in the Society and they could no longer live under the illusion that things weren't changing. Kaira needed to learn about the Society in order to be protected - in their world and above ground - for their world was about to change...

Casper Renn locked the door to 12 Spyndall Street and crossed the road, joining his sister and Kaira on the corner of Market Lane. Kaira watched as her dad turned up the collar of his coat to provide shelter from the harsh wind. Aunt Phee then took a scarf out of her handbag, encouraging her niece to wear it over her red coat. Kaira, not feeling the cold today, was bursting with questions although quickly learnt that no mention of the Society was made above ground so, having no idea what 'above ground' meant, listened to her dad and aunt's discussion regarding the itinerary of the day.

"So," prompted Aunt Phee, "we're going to be on Leaning Lane soon, if you want to pop into Wimples."

Could this day get *any better*? thought Kaira. Wimples was, without question, the best sweet shop in the *whole world*!

Leaning Lane (also known as Shrinking Lane) was so called because of its unique structural architecture, causing each building to lean to the right. Equally unusual was the way each successive building was smaller than its neighbour, providing the observer with a striking and mildly humorous sight. Forming one part of Market Square, Leaning Lane was by far the most popular place in the small town of Bibsley Corbett for another reason: Wimples sweet shop.

Situated at the end of Leaning Lane in the smallest shop, the sound of children's laughter and yelps of joy could be heard ringing through Market Square - for Wimples had the finest, funniest, tastiest selection of sweets in the land! Sweets with the most hilarious names and equally hilarious impressions left on the buyer's tongue (impressions matching the name of the sweet, no less!) which became moving illustrations when you moved your tongue: Well I Nevers, Core Blimeys, Codswollops, Flaming Noras ... the list went on and on!

Adults were utterly bemused by Wimples; children adored it! There was, of course, the added benefit that most adults were too tall to enter the tiny building, making Wimples a haven for the young.

Hordes of children could always be found outside, squealing with joy as they stuffed sweets into their mouths and poked out their tongues to show off the miraculous impressions forming there. It was no different today as children tugged on their parents' arms outside the sweet shop, pleading for extra pocket money to go inside whilst others rushed in-and-out to partake of the many-coloured, uniquely tasting delights.

As Kaira got closer to the crowd outside Wimples, her dad placed a five-pound note in her hand.

"Have fun," he said, enjoying the sense of wonder on his daughter's face, "And don't forget to save me some."

Kaira bolted for Wimples, burning with excitement at the sight of the new box of sweets displayed on the shop counter, momentarily forgetting the incredible fact that she was about to enter her dad's secret world. She manoeuvred her way through the crowd of enthralled children, squeezing past the hordes reaching for their favourite sweet jar. She finally managed to join the queue, impatiently waiting to get their hands on the new sweet box displayed on the shop counter.

Although the walls of the tiny, leaning Tudor building were lined from floor to ceiling with sweets of all shapes and colours (Flipping Nuisances, Who Would Have Thoughts,

Over My Dead Bodies, Never You Minds, Over the Moons)
Kaira, though, only had eyes for the new arrival on the shop
counter: Flabbergasteds. She inhaled the sweet smell of
confectionery as she jostled for position in the queue,
desperately hoping the new sweets wouldn't sell out before
she reached the till. She finally reached the front of the
queue and snatched up the last box.

With the new box of Flabbergasteds firmly in her grasp,
Kaira stepped out of Wimples and found her dad and aunt
waiting outside Hazel & Mirch. The adults watched in
amusement as she ripped open the yellow box to discover
the multi-coloured, oval sweets, putting one in her mouth
and turning it over on her tongue to taste the bitter sherbet
lemon, apple, raspberry and cinnamon flavours.

She watched the impression form in the reflection of
Hazel & Mirch's shop window: a hilarious illustration of an
open-mouthed woman with her hands pressed against her
shocked face, eyes bulging in utter disbelief, eyebrows
arched ridiculously high on her forehead, moving ever-
higher the faster your tongue moved!

The sound of children's laughter rang through Market
Square as the enthralled, young faces outside Wimples
sweet shop displayed the moving illustrations on their
tongues. Casper Renn and Aunt Phee looked on, relieved
that Wimples had momentarily taken Kaira's mind off what
was to come - for she was soon to find out that, unlike
Wimples, their secret society contained both light and
dark...

As the wonderment of the Flabbergasteds begun to wear
off, Casper Renn, Kaira and Aunt Phee crossed to the opposite side of Market Square towards Cribbe & Corrow, a
black-fronted building with an elegant bay window and
gold signage, specialising in hand-made jewellery.

Situated on Pimion Place, Cribbe & Corrow was the very opposite of Wimples: rarely busy, stuffy and expensive - not a place Kaira could imagine her dad or aunt visiting. She glanced at the silver jewellery on display in the windows before they entered: necklaces, bracelets, brooches and rings all with different coloured gemstones. It was certainly a sight to behold. The shop-bell rang to signal their entry and a portly gentleman in a dark blue, three-piece suit appeared from behind a green, velvet curtain.

"Mr. Renn," said the man respectfully, shaking Casper Renn's hand as if he were an important client. "Ms. Renn," came a similar pleasantry to Aunt Phee which was followed by an odd bowing motion. The well-dressed man, whose hair was brushed upwards into a large quiff, then looked over to Kaira and repeated the bowing motion, this time pausing in mid-bow.

Kaira had to stop herself from laughing, realising this would be incredibly rude, having never met the man before.

"And this is...?" asked the man, still in mid-bow.

Kaira looked at her dad, uncertain who this strange character was addressing; Casper Renn's furrowed brow was a signal for her to reply.

"Kaira," she said politely, immediately seeing her dad's expression cloud over: a sure sign she had been rude. "Sir," was added quickly to correct her error.

The man, still in mid-bow, uttered, "Kaira. Yes..." before regaining an upright position to introduce himself: "Morlan Corrow: proprietor."

Kaira guessed 'proprietor' meant 'owner' and looked on as Morlan Corrow bowed again.

"Kaira's here earlier than I had anticipated, Morlan," her dad then said. "Nevertheless, we need a fitting for her today."

"Very well, Mr. Renn," Morlan Corrow replied, glancing at Kaira somewhat knowingly. "One moment, please." The strange proprietor then stepped towards the shop entrance and turned the Open sign to Closed, placing his hand on the shop door whilst doing so and uttering "Mirriul". The shop seemed to darken as he said this, and Kaira could have sworn she saw images appear on the windows.

Casper Renn then tapped Kaira lightly on the shoulder and nodded towards the green, velvet curtain at the end of the wooden counter. Aunt Phee moved the green curtain aside, ushering Kaira to follow her dad through into the back of the shop.

Behind the curtain was a small, dimly lit hallway leading to a black-framed door with a brass door handle. Morlan Corrow placed his hand on the handle and, rather unusually, turned it upwards until it was pointing towards the ceiling. He opened the door to reveal another hallway, but this one was much longer - *impossibly* long in fact.

Kaira looked along the seemingly endless corridor lined with different coloured doors in various states of repair. She blinked a number of times as she tried to comprehend its bizarre length whilst wondering what she was being fitted for and, also, what "Mirriul" meant. There were so many things she was trying to remember. Above each door was a small, brass lamp and the polished, wooden floor was lined with a patterned rug which also seemed to go on forever.

Kaira shook off a mild sense of dizziness whilst trying to work out the illusion being used to create the impression of this never-ending-corridor for, after all, Cribbe & Corrow's dimensions certainly didn't accommodate this! They stopped outside a green door and Morlan Corrow placed his hand on the brass handle, repeating the action of lifting it upwards until it pointed at the ceiling. Kaira noticed the small, brass lamp above the door flicker and a mild wave of excitement grew as she sensed the endless, dimly lit corridor wasn't an illusion at all but, rather, a part of her dad's secret world.

They entered a well-lit room with a long, oak table at its centre and numerous, wooden drawers lining the walls. Kaira noticed two things as she stepped inside the room: a large, circular window which provided no view of Market Square and a small, black door at the end of the room. Morlan Corrow peered along the wooden drawers lining the walls, tapping his forefinger on each brass name plaque until he reached RENN.

He slowly slid the drawer out and placed it onto the oak table. Kaira moved closer to the wooden drawer on the table, enthralled by the beautiful, purple gemstones inside.

"The amethyst gemstone, Miss Renn," Morlan Corrow stated. "The gemstone chosen by the Renn family centuries ago."

Chosen for what? Kaira wanted to ask as she studied the different shapes and shades of purple - the same gemstone in her dad's signet ring on the little finger of his right hand, and Aunt Phee's necklace.

She felt her dad's presence behind her. "Before we go further, you need a penchant; an item of jewellery including a gemstone of your choice from this collection."

Kaira, who was literally lost for words by this point, watched as Morlan Corrow lifted the tray of gemstones from the drawer to reveal a collection of silver jewellery below: necklaces, bracelets, brooches and rings. How could they afford to pay for this?

"Charged to the Society, of course," chimed Morlan Corrow as if reading her mind.

After much deliberation and reassurance from her dad

and aunt that they *really didn't* have to pay, Kaira chose a silver bracelet and four gemstones to fit the empty clasps within it. As she studied the silver bracelet decorating her wrist, Morlan Corrow returned the RENN draw of gemstones and jewellery to its home, bid them farewell and exited the room with a bow - and soon they were standing by the small, black door.

"You might want to hold onto Aunt Phee now," her dad said as he placed his hand on the brass door knob.

Kaira frowned and looked **up** at her aunt who offered a reassuring smile.

"You might get a little dizzy in a moment, that's all," her aunt explained.

Kaira, feeling a sudden sliver of anxiety, took her dad's advice and held onto her aunt's arm.

He looked back at her and said, "Ready?"

Kaira paused momentarily, then nodded, knowing how deeply she would regret it if she turned back now.

"Welcome to our world, young lady..."

Her dad pulled the brass door knob and a clunk of locks reverberated in the room. The dizziness Kaira had been warned of immediately took hold. She grabbed onto Aunt Phee and repeatedly shook her head to regain her equilibrium, doing so just in time to see something truly wondrous.

As her dad turned the brass door knob, three things happened: the door got *bigger*, words formed on the black paint above the door handle and reflections began to appear in the circular window. Not a reflection, Kaira quickly gathered, but a representation of an *actual place* full of people milling around inside with tiny, luminous insects buzzing below a large skylight. She tried to read each word above the brass door knob, the gold lettering fading almost as quickly as it formed: *Tauvin Hall, The*

Hideout, Leverin, Feleecian, Pancithon, finally stopping at *Cendryll.*

The loud clunk of locks reverberated in the room again as Casper Renn pushed the brass door knob back into place, opening the door into what could only be described as a place like no other...

~

THE BUILDING KAIRA followed her dad into was, unquestionably, the most incredible thing she had ever seen! It was a vast, circular-shaped structure with a large skylight, seeming to touch the sky. An array of brightly-coloured insects hovered above, their colour changing as they carried books to and fro, operating in small armies to manage the heavy volumes. Kaira watched them float up and down, past each floor, some delivering books to the circular seating area near the lift, and others returning discarded ones to various shelving which stretched from the third floor upwards.

"Quij," Aunt Phee whispered to Kaira. "Aren't they beautiful?"

Kaira nodded: they were *magical.* She watched the Quij float above her until the dizziness returned, causing her to squint in pain.

"Here," prompted her aunt, taking the lid off a small bottle containing purple liquid. "Drink this; it will help with the dizziness."

Kaira looked at the bottle uncertainly.

"It's perfectly safe," her dad interjected, taking a sip to reassure her. "See ... harmless."

"What is it?"

"Fillywiss. Try to drink it in one go: it works better that way."

Having no reason to distrust either of them, and with the dizziness worsening, Kaira took the small bottle and gulped it down, surprised by the sweet aftertaste. The dizziness evaporated almost immediately.

"Better?" her dad queried.

She nodded.

"Good. Why don't you have a look around," her dad encouraged as he caught the attention of a woman dressed in light blue who acknowledged him with a stern nod. "We'll be back in a few minutes."

Kaira stood in the centre of the vast building, taking in her surroundings whilst getting used to the silver bracelet on her right wrist. She briefly studied the triangular pattern on the marble floor before turning her attention to the numerous doors lining the walls. She looked back at the door they had entered through, keen to open it, but deciding instead to read the brass plaques on the neighbouring ones, each name as bizarre as the next: Fumbunctions, Fimiations, Follies, Bovies.

It was then she noticed the letters engraved on each brass door knob: the letters S. P. M. A. formed on top of one another - each letter bigger than the previous one so the S could be viewed through the space in the P.

"S. P. M. A," Kaira muttered to herself, guessing the 'S' stood for the society her dad had referred to.

Next was the spiral staircase at the west-end of the building, stretching ever upwards, before her attention was drawn to a group standing by the circular seating area, looking in her direction. There was also a girl sitting on her own in the far corner behind the circular seating area, staring at her...?

Feeling a little self-conscious, Kaira turned to look for her dad and aunt but saw they were still talking to the stern woman dressed in light blue so she decided to keep looking around, and promptly tripped over the feet of a figure asleep against the wall.

The figure - a tall, slender young man - woke immediately and clambered off the floor, tucking his oversized, white shirt into his grey trousers. He glanced around him before seeing Kaira rubbing her knee in some discomfort.

"Sorry ... Are you okay?" the young man asked, a nervous mannerism evident. "Good thing you woke me. I'd probably get into trouble if I got caught asleep."

Kaira, flushed with embarrassment, studied the young man and saw genuine worry in his expression. "It's my fault. I wasn't looking and didn't notice you behind me. I'm sure you won't get into trouble."

"Hope not," said the young man, rubbing his face to improve his alertness. "I'm Jacob, by the way. Jacob Grayling."

"Nice to meet you. I'm Kaira."

"Kaira ..." The tone implied it was courtesy to provide a surname.

"Renn. Kaira Renn."

Jacob Grayling's unease returned. "Ahhh... Would you mind not mentioning the 'sleeping bit' to your dad?"

"Of course," said Kaira, wondering why her dad mattered in this.

"I haven't had the best of introductions here and my mum's always on my case, saying I need to improve."

Kaira had an inkling that, like her, Jacob Grayling was quite alone here, not knowing where he belonged, and she felt a little sad for him.

"Do you know what they are?" she asked, pointing to the Quij high above. She already knew, of course, but thought averting his attention might ease his worry.

"Quij," he said, looking up at the luminous, coloured

insects and moving away from the wall.

"How can they carry such heavy books?"

"They can carry over a hundred times their weight. Amazing, aren't they?" He then held out his hand and made a faint whispering noise, looking up as a small group of turquoise and orange Quij floated down towards them. Kaira noticed how the small, luminous insects seemed drawn to the ring on Jacob's forefinger containing a light-blue penchant stone.

"Hold out your hand," he prompted, watching the Quij buzz closer to them.

Kaira did so, looking in wonder at the beautiful insects as they rested gently in the palm of her hand. "They're beautiful," she whispered, smiling in wonder.

"Looks like you've got some new friends."

"I love this place already."

Jacob laughed and added, "Not bad for an old building, is it?"

"What's it called?" asked Kaira, studying the wondrous insects in her palm.

"The Cendryll."

"Why's it called that?"

"Because it's the centre of things."

"Do you know what the logo stands for? The one on all of the door handles?"

"The S. P. M. A. logo?"

"Yes."

"The Society for the Preservation of Magical Artefacts," replied Jacob before blowing softly over his hand and watching the Quij float away towards the skylight.

Kaira looked at him, stunned ... *magical* artefacts? She remained silent for some time, struggling to accept this could be true. After all, *who* believed in *magic*?

"Don't worry," said Jacob, seeing the disbelief etched on her face. "You'll get used to the idea in time. It's always a bit of a shock at first."

"*Magical artefacts*...?" Kaira queried, almost in disdain.

"Probably not my place to say much more. Your dad will fill you in soon, I expect."

"How long have you known ... about here, I mean?"

"I was told six months ago - not long after my eighteenth birthday. My sister was told at the same time, which was pretty annoying since I had to wait until the proper time."

"Proper time?"

"Eighteen ... if you're told at all. Not all families want their children to know."

"Why?"

"Suppose it's not for everyone."

"So your sister's younger than you?"

"Thirteen and already knows more than me; she's a bit obsessed, if you ask me."

Kaira looked at Jacob, puzzled. "Your sister works here too?"

"No. You have to be eighteen to work here but she comes with me and mum because our dad isn't around."

"Oh," she uttered, realising she had touched on a sensitive subject and needed to retreat a little.

"Not a big deal. He's never been around so Guppy comes along with us each day. She doesn't mind: says she prefers it to school."

Who wouldn't? thought Kaira. "Is she with your mum now?"

"No; she's over there, sitting in Quandary Corner." Jacob nodded towards the girl sitting alone behind the circular seating area: the girl who had been staring at Kaira earlier.

3. The Girl in Quandary Corner

THE GIRL IN QUANDARY CORNER

On realising the girl sat in Quandary Corner was the younger sister of Jacob Grayling, Kaira was intrigued to find out more, not least because Guppy Grayling was practically the same age as her and might feel the same sense of disorientation which Kaira currently felt. This feeling had only been heightened by her dad and Aunt Phee entering one of the rooms underneath the large, spiral staircase accompanied by the lady in light blue.

"Society business," explained Jacob. "Mum spends her life in-and-out of those rooms. Out-of-bounds to everyone except for senior Society members."

"That's your mum with my dad and aunt?"

"Yep. Not that you'd know as she barely speaks to us at work."

"Why not?"

"We're a distraction."

"From what?"

"From whatever's more important."

A brief silence fell between the two.

"So, do you look after some of the artefacts?" asked Kaira, thinking it a good idea to try and change the subject.

"I catalogue creative charms - established ones and the hundreds with potential."

Creative charms, thought Kaira, wondering if she had heard Jacob correctly.

"Just means keeping a record of all creative charms: their name and function. Everyone starts at the bottom, doing the boring stuff until you become more experienced."

"So creative charms are a type of magic?"

"Yes. Fun and harmless."

"So why is it called The Society for the Preservation of Magical Artefacts?"

"Because it's a peaceful society and a way of keeping our existence under wraps. People don't respond well to magic when they find out it's real. The Society has protected, restored and studied magic for centuries."

"It's a secret society?"

"Yes," replied Jacob. "Very."

"Okay ... but you don't use the artefacts?"

"Yes, we use them along with everything else but keep it under wraps. If you think of the Society as a secret world with its own rules and way of doing things, it will probably help."

"Do you think I'll learn about the artefacts and how to use charms ... being under age, I mean?" asked Kaira, keen on proof that this fascinating building was, in fact, a magical society.

"Well, Guppy's under age and she's found a way to learn about them so I'd say she's your best bet." Jacob rubbed his face again, blinking to fight off another bout of tiredness. "Come on," he prompted. "Let's get the two of you acquainted."

Guppy Grayling looked up as her brother and Kaira approached.

A slight girl with an oval face and long, brown hair down to her waist, Guppy could be typically found perched in Quandary Corner, studying magical artefacts 'borrowed' from her mum's office or reading Society books on topics as varied as charms, remedies, buildings, histories and creatures.

Quandary Corner was named so after one of the Society's founders adopted it as the place in which to sit to solve important problems, not leaving the small corner of The Cendryll until he did.

Legend has it that Eran Tallis once spent four solid days in Quandary Corner, trying to identify the magical properties of a Bovie (the term used for an artefact with complex magical properties) until, exasperated, he threw the small, metal object on the floor, crying "I need my bed!" only to see the object transform into just that. An object now known in the Society as a Vaspyl or morphing steel.

Guppy put down the small book she was reading, keeping her legs tucked under her. She offered her brother a brief smile before giving Kaira the once-over. Guppy was glad to see that, like her, Kaira was dressed informally in jeans, an old jumper and red coat, going against the Society's formal dress code. Also the warm expression, intelligent eyes and respectful manner made Guppy certain she was going to like Casper Renn's daughter.

"Hello," she finally said as she stood away from Quandary Corner, picking up the book as she did so. Kaira noticed that Guppy's penchant was similar to hers: a silver bracelet with four gemstones, although Guppy's was light-blue as opposed to Kaira's purple amethyst stone.

"Hi," replied Kaira, feeling a sudden shyness. She caught

the title of the book, *Symbols, Runes and Omens* before Guppy placed it into the pocket of her jeans. Was it Kaira's imagination or did the pocket still look empty?

"Well, I'll leave you girls to it," said Jacob. "I should get back before I'm caught slacking off."

"No more naps," teased Guppy with a smile, giving her brother the briefest of hugs.

"Maybe give Kaira the tour," suggested Jacob. "Although not your 'unofficial' version."

Guppy offered a mischievous smile: "I wouldn't want to miss out the juicy stuff."

"The off-limits stuff, you mean," said Jacob, raising an eyebrow.

"Don't worry. I'll be on my best behaviour."

"Okay. Well, have a good first day, Kaira, and don't let my sister lead you astray."

Kaira and Guppy watched Jacob walk towards the lift behind the circular seating area.

"Right," said Guppy, a glint of excitement in her eyes, "Do you want to hear what's going on in there?" She nodded towards the room that her dad, aunt and Meyen Grayling had entered a few minutes ago.

Kaira looked at Guppy. "Your brother said those rooms are out-of-bounds."

"We don't need to go in; we just need to find a vacant room. The third floor's usually the best."

Kaira hesitated, quickly picking up on Guppy's lack of concern for rules. "What about the tour?"

"We can do that after."

Kaira looked over at the room in question with the green door partially hidden behind the vast, spiral staircase and wondered what was so important to take her dad and aunt away as soon as they had arrived. After all, wasn't this supposed to be her introduction to their secret world? Or was she going to be left on her own like Guppy and Jacob ... on the margins of the Society until she was old enough or important enough to be allowed behind the veil?

Feeling a sense of frustration building in her, she turned to Guppy: "Okay, what's happening that's so important in there?"

"This," said Guppy picking up a piece of paper from the floor. She flicked at the blank pamphlet as if this should explain everything.

Kaira looked at Guppy, puzzled: "There's nothing on it."

Guppy then pointed at the title of the pamphlet - the only writing on the piece of paper: *No News is Good News.*

"What about it?"

"It's a Society Pamphlet which is always blank because there's been no danger or threats for over thirty years."

"So why do they print it...?" "It reassures people."

"And what's that got to do with the room my dad and aunt are in...?"

"Well," said Guppy, "that's the interesting bit... You arrive today with your dad. You're only twelve, under-age like me, and your dad, aunt and my mum head straight into the room under the spiral staircase which is only used for important meetings."

"And...?"

"*And* the rumour is that, last night, two men brought a senior Society member here and he's been in that room ever since."

"They arrested someone?" asked Kaira.

"Mum likes to call it 'invited'," replied Guppy with a hint of irony.

"Why?" said Kaira.

"Because something's happened and it's not showing

on here ..." Guppy tapped the blank pamphlet again. "Which means the Society is trying to keep a secret about someone or something which they think would worry people."

Kaira suddenly remembered the sign she had seen last night from the bedroom landing ... on a piece of paper in Smyck's hands ... and her aunt's worried tone: The Sign of the Symean. The tour was no longer a priority. "Okay. How do we listen in?"

THEY WALKED past the circular seating area - which Kaira learnt was called The Seating Station - ignoring the suspicious looks of the men and women located there, some in deep discussion and others waiting for their books to be delivered by the Quij. The lift took some time to arrive, giving Kaira a moment to wonder how many floors were in The Cendryll; after all it was less than twenty minutes ago that she had entered this wonderful building via the two-storey structure of Cribbe & Corrow ... a thought which still befuddled her.

They stepped into the lift, its shape matching The Cendryll's circular form, and Guppy pressed the button for the third floor. Kaira held onto the brass handle as the lift began to revolve before rising slowly.

"So, Calamities is probably the first room to try," Guppy said, clearly used to the lift's revolving motion and the bizarre names given to rooms in The Cendryll. "It's rarely used at the moment."

Kaira nodded, fixing her attention on the S.P.M.A. crest carved into the wooden floor to avoid dizziness.

They stepped out of the lift onto the third-floor corridor

which, like the other floors, formed a circular perimeter around the vast central space of The Cendryll.

"This way," whispered Guppy as she moved along the corridor with a sudden sense of urgency. Guppy knew that although Kaira's arrival was an ideal excuse for exploring, the adults had little patience with children - least of all those who were about to enter a locked room which was strictly off-limits.

They stopped outside a dark, blue door with 'Calamaties' engraved on the brass plaque, glancing back along the corridor to ensure they hadn't been seen. Guppy put her hand into the pocket of her jeans and whispered, 'Comeuppance', placing the key she took out into the lock.

Kaira had a sudden moment of panic, convinced being caught up here would mean her first-and-last day in her dad's secret world. "Are we supposed to enter locked rooms?"

Guppy put a finger to her lips, placed the palm of her hand on the door (much like Morlan Corrow had done in Cribbe & Corrow) and whispered 'Pryal', listening intently as she did so. "Okay, it's empty," she said, turning the key in the lock: "Let's go."

They entered a mid-sized room, mainly furnished with wooden display cabinets housing strange objects - none of which Kaira had ever seen before. The other furnishing included four leather chairs set around a small, circular table and a drinks tray containing a few glasses.

Next to the glasses was the object Aunt Phee had brought with her to Kaira's house last night when she was secretly listening in on the bedroom landing - the glass object filled with a strange green liquid: the stuff Farraday called Jysyn Juice.

Guppy locked the door behind them and placed the key back into her jeans' pocket, whispering, 'Keepeasy'.

Kaira wanted desperately to know what all these whispered words meant, hoping they were proof that this really was a magical Society, but thought better of it as Guppy moved over to the four leather chairs and motioned for her to follow.

"Okay," whispered Guppy, sitting in one of the leather chairs surrounding the circular, wooden table. "You've probably got a million questions about the Society and all of the strange objects in all the cabinets so I'll do you a deal: we listen in on the meeting downstairs to find out what's happening and then I'll take you on the tour and answer all your questions."

Kaira nodded, a mixture of admiration for Guppy's fearlessness along with a keen awareness of the trouble they would get into if they were caught.

The next thing to happen made Kaira more certain than ever that this truly *was* a magical Society as, once again, Guppy reached into her jeans' pocket and whispered 'Comeuppance', this time bringing out a small glass, hexagonal object with a silver clasp. Guppy placed the glass object onto the table and suggested Kaira sit in the chair opposite.

"Okay," whispered Guppy, "This is a Looksee: it allows you to see into any space within the same building. The preservation part of the Society's name really means secretive: i.e. making sure artefacts don't get into the wrong hands. Everyone uses artefacts inside the Society and above ground, but it's against Society law for any artefact to be seen by above-ground people which is where the Keepeasy comes in."

Kaira stared at Guppy, questions fizzing in her mind but remembering their agreement: questions later.

"We haven't got a lot of time so I'll explain quickly. When I open the lid, it will fill with colour and images you won't be able to decipher. You'll also hear a humming sound before the images start to spread across here." Guppy made a circular gesture with her hand, signalling where the image would form. "As the image spreads across the table, you'll be looking into the room below: you'll see and hear everything."

"*Impossible*," blurted Kaira.

Guppy looked at her impatiently as she undid the silver clasp on the lid of the Looksee. "Here we go," she whispered and lifted the lid, sitting back in the leather chair to watch Kaira's stunned expression as the Looksee indeed filled with colour, humming sounds and indecipherable images...

As the images began to spread across the table, they formed precisely what Guppy had said they would: a bird's eye view of the room Casper Renn, Aunt Phee and Meyen Grayling were in. Kaira watched enthralled, peering down through the image on the wooden table into the room.

Farraday was in the room as well, and Smyck ... along with a man Kaira hadn't seen before. With the exception of the seated stranger, the adults were standing in front of a fireplace, asking the unknown man questions about "excessive amounts of Laudlum ... black market trading ... breaking Society protocol". Her dad was the quietest, turning the ring on the little finger of his right hand (his penchant, Kaira assumed) whilst studying the stranger's awkward responses.

"Tell us why, Theodore," came her dad's voice.

"We know why," interjected Meyen Grayling. "Greed."

"I want to hear from Theodore," Casper Renn insisted, maintaining his gaze on the stranger and ignoring Meyen Grayling's statement. It was clear from studying the room below via this magical device that her dad had authority in the Society.

"As I say, it started out harmlessly enough," the stranger began nervously.

"Theodore Kusp," Guppy whispered for clarification. "Works in Restrictive Charms on the fourth floor. Obviously, been caught selling Laudlum on the black market." Guppy then knelt to get a closer look at the tension brewing in the room, keeping a particularly close eye on her mum who was whispering something to Smyck. "But that can't be all ... black market trading isn't a reason to drag someone in."

"Who dragged him in?" asked Kaira. "Farraday and Smyck."

Kaira stared up at Guppy. "They were at my house last night talking to my dad and aunt..."

"*Told* you something was going on."

They turned back to the image, their noses almost touching the table.

"But now it's out there," growled Smyck, "above ground in God-knows-whose-hands."

"Above ground?" queried Kaira.

"Non-Society world," said Guppy impatiently, trying to gather the true reason behind this secret meeting.

"You know the harm it could do us," Meyen Grayling added, her contempt for Theodore Kusp apparent.

"You're sure you only sold it on the black market using Kyals?" asked Aunt Phee.

Theodore Kusp nodded, looking increasingly concerned.

"Society money," explained Guppy, pre-empting Kaira's question.

"Well, that's a start, at least," added Farraday, a compassionate tone entering his voice as he walked over to

Theodore Kusp and placed a reassuring arm on his shoulder. "Worse things have happened, my friend."

Meyen Grayling was the next to speak - words which confirmed Kaira's dislike of Guppy and Jacob's mother:

"We'll discuss the necessary consequences of your actions in due course, Theodore. Whilst we're aware of your difficult personal circumstances..."

"Meyen, for goodness sake," came Casper Renn's angry interjection. "The man has just lost his wife!"

The bitter resentment on Meyen Grayling's face was unmistakable. "I was just following Society procedure."

"Well, sometimes compassion is more important than procedure," replied Casper Renn as he joined Farraday in offering Theodore Kusp his reassurances.

"And what about this?" came Meyen Grayling's voice again - clearly not one to miss out on an opportunity to wield her power.

Casper Renn and Farraday turned back towards her, looking at the piece of paper in her hand - the same piece of paper which Smyck had been holding the previous evening during the secret meeting at Kaira's house. "I suppose this can be ignored as well - viewed as the oversight of a grieving man...?"

"The Sign of the Symean," whispered Kaira, recognising the drawing immediately.

"The *what*?" asked Guppy, her eyes shining with excitement.

"Smyck was holding it last night ... I was listening in. I'll explain later."

The girls turned back to the image, looking into it intently.

"Yes, Meyen; I've already seen it," replied Casper Renn.

"But where did you get it, Theodore?" she persisted.

Theodore Kusp hesitated, blinking repeatedly, his grief-stricken mind increasingly fragile as the questioning continued. "I ... I drew it," he mumbled. "It wasn't a symbol I had seen before so I thought I'd go to The Pancithon to research it when I had time."

Farraday, keeping his reassuring hand on Theodore Kusp's shoulder whilst glaring in disgust at Meyen Grayling's stunning lack of compassion, asked, "Do you remember where you saw it, my friend?"

Theodore Kusp blinked again, wiping his eyes with a handkerchief. "Yes. I saw it on the back of someone's neck ... a sort of branding on the skin. I thought it rather unique so drew it, you see."

"Who was it, Theodore?" asked Aunt Phee gently.

Theodore Kusp hesitated again before replying, "Prium Koll."

The silence in the room rested heavily on its inhabitants, each realising that the mention of Prium Koll's name added a different level of gravity to the situation. Trading on the black market was one thing - selling remedies to a Melackin was something else for Melackin were rehabilitated criminals, ex-Society members turned bad who now roamed the alleys of Society Square and Dyil's Ditch forging a living.

It was a silence shared by Kaira and Guppy ... a silence broken by Casper Renn's next statement:

"Theodore, I'm going to leave Farraday and Smyck to look after you for a moment. As you know, it's Kaira's first day and tradition for parents to show their children around, so if you'll excuse me."

The lid on the Looksee was closed and taken off the wooden table. Guppy and Kaira looked at one another, amazed with what they heard and desperate to discuss every detail, but their parents were about to leave the room beneath the spiral staircase downstairs, expecting to see them, and they weren't going to be there. They needed to get back to the ground floor quickly. Guppy put the Looksee back into the pocket of her jeans, uttering 'Keepeasy' once more and they moved towards the door of the room named Calamaties.

Kaira glanced at the strange objects in the display cabinets, reminding herself of Guppy's deal to tell all she knew: all about other magical things like the Looksee, the creative charms Jacob mentioned, the Protective Charms department where Theodore Kusp worked, the Melackin and why they had turned bad ... but this would all have to wait.

Guppy knelt beside the door, placing the palm of her hand on it once again, whispering 'Pryal'. Confident there was no-one outside in the hallway, she opened the door and they exited the room, being sure to lock it.

"What if they ask us where we've been?" asked Kaira quickly, already worried she was in trouble.

"Just say I took you on the tour," replied Guppy confidently.

"Will my dad believe that?"

"If you sound like you're telling the truth."

"How do I do that?"

"Let me do the talking," said Guppy.

THANKFULLY, the lift was still on the third floor so sticking to the story that they were returning from the tour should be straightforward, thought Kaira. It briefly occurred to her on their way down to the ground floor that if Guppy had a Looksee, it was perfectly reasonable to think that other people had them too. What if one of the adults in The

Seating Station had used a Looksee to see where they were really going? Kaira reminded herself that this mild paranoia wouldn't help her pretence of innocence.

"Relax," said Guppy as the lift arrived on the ground floor. "If you look nervous, they'll know we've been up to something."

"It's just my dad knows when I'm not telling the truth."

"Which is why I'm doing the talking." Guppy gave Kaira a quick nudge on the arm. "Just look at me if they ask you any questions, okay?"

Kaira nodded.

They exited the lift, turning towards The Seating Station and the suspicious faces of Casper Renn, Aunt Phee and Meyen Grayling...

The crowds who had been gathered at The Seating Station earlier had thinned out and now only a handful were reading on the wooden benches. The older members had no-doubt discussed why Kaira Renn was in The Cendryll at all as Society law clearly stated eighteen to be the age of induction. Special treatment, some would conclude in their whispered conversations, pointing to Guppy Grayling as another example of this. Protection, others would offer as an explanation, however from what they could not say.

Guppy's mum spoke first, the light-blue of her skirt and jacket in stark contrast to the lack of warmth emanating from her: "Well, are you going to introduce your friend?" she asked, looking at her daughter rather coldly.

Guppy returned the cold expression and played along with her mum's attempts to make them uncomfortable. "This is Kaira; she arrived today with her dad." Guppy then turned her glance to Kaira's dad and added, "Hi, Mr. Renn" with significantly more warmth.

"Hello, Guppy. Thanks for looking after Kaira." Casper Renn stepped forward, ignoring Meyen Grayling's inquisitorial glance at the girls. "And sorry we had to go off straight away, Kaira. We obviously want to make your first day special."

"It's okay, Mr. Renn. I showed Kaira around a bit; we didn't finish the tour but we got started."

"That's very kind of you, Guppy," added Aunt Phee whose dislike of Meyen Grayling was evident. "Well, what would you like to do first. Kaira? We could finish the tour, look around Founders' Quad or we could start with questions, which I'm sure you've got lots of." Aunt Phee sat down at The Seating Station and patted for Kaira and Guppy to join whilst her dad looked on, happy Kaira had made a friend.

"Maybe questions," replied Kaira, remembering not to mention the Looksee or the artefacts in the room named Calamaties.

"Okay," interjected her dad as he sat down alongside them: "Fire away."

"Casper." Meyen Grayling, now standing alone, motioned behind her to Smyck whose balding, burly figure was running across The Cendryll towards them.

Casper Renn stood, noticing the look of panic on Smyck's face.

Smyck stopped beside Meyen Grayling, bending to catch his breath before whispering in her ear.

"What is it, Smyck?" Casper Renn asked impatiently.

"It's Theodore."

"I did say I needed some time with my daughter."

Smyck hesitated ... a moment of uncertainty in his expression. "Sorry, yes ... but you probably need to come. Sorry, Kaira."

Kaira looked up at Smyck and thought of the drawing on the piece of paper he had been holding last night: The Sign of the Symean. Who was Smyck and what did he know? she wondered as she smiled in recognition of his apology. As much as she loved her dad and aunt, it was clear to Kaira that they were important in The Cendryll and there were undercurrents of unease - just as Guppy had suggested.

"Find Jacob," Kaira's dad instructed Smyck.

"I don't think Jacob's the right person..."

"I need Jacob to stay with the girls so they can go above ground," Casper Renn continued, ignoring Meyen Grayling's protest regarding her son's capacity to be trusted. He turned to Kaira, a sign of regret on his face. "It's still going to be special just not quite the way I'd planned."

Kaira gave her dad a hug and whispered, "It's okay. It will still be special; Guppy and Jacob can show me around and we can meet up and look around more later."

Her dad nodded. "I need you to stay with Jacob - no wandering off."

Kaira nodded and offered a reassuring smile. Yes, it would have been special for her dad and aunt to introduce her to everything and everyone, but she knew Guppy would answer questions her dad wouldn't, go to places they shouldn't and listen in on things they weren't supposed to. And just to think, less than an hour ago she had been standing in Wimples sweet shop, staring in wonder at the new Flabbergasteds, thinking the sweets to be the most magical thing in the world!

~

AFTER A FEW MINUTES of further apologies from her dad and Aunt Phee and a final glare from Meyen Grayling, Jacob appeared through the crowds, looking far more alert and a little less worried.

"You asked for me, Mr. Renn?" he uttered as he reached The Seating Station.

"Jacob, yes. Something has come up which means the traditional introduction for Kaira needs to be postponed. So to ensure she enjoys her first day, I'd like you to go with her and your sister above ground."

Jacob nodded, clearly surprised that he had been chosen as the responsible adult. "Of course, Mr. Renn."

"Founders' Quad, Society Square and its boundaries - particularly its *boundaries.*" Casper Renn passed a knowing glance in Guppy's direction.

"Perhaps some of the history, Jacob," added his mother in her usual, cold manner.

"And remember to stay together," Aunt Phee reminded them with a smile, her eyes emitting a maternal concern.

The three headed to the revolving lift, Jacob leading the way. Kaira noticed a sense of pride in his mannerisms, realising how important this simple act of recognition was for him.

"Okay," said Jacob as they stepped inside the lift, "Where do you want to go to first, Kaira? Or maybe you've got some questions?"

"What about if you do the information on Founders' Quad and I answer questions?" suggested Guppy, a clear plan already formulating in her mind.

"Whatever you think, sis," replied Jacob, clearly happy to be included rather than being on the margins of things. "That okay with you, Kaira?"

Kaira nodded, observing the closeness between them. "Well, fire away," said Guppy, pushing her hands into the pockets of her jeans.

Before Kaira could ask a question, Jacob leaned over and pushed one of the numerous buttons - this one with the letter Z on it. The lift then began to revolve anti-clockwise, continuing its ascent until it jolted to a standstill.

Kaira grabbed onto the lift's brass handle, trying to hide her fear of heights.

"Just a little detour," explained Jacob, his smile a sign that this sudden jolting motion was perfectly normal.

Kaira studied the darkness through the lift's glass panels, wondering if, in fact, this was a normal occurrence. Moments later, the revolving motion began again and the lift began to move, but not upwards... sideways! Kaira kept a firm grip on the brass handle, terrified that they were going to suddenly descend at rapid speed, for how could a lift go sideways!?

"You okay?" asked Guppy, noticing the growing fear in Kaira's face. "It's just another route the lift takes. It's perfectly safe."

Kaira managed a grimace as the lift continued its horizontal journey.

"Probably should have mentioned the lift can take you to the buildings within the Society; a better option than Periums if you need to talk on the way. Jacob's chosen Zucklewick's to go to first," explained Guppy. "It's the book shop in Founders' Quad ... run by Ivo Zucklewick who works in The Pancithon in the evenings: the Society library."

Kaira tried to keep up: "Isn't Zucklewick's in Market Square?"

"That's the 'above ground' name for it," continued Guppy. "What's known as Market Square was built by the Society founders over five hundred years ago: Eran Tallis, Riamina Mirch, Thoran Follygrin and Kylan Koll. Founders' Quad was built to symbolise the foundations of the Society - where it all began. The underground stuff came later."

The lift then came to a slow halt in the darkness, the only light a small lamp directly above a black door with the letter Z on it. "Here we are," said Jacob. "Zucklewick's: the best bookshop in the world, if you know what you're looking for."

KAIRA WATCHED as the door opened to allow the lift to move forward into the space within. Jacob opened the lift-doors and stepped into an indistinct, dark space - as if stepping into a self-opening door in mid-air was the most natural thing in the world! Noticing that very little could be seen ahead or under foot, Kaira waited for Guppy to follow.

"Quickly, Kaira," prompted Jacob. "Just step forwards and close the lift door behind you."

Kaira hesitated once more, feeling nauseous in the knowledge she was very high up with no clear sense of her surroundings.

Jacob extended his hand: "Grab on."

Kaira did so and closed the door as instructed, her fear of heights not allowing her to look down.

"Okay," added Jacob with a quick glance at his sister. "My turn to be the tour guide. The lift has thirty buttons. Apart from floors one to six, the other buttons are letters: each letter represents a building so Z for Zucklewick's etc."

"How am I going to know what each letter stands for?"

"You'll get the hang of it. Anyway, the important thing to remember when using the lift is to only step out when the door of your chosen location opens: otherwise ..."

"An uncomfortable tumble," Guppy interjected with

profound understatement before adding, "Do you know how the Periums work?"

Kaira shrugged. "Sort of. My dad and aunt took me to Cribbe & Corrow to get this bracelet; they said I needed a penchant then my dad turned a door handle and sort of pulled it. I remember feeling dizzy when he pushed the handle back in before we entered The Cendryll."

"Your penchant allows you to go through Periums," explained Guppy.

"And Periums are like portals in the Society...?"

"Right," added Jacob, placing his hand on the brass door knob before pulling it towards him as Kaira's dad had.

Kaira watched the words appear above the brass door knob as Jacob turned it, the same words she had witnessed in Cribbe & Corrow: Tauvin Hall, The Hideout, Leverin, Feleecian, Pancithon, Cendryll ... appearing and fading until Zucklewick's appeared and Jacob pushed the door knob back in, causing Kaira to feel as if everything was spinning again. "Think of them as doorways to parallel worlds," added Jacob before opening the door into Zucklewick's - a quaint, ramshackle bookshop with a peculiar charm.

Parallel worlds ... Jacob's words resonated in Kaira's mind as she followed him through the door into the bookshop. It seemed this secret world was vast and not just a building her dad worked in. She could never have dreamed that something so incredible existed nor that she would ever find herself within it, and perhaps the most exhilarating part was she had barely touched the surface.

"Fillywiss?" Guppy closed the door behind her, holding out the small bottle of purple liquid - the same one Aunt Phee had given her when they entered The Cendryll. Kaira drank it quickly, feeling the dizziness evaporate.

Guppy then sat on the floor of the shop, motioning for

Kaira to join her away from the crowds. "Anyway, changing the subject for a minute, I was thinking about that sign you mentioned; the one you saw on a piece of paper at your house last night."

Kaira remembered her dad's stern words when she tried to question him about the Society above ground this morning. No mention was made of the Society above ground, which was exactly where they were now - surrounded by eager customers searching amongst the dusty piles.

"Don't worry, I've used a Worble charm; they can't hear us."

Kaira frowned, wondering if this was just another example of Guppy disregarding Society rules.

"It's a protective charm which turns all conversation into muted sounds even when people are up close. I'll teach you it later."

Happy that she was considered worthy enough to learn charms, Kaira gave in.

"I think the sign I saw is connected to what's going on in the Society," explained Kaira as she watched people hunt through piles of dusty books, oblivious to their conversation.

"Agreed. The Sign of the Symean they called it, right?"

Kaira nodded. "Branded onto the back of someone's neck, Theodore Kusp said." She watched Jacob shake hands with a middle-aged man whose wild, auburn hair and thick-rimmed glasses gave the impression of an eccentric academic. "Who's Jacob talking to?"

"Ivo Zucklewick," replied Guppy impatiently. "Anyway, before we left The Cendryll, Smyck came running out, saying something about Theodore: they're definitely hiding something."

"Maybe if we use the Looksee again."

"It only works if you're in the same building. We could

try again later but your dad and aunt will want to spend time with you and Jacob doesn't know I've got one, strictly speaking. There's another way but it's tricky, and it'll almost certainly get us into trouble."

"Well, if we get into trouble, Jacob gets into trouble. Maybe we should stick to the tour for now; he seems happy he was asked."

Guppy studied Kaira, impressed by her sensitive nature, something she often lacked. "You're right. It wouldn't be fair on him."

"Is it because he's new?" queried Kaira. "He mentioned he hadn't had the best start in the Society, and that people are on his case."

"Jacob's shy," began Guppy, a protective tone apparent in her voice, "and he doesn't always stand up for himself but we've got each other ..."

Kaira sat quietly, wondering if she had overstepped the mark. She watched Jacob converse happily with the wild-haired, bespectacled man called Ivo Zucklewick - a discussion regarding a pamphlet the man was holding, it seemed.

"Let's just say some people in the Society get a kick out of belittling others," continued Guppy, picking at something invisible on the floor. "The thing that makes me angry is Jacob's one of the nicest people you could meet: kind, caring and loyal. Obviously, I'm biased but no matter what he does, he's treated badly by some of the adults in the Society." Guppy then stood, a mark of emotion in her eyes and the flush of her skin. "Anyway, today's about you. Like your dad said, your first day in the Society should always be special so let's make sure it is."

Kaira stood alongside her new friend, glancing over the stacks of books on the floor - old, leather-bound volumes on things she'd never heard of but generating interest among the swell of customers. "So, Founders' Quad?"

Guppy nodded, uttering 'Undilum' as she did so. She noticed Kaira's intrigue as she spoke the word and added somewhat mischievously, "Don't worry, I'll teach you that one too. Right, let's get Jacob away from Ivo or we'll be here all day."

After briefly introducing Kaira to Ivo Zucklewick, Jacob made his apologies to the wild-haired proprietor and led the way out of the bookshop and onto Founders' Quad.

4. Above Ground

ABOVE GROUND

They stepped out of Zucklewick's onto the Market Square Kaira had frequented throughout her young life, only now she knew it as something else: Founders' Quad. She remembered Guppy's brief summary of the history of Founders' Quad and wanted to know much more but, once again, before she could ask a question, Guppy had whispered 'Worble' into her hand and proceeded to point out familiar shops to Kaira and their role in the Society.

Jacob happily let Guppy do the talking, watching his sister's conversation and interaction resonate with warmth and, more importantly, trust - something which didn't come easily to her.

"Okay," began Guppy, manoeuvring through the usual crowds enthralled by the peculiar and equally wondrous buildings. "Founders' Quad is important, because, like I said, it was the first building in the Society and symbolises our origins and continued existence. Each shop has its own role and link to the Society." Guppy received a few sympathetic glances from some concerned faces in the crowds, feeling sorry for the girl who could only form muted sounds rather than words - the Worble charm shielding their conversation from above-ground ears.

"They say that if you could see underground from here," continued Guppy, stamping her foot on the pavement, "you'd see all of the faculties floating in the space below, all connected although they're hundreds of miles apart. The Cendryll, Leverin, Orium, Feleecian, Velnyx..."

"You might want to take a breath there, sis," interjected Jacob as he gained pace to keep up with them. "Maybe if we take one shop at a time and give Kaira a chance to *ask questions.*"

Kaira tucked her hands into the pockets of her red coat, thankful that Jacob had introduced a pause to Guppy's rapid-fire Society history. What she really wanted to learn was how to use charms which Guppy had promised to teach her later, and to talk more about the Periums: the magical stuff. Yet it was clear how much Guppy and Jacob were enjoying the opportunity to show her around and she didn't want to spoil it for them, so, instead, she decided to lead with a question.

"So Zucklewick's is a normal bookshop which links to the Pancithon which is the Society library?"

"Right," replied Jacob. "Zucklewick's sells rare books; the Pancithon holds all Society books."

"And there's a Perium in every building in the Society?"

Jacob and Guppy nodded again.

"And all Periums lead to all parts of the Society?"

"Not quite," said Guppy. "Certain parts of the Society have limited access."

"Such as?"

"The Velynx, Quibbs Causeway and a few other places."

"Why?"

"The Velynx deals with security with a particular focus on Gorrah."

Kaira waited for a translation of Gorrah as a crowd of excited children pushed past them to get to Wimples sweet shop, situated on Leaning Lane.

"Dark magic," added Jacob. "The Velynx is accessed via Quibbs Causeway: a long, narrow stretch of land that appears when the tide is out, a weird place that they say causes hallucinations, like it's trying to stop you getting there."

"A tide? Close to here?" asked Kaira, referring to the market town of Bibsley Corbett which was very much on land.

"Parallel time and space," re-asserted Guppy with an impatient tone as if this was the simplest concept to grasp. "Think of the Society as an alternative reality - that's how I finally got my head around it."

"Anyway," interjected Jacob, deciding that a metaphysical lesson was not what Kaira needed right now. "The Velynx is hidden within a cliff on the edge of a body of water beyond the Society boundaries, but that's for later. Let's stick to Founders' Quad for now otherwise your head will probably explode."

They carried on walking along Leaning Lane, past the chaos of Wimples sweet shop, children's screams of joy echoing in their ears. The architectural wonder of Leaning Lane never failed to impress, each Tudor building successively shrinking and leaning into the next, concluding with the tiny sweetshop famous across the land: Wimples.

"Wimples has a Perium too?" asked Kaira.

Guppy nodded. "All the shops do."

"How do you get to the Periums?"

"You ask for a specific thing in each shop until you're a regular."

"What do you ask for in Wimples?"

"Half a pound of Up Yours and two Put a Sock in Its," added Jacob without a trace of humour.

"Why can't anyone just ask for that - if they overheard it, I mean?"

"They can," added Guppy. "But you need a penchant to access Periums, and there are always loads of doors and corridors to go through before you access any Society building - to stop impostors."

Kaira looked back at Wimples, smiling at the wondrous expressions on the children's faces as they exited with their bags of sweets. "And every family's got a penchant stone?" she asked, remembering Morlan Corrow taking out the RENN tray of amethyst gemstones from the line of labelled drawers in the room with the large, oak table and strange, reflecting window.

"That's right," added Jacob. "The Grayling penchant stone is topaz: light blue. Not as nice as amethyst, if you ask me."

They managed to squeeze past the army of children outside Wimples and onto Pimion Place which had its own unique establishments, including Merrymopes, Tallis & Crake and the shop Kaira had entered earlier: Cribbe & Corrow. Kaira observed the chaotic excitement outside Wimples a little longer, momentarily wondering if the magic of the sweet shop was, in some way, better than the knowledge of an entire magical world.

The innocent wonder of Wimples and the blizzard of colour and scents seemed both an age away yet still within reach. Did she really want to enter further into this secret society now she knew more? Faculties connected in parallel time and space, charms, books, Gorrah, Quibbs Causeway, Periums, penchants...

As fascinated as she remained, Kaira was equally clear that this was no longer a mere exercise in innocent wonder: The Society for the Preservation of Magical Artefacts was a world with all of the complexity, mystery and darkness like any other.

Jacob, sensing Kaira was overwhelmed, nodded to the red-and-white themed shop ahead: Merrymopes.

"Ice cream?"

Merrymopes sat adjacent to Wimples sweet shop on the corner of Pimion Place, three doors down from Cribbe & Corrow. Run by eccentric twin brothers in their sixties, it was famous for its ice-creams and milkshakes, all of which were spectacularly bizarre.

Legend had it that the ingredients used in the ice-creams and milkshakes were sourced from Wimples, however mentioning this in Merrymopes was not the 'done' thing. Wimples, you see, was considered the enemy of the twin brothers' ice-cream and milkshake emporium for Merry-mopes was longer established, had introduced wonder into Founders' Quad earlier and didn't take lightly to a competitor setting up in such close proximity.

"Impostors!" the twin brothers, Henkle and Boven Merrymope, would yell at the mention of Wimples, waving the culprits out of their shop who had dared insult them by uttering the name of their bitterest rivals. Thankfully, Jacob and Guppy had learnt long ago not to mention Wimples in the presence of the twin brothers and entered with a polite wave, sitting at one of the window tables.

Guppy whispered 'Undilum' into her hand to undo the Worble charm, knowing it rude to mute conversation in

Society establishments unless entirely necessary, and as there was only one other family sat on the other side of the shop, she considered it both safe and polite to talk without protective charms.

Merrymopes had a number of quirks evident to the uninitiated customer. Firstly, the red-and-white theme ran throughout the shop, on the furniture, floor, ceilings and doors. The second oddity was the lack of menus; there was no reference to ice-creams or milkshakes anywhere in the establishment and many a customer had walked in out of sheer curiosity to be met by the tall, imposing figures of Henkle and Boven Merrymope who would proceed to rattle off a menu before impatiently waiting for their order.

The most fascinating aspect of the ice-cream and milk-shake parlour was, without doubt, the twin brothers themselves who did everything in tandem: every movement, gesture and word carried out in perfect synchronicity. They were identical twins, even in their sixties, and their mirroring permeated every aspect of their being. To say it was a little off-putting on first experiencing the Merrymope brothers would be an understatement although Kaira would soon learn that, along with Ivo Zucklewick, Henkle and Boven Merrymope were Society members you could rely on.

Kaira sat in the window of Merrymopes, looking across at Wimples once more. She wondered what her dad and Aunt Phee were doing now and if they had gotten to the bottom of events involving Theodore Kusp.

She thought about Churchill, her beloved cat, curled up somewhere at home and had a momentary desire to return to a life of ignorant bliss - but this fleeting feeling soon passed as all of today's information floated in fragments in her mind: disconnected particles of a secret universe which had a firm hold on her.

Aunt Phee had often said that she looked most like her dad when she was preoccupied; the frown and 'elsewhere' stare. Her dad, in turn, had inherited it from his father, Isiah Renn, a tall, imposing Jamaican who existed on the margins of Kaira's life and memory. It was rare for Kaira to be able to form more than shades and outlines of her grandfather ... an impression less distinct than her mother who had died before Kaira's memory of her could form. Photographs of her mother were the closest thing to memory she had; there were no equivalent photographs of her grandfather, Isiah Renn, after a feud her dad refused to discuss.

The Merrymope brothers brought Kaira out of her reverie, their synchronised movements entering her peripheral vision. She already knew what she wanted: The Bottomless Pit and Mud Never Tasted So Good: the first her favourite ice-cream and the latter a milkshake she had never dared taste.

"Miss Grayling. Master Grayling. Miss Renn," the twin brothers said in welcome, their traditional all-white attire off-set by the red bow tie complimenting the shop's red-and-white theme.

Kaira was glad to hear that The Bottomless Pit and Mud Never Tasted So Good were both available and, after placing her order, returned her attention to the fragments of knowledge floating around in her mind.

"Sorry if I've gone too fast," Guppy said, sensing that Kaira's detachment was due to being overwhelmed with information. Guppy, for the first time in years, wanted someone else's approval - an emotional need she had long abandoned after realising her mother was never going to provide it.

Kaira looked up with somewhat of a forced smile.

"You've both been great. It must be annoying to have to go over everything again."

Jacob was busy studying the pamphlet he had acquired from Ivo Zucklewick, the faded writing barely legible on the dull parchment. "Not at all; it's our pleasure. I remember wondering if it had been better not to find out."

"It just seems so enormous, and you both know so much. I remember you saying it's not for everyone ... that some parents don't tell their children."

"You're wondering if you're cut out for it ... living in two different worlds?"

"Yes. Don't you ever wonder that?"

"Of course. Just hold onto the *wonder* of it all, Kaira. Thinking of the most beautiful thing always helps me when it gets too much. I always think of the Quij and how I felt the first time I saw them - their luminous, multi-coloured forms floating down towards you like snowflakes. It's natural to be overwhelmed at first but think of the alternative - a world of strangers staring at screens."

Jacob nodded over to the family at the far end of the shop: a mother, father and two teenage children all glued to their phones.

Technology had been absent from Kaira's upbringing and it was clear that this applied to Guppy, Jacob and the Society as a whole.

"I'm gathering there's a reason Society families don't have technology?"

"It's not as harmless as above-ground people think," replied Guppy without offering further explanation. "Anyway, I need to pay a quick visit to Tallis & Crake. I'll be back in no time."

And before they could protest, Guppy was out of the door of Merrymopes and amongst the bustle of Founders'

Quad, walking to the nearby, peeling-white structure Kaira knew very little about: the theme of the day, she concluded.

"SHE DOES THAT," explained Jacob as he watched Guppy ease her way through the bustle of Pimion Place, losing sight of her as she reached the entrance to Tallis & Crake. The peeling, white frontage gave the impression of an establishment weary of business - an impression reinforced by the dirty, tinted windows and lack of identifiable trade.

On glancing in the window of Tallis & Crake, you would be as likely to see a tatty comic as you were a pocket watch; a landscape painting alongside a cheap, wooden toy. However, this was merely the facade adopted by the proprietors because, like all other Society buildings on Founders' Quad, Tallis & Crake had its own unique function.

Kaira watched as Jacob continued to study the pamphlet he had acquired from Ivo Zucklewick, attempting to read the faded writing on the front and back whilst slurping his milkshake, the interestingly named Belly Blitz.

"Do you think she'll be long?" asked Kaira, keen to get to the exciting stuff: charms and magical artefacts.

"You never know with Guppy; it depends who she gets talking to."

"Wouldn't it have been easier to go together?"

Jacob scooped up a big gulp of ice cream. "Probably not, to be honest." He paused whilst the family who were at the other end of the shop paid and left. "Tallis & Crake is a place you go to get stuff."

"Society stuff?"

Jacob nodded. "Artefacts mostly; stuff that isn't supposed to be above ground."

"Is that allowed?"

"The Society turns a blind eye to black market trading as long as you don't expose the Society or cause harm."

Kaira thought back to the conversation she and Guppy had heard earlier with the Looksee: Theodore Kusp's black market trading in Laudlum to someone called Prium Koll and the trouble he seemed to be in. "And Guppy's allowed to trade on the black market ... being under eighteen, I mean?"

"Anyone affiliated with the Society can trade at their own risk."

"Why would Guppy take the risk?"

"Risk-taking is in her nature. Also, she has a knack of 'acquiring' magical artefacts from our mother when she's not paying attention, which is most of the time. She uses her Keepeasy to hide them from her but 'acquiring' too many at once makes it obvious things are going missing. Guppy uses Tallis & Crake to trade artefacts so when our mother searches her, what's gone missing isn't there because she's traded it for something else."

"A Keepeasy?" queried Kaira.

"A pocket or pouch made of Hemppla. Anything you put into it vanishes, evaporating until you need it again."

Kaira now understood why Guppy had whispered 'Comeuppance' before taking out the Looksee earlier and assumed the second utterance, 'Keepeasy', was the command to make the Looksee vanish when returned to the pocket.

This would also explain how the book Guppy had been reading when they first met earlier today, *Symbols, Runes and Omens*, had appeared to take up no space in the pocket of her jeans. She bit the straw in her milkshake, containing her desire to get up and follow her friend into Tallis & Crake. "How long before I learn about charms and artefacts?"

"As soon as you find a teacher."

"Guppy said she'd teach me some charms."

"There you go then," said Jacob with a smile.

"Can we look around Society Square and its boundaries now?"

"Of course," said Jacob, taking a final slurp of his Belly Blitz milkshake. "I should probably warn you that Guppy will do her very best to talk you into going beyond the boundaries of the Society."

"Is that a bad thing?"

"*Definitely*. Going beyond society boundaries is *serious*."

The uneasy look on Jacob's face signalled that he wasn't going to elaborate.

"Is there a boundary close to here?"

"Yes. The Hideout."

THEY EXITED Merrymopes with an overt thank you to Henkle and Boven Merrymope who bowed in perfect synchronicity. The streets of Founders' Quad were as busy as ever and they were quickly caught up in the pace of the crowds whose attention was either diverted to the architectural puzzle of Leaning Lane or the wonder of Wimples sweet shop.

"Okay, this way," instructed Jacob as they moved through the crowds away from Founders' Quad and onto Paupers' Alley. "This is probably the best place to show you the Society boundaries."

Kaira stepped off the pavement as a couple, huddled up against the chill wind, bustled by. They were standing at the foot of The Cross, named so because of the cross-shaped design of lanes leading to St. Salonius Church.

"This is one of the boundaries?" she asked, pushing her hands into her coat pockets.

Jacob shook his head. "The best view is from the church roof."

"Are we allowed up there?"

"Not allowed, as such." Jacob raised his eyebrows mischievously, making Kaira wonder if a rebellious streak ran in the Grayling family.

An old lady, hunched over with the weight of her bags, was the next person to appear on Paupers' Alley, glancing suspiciously at them before shuffling on.

"Will Guppy know where to find us?"

"She'll know we're here or near The Hideout. If not, we'll head back towards Tallis & Crake and Merrymopes. We always wait in certain places for each other above ground. You'll choose your meeting places in time."

Kaira returned her attention to the issue of getting to the church roof. "So we just sneak into the church and find our way up to the roof?"

"That's the general idea."

"And there's no-one watching who comes-and-goes through the door?"

"The door's locked from the inside so it's just a case of unlocking it."

Kaira was getting used to statements like these which, only a few hours ago, would have seemed bizarre. Unlocking a door from the inside when you were on the outside was, obviously, *impossible* - without magic.

"Undilum?" queried Kaira, guessing the charm to unlock the door, the one Guppy had used to undo the Worble charm earlier.

Jacob smiled as he buttoned his dark, blue jacket. "Something like that. Come on."

They made their way along The Cross as the echoes of voices from Founders' Quad filled the cold air. It was striking how rapidly the crowds thinned once you stepped beyond Founders' Quad ... as if an invisible boundary existed which people dared not step beyond.

Kaira would soon learn the real reason for this distinct divide in congestion and why Paupers' Alley and beyond was almost exclusively populated by Society folk. Society Square, the lanes, alleys and streets beyond didn't share Founders' Quad's quaintness nor touch of the eccentric. It was dingier, greyer and more down-at-heel with a less-friendly clientele who shared its washed-out character.

The reason for above-ground people's fear of what lay beyond Founders' Quad was not entirely clear, however legend had bestowed many tales of hauntings in Dyil's Ditch and vanishings near Blindman's Point not to mention the tale of 'the grey lady' found screaming in the middle of night in Hangman's Court, never to utter another word. In any case, the madding crowds of Founders' Quad didn't take it upon themselves to explore Society Square and its boundaries with the same vigour.

The church was almost empty when they entered except for a single figure lighting candles below the stained-glass windows at the north end. The figure, a white-haired man dressed in grey trousers and a blue cardigan, offered a brief smile as they entered before returning to the business of candle-lighting.

"How do we get to the roof?" whispered Kaira, wondering how her first day in the Society had become so convoluted.

Jacob nodded to a wooden, arched door they were walking towards with little concern for being seen. Kaira kept pace with a greater degree of self-consciousness. She sat next to Jacob on the church pew near the door, watching as he bowed his head as if in prayer.

"What are you doing?"

He ignored her, lifting his gaze just enough to check if the church attendant was watching them: he wasn't. With his head still bowed, he whispered 'Entrinius' whilst coughing loudly at the same time.

Kaira instinctively patted him on the back to help with his coughing fit, knowing it was done to disguise the sound of the door being unlocked by the Entrinius charm; another one to remember.

As the coughing performance ended, Jacob whispered, "Follow me..."

They were through the unlocked door in no time, entering and re-locking it as quietly as possible before taking the spiral stairs to the roof.

The panoramic view from the church roof was not only, as Jacob had suggested, the best way of seeing the boundaries of Society Square but a perfect point from which to study the maze of streets and landscape beyond. The battlement design of the roof meant that, as long as you sat or knelt below the parapet and peered through the narrow hollows cut into the stone, you were unlikely to be spotted.

Kaira buttoned her red coat against the wind as Jacob pointed out all the boundaries in the square: The Hideout, Tauvin Hall and The Bull & Bladder to the North; The Blind Horsemen to the South; Long & Little marking the east boundary and Ramshackle Alley the west.

She looked over the maze-like structure, wondering how little she had ventured beyond Founders' Quad in all the times she had visited, Wimples being her primary concern on almost every occasion. The contrast of the marauding masses of the Quad and the lightly occupied streets of the

Square was even more distinct from this high vantage point, as was the mood: a contrast between joviality and excitement in the Quad compared to the more secretive, purposeful movements in the Square as if each person had a specific quest or task to complete.

Kaira used the time on the church roof to ask about the expanse of land visible beyond Society Square, starting with the stretch of marshland beyond The Hideout and Tauvin Hall.

"Dyil's Ditch," explained Jacob, sitting cross legged alongside Kaira. "Known in the Society as No Man's Land. Wild. An absolute no-no. Above ground, it's just marshland, leading to a ditch shrouded in fog but if you access it through a Perium, it's something else altogether."

Other buildings pointed out included The Argy Bargy, enticing further knowledge she attempted to store amongst the many other floating fragments. "A pub mainly used by Society people although some above-ground people go there if they're desperate to acquire some 'miraculous invention'."

"So above-ground people know about the Society?"

"Very few. Any attempt to expose the Society gets you kicked out. Above-ground people who buy things on the black market think the traders are mad scientists. It's surprisingly easy to discredit those who mention the Society above ground."

"And it's allowed? To sell to above-ground people?"

"If it's harmless and helpful."

"Like what?"

"A Sootheral; a small, brass object which chimes softly and hypnotically. Frazzled parents desperate for sleep risk entering places like The Argy Bargy to get their hands on one. No child has ever lasted more than sixty seconds once they hear its chimes: harmless and helpful.

Anyway, The Argy Bargy got its name because people used to always come out of the pub fighting drunk. Society members had a word, insisted only the weakest ale with 'a Society twist' was served, and now everyone sings at the top of their voice all night. You can hear it if you live close by, which must be pretty annoying."

Kaira also learned the history of The Spinning Shoe, something she had always wanted to know.

"The huge spinning shoe on the roof was the invention of the shop's original owner - Erina Blin." explained Jacob, "who, on her first visit to Society Square, 'saw a sea of grey faces only magnificence could heal'. From that day on, she set out to make the people of the square 'sigh in horror or scream in joy' and that's what happened. The Spinning Shoe is one of the places above-ground people will venture away from Founders' Quad for."

"Why?"

"You'll have to pay a visit to find out."

The rhythm of Kaira asking and Jacob responding with legends of Founders' Quad and Society Square went on until the cold air begun to win the battle.

Jacob got up first. "Time to find Guppy. She'll be wondering where we've got to, and your dad and aunt will be expecting us back soon."

Kaira took one final look over Founders' Quad and Society Square, her gaze hovering over The Hideout ... a low-lying building with shutters on each window and smoke billowing out of the chimney. Was the name synonymous with the place? Would Guppy suggest they go beyond the society boundaries? Why was Dyil's Ditch so feared and strangely enticing? And what had Guppy needed so urgently from Tallis & Crake?

Kaira believed the answer to the last question was linked to something Guppy was planning ... something the Looksee couldn't help with but which was linked to what they had seen earlier when using it to spy on the adults' secret meeting ... and it was barely mid-day.

∾

THEY FOUND GUPPY EXITING TALLIS & Crake as they made their way through the bustling streets of Founders' Quad. Kaira couldn't help glancing in the window of Cribbe & Corrow which occupied the building adjacent to Tallis & Crake; no sign of Morlan Corrow ... just the empty shop counter and the green, velvet curtain drawn to hide the mysteries beyond.

"Hey," said Guppy as she finally got through an excitable family making their way to Wimples. "Did you get to see much of Society Square?"

Kaira read this chirpy, upbeat tone to mean Guppy had gotten her hands on the desired artefact.

"We chose the church-roof version," replied Jacob, letting out a mild shiver, his reddening face a sign he needed to get out of the cold.

"Did you get what you wanted?" asked Kaira, surprising herself with her forthrightness.

Guppy paused before answering, a squint of suspicion returning. "Yep. Not the easiest place to get your hands on things."

"Good." Kaira smiled and pushed her chin down into the collar of her red coat in an attempt to limit the impact of the biting wind. She saw the figure before Guppy and Jacob did, standing on the corner of Willisp Way to the west of Founders' Quad. She had first noticed the man when they were in Merrymopes and noticed him again for the same reason: he appeared to be watching them... unkempt, unshaven and staring intently in their direction.

"Kaira." Guppy waved a hand in front of her face to get her attention.

Kaira kept her gaze on the man who was now walking in their direction, manoeuvring his way through the crowd. "Do you know that man there?"

Jacob and Guppy looked in the general direction Kaira was surveying.

"Where?" Guppy asked.

"The one walking this way ... scruffy with a beard; I noticed him earlier when we were in Merrymopes."

They looked again before Jacob said. "I see him. Time to head back."

"Why?" asked Guppy. "Who is he?"

"Prium Koll: Melackin."

Kaira and Guppy stared at each other: Prium Koll ... the Melackin Theodore Kusp had admitted selling Laudlum to on the black market! The man with The Sign of the Symean branded on the back of his neck ... and now he was following them!

"Okay, *let's go*," prompted Jacob, directing Guppy and Kaira in the direction of Merrymopes as Prium Koll notice-ably picked up his pace, now pushing through the crowds on Founders' Quad.

The wall of people made it impossible to move quickly, forcing them to negotiate each space.

"*Faster*," urged Jacob, struggling to manage his anxiety.

"We're not going to make Merrymopes through these crowds," Guppy stated, before grabbing Kaira's arm and adding "this way". They cut down a narrow passage off the crowded streets, leading to a narrower lane: Bayun Passage.

"*Quickly*, Guppy," urged Jacob.

Kaira turned at the sound of Guppy uttering 'Cympgus' and watched a tiny ball of light appear from a penchant stone on her bracelet before she added 'Whereabouts', the second command making the ball of light morph into numerous shapes until it took the form of an archway just big enough for them to walk through.

Bayun Passage was no longer visible through the archway of light hovering a few yards ahead, utter darkness taking its place.

At the sight of Prium Koll entering Bayun Passage and running towards them, Guppy shouted "Go!" and pushed Kaira through the light-based archway which promptly swallowed her into darkness. Guppy and Jacob joined her moments later before the Cympgus vanished from view.

"Watch your step," said Guppy as she led the way.

Kaira had a distinct feeling they were walking down invisible steps in this dark space which was obviously a different type of Perium ... one which didn't transport you directly into a Society space but, instead, placed you temporarily in a dark limbo between worlds.

"It's a Cympgus," explained Jacob who was following close behind. "A portable Perium used for emergencies."

Kaira kept time with Guppy, beginning to realise that you simply had to imagine you were walking down invisible steps in darkness - not something which came naturally. Asking more questions seemed unnecessary because she had already heard the name Prium Koll today; she also knew he was a Melackin and that those two things were synonymous with danger. The only thing on her mind at present was getting back to the safety of The Cendryll, her dad and Aunt Phee.

THE UNSHAVEN PURSUER, Prium Koll, slowed when he saw the Cympgus vanish as Guppy and Jacob Grayling stepped through the archway to safety. Using a Cympgus to escape was clever and also dangerous ... watching someone vanish through an outline of light above ground wasn't an everyday occurrence. It was an insight into the Grayling girl's attraction to risk which meant she would bring Kaira Renn back above ground soon.

Allowing children to go above ground so uninitiated was a mistake, Prium Koll mused, even when they were accompanied by an older companion. The young couldn't resist the wonders The Society for the Preservation of Magical Artefacts offered. They would return above ground soon enough.

Prium Koll turned and walked back along Bayun Passage, keeping to the side streets, his coat collar turned up to hide the sign branded on the back of his neck. He moved along Malens Lane, past Long & Little and Ockly & Co until he had reached the boundaries of Society Square where the large, derelict structure of The Sylent stood in the distance.

The pain in his chest lessened as his heartbeat slowed, a sure sign the Laudlum was wearing off. The steep incline of Horsel Hill would increase the chest pains again but resting now was little use, and there would be no more medicine to heal his pain if he kept the figure waiting in The Sylent too long, keen to hear of his granddaughter's entrance into the Society.

ISIAH RENN STOOD at a top floor window in the building on top of Horsel Hill, looking out over Society Square. The Sylent's facade had been sorely neglected, giving the impression of a once-grand house left to gradually collapse in on itself. The imposing structure had been a talking point for many years ... from its origins to the reasons for its decline.

The Sylent was infamous in the Society for it was in this house that the practice of Gorrah (dark magic) began above ground - a practice which soon swept across the country until swift retribution was taken by the Society in one of the bloodiest chapters of its history: retribution which led to the abandonment of the building and the practices within it.

Since then, numerous protective and restrictive charms made The Sylent inaccessible to most. The building's name, originally Horsel House, became unofficially known as The Sylent during the time of the secret, illegal practice of Gorrah, the term 'Sylent' a reference to secrecy, cruelty and betrayal.

Isiah Renn adjusted his black tie in the reflection of the window, studying the lone figure of Prium Koll making his way up Horsel Hill, his hunched figure a sign that the Laudlum was rapidly wearing off. He brushed a hand over his grey waistcoat to remove a stray hair before glancing at the deepening lines around his eyes and the grey streak running through his afro hair.

The tall stature, formal dress and serious disposition had been passed on to his son - a son he no longer had any contact with. The accusations against him were numerous and merely being in The Sylent was a risk.

He was a wanted man, after all, amongst the group discovered in The Sylent all those years ago when rumours of dark practices spread. Rumours of his role in the secret teaching of Gorrah (dark magic) were now part of the myth of Isiah Renn: a ghost hovering on the Society margins.

The irony of standing alone in The Sylent, the place which had led to his downfall, was not lost on him but there was no easier place to enter without being seen at night and no better position to overlook Society Square, waiting for the appearance of his grand-daughter. Although the building was protected by charms, they were little trouble to a man of his powers.

He had long wondered when Kaira would be introduced to the Society, certain that his son's belief that his grand-daughter would neither be aware nor interested a mere delusion. Secrets were hard to keep, after all, and something so incredible as The Society for the Preservation of Magical Artefacts was always going to fascinate her.

News of Kaira's entrance into The Cendryll this morning came quickly as did Isiah Renn's movements thereafter. Although Society Periums were inaccessible to those who had practised Gorrah, other Periums existed outside of the Society's control - ones which allowed move-ment on the margins of the Society via abandoned build-ings such as The Sylent which had long been deemed unfit and unsafe.

And here he had stood, waiting to see his grand-daughter appear on Founders' Quad with her new friends: guides for the day. Twelve was very young to be inducted which could only mean one thing: Kaira's safety and protec-tion. Yet safety and protection within the Society was dependent on a recognition of the darkness surrounding it: a darkness Isiah Renn knew only too well.

He watched the clouds merge above Horsel Hill, their grey hue a sure sign of rain - the first drops flecking the small windows of the dilapidated building as the familiar sight of Prium Koll reached the top of the hill, the pale figure struggling to catch his breath, bringing news which would benefit or cost him...

5. The Pancithon

THE PANCITHON

As Kaira's eyes adjusted to the darkness, she could see the faintest outline of steps stretching out below; they seemed to go on for an eternity, stretching across the entire width of the darkness encompassing them. She kept to Guppy's rhythm, jumping at every noise whilst wishing they would reach a door and step through it back into The Cendryll.

"Almost there," said Jacob reassuringly from behind. "Cympgus' aren't as direct as normal Periums; they're more an emergency exit."

"Still ace, though," Guppy chipped in ahead.

They *were* ace, Kaira thought. Everything was ace in the Society but it was all going so fast and now there was a Melackin following them ... first hovering outside Merry-mopes then chasing them through Founders' Quad before Guppy found an escape route. Kaira couldn't shake the feeling that there must be a link between Prium Koll and the artefact Guppy had sneaked off to Tallis & Crake to get. Why else would he have been following them?

Whatever the reason, and whether it was linked to Guppy's secret transaction in Tallis & Crake or not, Kaira needed answers to lots of things - to why Guppy was being so secretive, who the Melackin actually were and why there had still been no time for her to ask questions about her dad's role in the Society or how to use charms and vanish through a Cympgus.

The day was getting away from her as she got increasingly caught up in the whirlwind which was Guppy Grayling. Getting back to the safety of The Cendryll would be a perfect time for Kaira to be a little more insistent on getting Guppy and Jacob to teach her things: about magic ... where it all started and her family's role in The Society for the Preservation of Magical Artefacts.

"Here we go," said Guppy, pointing to the faint outline of a door ahead which opened of its own accord into a vast, well-lit space of moving bookshelves and the busy traffic of books, moving in mid-air. The books were carried by a multitude of Quij, their luminous bodies a sign they had returned to the safety of the Society, although somewhere other than The Cendryll.

THE PANCITHON STRETCHED out before them as the door symbolising their safe return closed. Earlier in the day, Kaira would have looked back at the door to study its shape, wondering about its magical ability to transport people elsewhere, but this was of less interest now than the building they were standing in: a long, rectangular building stretching over an implausible distance dominated by large, wooden bookshelves which moved of their own accord. The Quij were in greater number here, fluttering between each bookshelf, gathering and tidying together, their shimmering colours an infinite wonder.

The building they had entered via the Cympgus was the Society library, holding a copy of every book ever written by a Society member except for a few rare items housed elsewhere.

Kaira looked up at the low-hanging lamps which lit the wooden floor running the length of the building towards the grand clock on the north wall. The floor was decorated by gold letters on either side which spun each time the accompanying bookshelf moved outwards onto the central walkway.

Situated on the edge of the walkway, each letter formed an alphabetised system for visitors, allowing for easy navigation of book titles. The spinning letters acted, to some degree, as a warning to those who were standing in line of a moving bookshelf to avoid getting hit.

Standing on the central walkway, as they were now, also gave you the best view of the seemingly rhythmic motion of the moving bookshelves, easing out before stopping under the low-hanging lamps, as if sensing this provided the best light for visitors.

"Careful," said Jacob as the gold-letter K began to spin on the wooden floor near their feet. The bookcase began to move outwards onto the central walkway ... clearly no-one pushing or controlling it as far as Kaira could gather: another Society wonder.

"So this is The Pancithon," said Kaira, stepping back as the bookshelf moved passed her.

"Yep," replied Guppy, browsing the shelves with her forefinger. "I was planning on coming here tomorrow but then we made friends with that Melackin so it seemed like a good idea."

Kaira was struck by how fearless Guppy seemed ... as if being chased by a Melackin was entirely normal and absolutely nothing to worry about. In contrast, Jacob was the one on edge, repeatedly brushing his dark hair out of his eyes and surveying the Pancithon for any prying eyes.

"Why did you want to come here before going back?" asked Kaira, wondering what Guppy was looking for on the long, wooden shelf dominating the space in front of them.

Guppy raised her eyebrows in mock disdain: "The Sign of the Symean, of course."

She then uttered 'Comeuppance' and reached into the pocket of her jeans for the book she had been reading this morning. "Look, one of the reasons I took so long in Tallis & Crake was because I was looking through this," she said, tapping the cover of Symbols, Runes and Omens. "There's no mention of it in here which means it can't be just a sign or omen: it must be a creature or something else."

"So there are different types of signs?"

"Have I missed something?" interjected Jacob, looking mildly annoyed that he had been excluded from the secret knowledge they shared.

"It's just something Kaira heard the other night," added Guppy, turning her attention from the bookshelf to Jacob, sensing his annoyance.

"The other night?"

"At home. My dad, aunt, Farraday and a man called Smyck were talking about Searings, Melackin and other stuff...."

"Smyck was at your dad's house?" Jacob's full attention was on Kaira now.

Guppy then motioned for them to lower their voices whilst peering through the gaps in the bookshelf to see if they had been heard. Confident that no-one was in earshot, she whispered 'Worble' and turned back to Kaira and Jacob, reassured that the protective charm now made their conversation indecipherable.

"You didn't mention them talking about Searings," Guppy said turning to look at Kaira whilst keeping an eye on the door they had entered through.

"Sorry. It was late and I was tired. They seemed worried; that's what stood out for me."

Jacob and Guppy exchanged a glance before Jacob added:

"You're sure you heard them mention Searings...?"

Kaira nodded, wondering if they were ever going to explain each new aspect of the Society or continue to forget this was still her first day. "So, what are Searings?"

"Gorrah," replied Guppy.

"Dark magic?"

"Yes. A type of attack but very rarely used although always reported."

"Which they haven't been," added Jacob. "Nothing in No News is Good News, no mention of it in The Cendryll or other faculties."

"Which means someone's trying to keep a secret," added Guppy with an inquisitive frown.

"Theodore Kusp?" offered Kaira. "The man we saw. You said Farraday and Smyck brought him into The Cendryll last night. They were at my house until late so they must have gone to him after they left. And remember Theodore Kusp explaining how he drew the sign after he saw it on Prium Koll's neck...?"

"Is there something you two *need to tell me*?" interrupted Jacob, his gentle expression momentarily darkening.

"Promise you won't tell mum," Guppy pleaded, realising Kaira had inadvertently let slip their secret trip to the third floor, listening in on the adults' meeting with the Looksee.

"You've been spying again."

"I knew there was something going on," began Guppy trying to explain their use of the Looksee to listen in on the secret conversation involving their parents and Theodore Kusp. "A senior Society member gets brought in late at night, Kaira sees a weird sign that her aunt calls 'The Sign of the Symean', a sign that Theodore Kusp draws after seeing it on the back of Prium Koll's neck, but No News is Good News is blank ... We thought listening in would help us find out what was going on."

"We? Prium Koll? The Melackin who just chased us!?"

"Okay, me. Anyway, we ... *I* was right."

"So, anything else? Broken any more rules in the last hour?"

Kaira sensed this sibling spat was going to escalate and at the sight of a tall, elegantly-dressed woman appearing through a door to their right, she thought it best to quell the rising tensions.

"Sorry; it's my fault, really. After I'd asked you what the S.P.M.A stood for, I didn't really believe the magical part. I pestered Guppy to show me something to prove it."

Jacob studied them both, doubting Kaira's explanation. "And Guppy showed you what, exactly?"

"A Looksee. I was being annoying, asking loads of questions about magic and charms so Guppy agreed to show me one artefact: more to shut me up than anything else."

"You know how serious spying on Society meetings is, Guppy. And wandering around above ground with this secret information which you're *clearly not supposed to know*. You could get us all into trouble."

"I know. It was the easiest way of showing Kaira something quickly that would stop the constant questioning. I didn't know we were going to hear what we did."

"And the trip to Tallis & Crake ... what was that for?"

"A Now-Then," replied Guppy a little sheepishly as her brother's annoyance grew.

"To do more spying?"

Kaira thought it best to leave questions about the Now-Then's purpose for another time, although she knew it had something to do with Guppy's ever-evolving plan to uncover the secret goings on in the Society.

"No more spying."

Guppy nodded in agreement.

"No offence, Kaira, but your dad and aunt aren't very sympathetic to people who break Society rules, and I'm the one your dad asked to keep you out of trouble."

"Sorry," Kaira and Guppy uttered in unison.

"Well, it's done now," said Jacob, watching the tall, elegantly dressed lady disappear quickly behind a book-shelf in the L section - as is if she didn't want to be seen. "And we're in the best place to find out what the sign means."

Kaira and Guppy were relieved to see the shadow of anxiety lift from Jacob's face, happy he had partially believed Kaira's relentless inquisitiveness was behind the use of the Looksee. Even better for them was the fact that Jacob's own intrigue outweighed his frustration and the danger they could have put themselves in.

Their excuse for using the Looksee was a white lie, of course, but a necessary one to navigate Jacob away from a sense of being marginalised and back to their reason for being there. The large clock at the north end of The Pancithon, above the reading-room doors, provided an additional reason for a collective truce: they had been gone longer than anticipated.

"Do you remember what the sign looked like, Kaira?" asked Jacob, realising that the role given to him by Casper Renn was to act as guide not parental figure.

"Yes. It looked like a winged figure ... some sort of creature, maybe."

"So, a creature with wings."

"I only got a glimpse of it. My aunt's voice changed when she saw it."

"To what?"

"Worry. They were all worried."

"And Theodore Kusp said it was branded on the back of Prium Koll's neck; that's why he drew it?"

Kaira and Guppy nodded.

"So if it's a sign of something it should be in here," added Guppy, tapping *Symbols, Runes and Omens* held in her right hand.

"Not necessarily," added Jacob, surveying the vast space of moving shelves and floating Quij for prying eyes, although the only figures currently in view were those moving in-and-out of the reading rooms at the north end, occupied in their own thoughts. "*Symbols, Runes and Omens* covers common signs and omens in the Society's history; it's not comprehensive."

"So, what doesn't it cover?" asked Kaira.

"Unofficial symbols, for example."

"Meaning?"

"Meaning symbols used by Society members past or present that are not recognised by the Society."

"So it could be a new symbol with no historical links?"

"Yes ... or a banned symbol with lots of links."

"So where do we start?" asked Guppy.

"I've got an idea," replied Jacob, reaching inside his jacket and taking out the pamphlet he had acquired from Ivo Zucklewick. "This might do the trick."

"What is it?" asked Kaira and Guppy, looking at the pamphlet marked only with a few faded letters.

"Blindman's Watch," replied Jacob, surveying ahead and behind them for any other suspicious figures. Their conversation couldn't be heard, he knew, but their odd behaviour could be, and if Prium Koll had been watching them he probably wasn't the only one. "It's a clever little thing; you put it into any book as a way of studying the area the book is in."

"Like a listening device?" asked Guppy.

"Not quite. It records books taken out, conversations had, notes taken and the physical description of each person active in the area."

"So you put it into a book to work out why weird people are acting weird?" added Guppy.

"Basically, yes."

"What stops it falling out when someone opens the book?" queried Kaira.

"It becomes part of the book, morphing into the shape and colour of the pages. It then adapts to the book's contents so it can, basically, morph into any part of the book or just form blank pages at the end."

"Cool." Guppy looked at the pamphlet in Jacob's hands, wondering how she could get hold of one.

"But how is it going to help us find out what the sign means?" asked Kaira.

"First we have to find out who's using the sign and where they came across it, and the most likely place they found it is here." Jacob nodded to the numerous moving bookshelves, a rhythm of activity complemented by the elegant array of

Quij busy at work, their multi-coloured forms decorating the vast space of The Pancithon.

"*So...*" Guppy said with a hint of impatience.

"So the reason Ivo gave me the pamphlet is because books have been disappearing recently which has coincided with some unfamiliar faces appearing - like the woman who came in a few minutes ago."

"The tall lady in the white coat?" asked Kaira.

Jacob nodded.

"So you knew something was going on?" asked Guppy. "In the Society, I mean, which they're trying to cover up?"

"Ivo knows something's going on but he has to be above ground in the day to run Zucklewick's, and I need to be in The Cendryll, but there's always the evenings..."

"So that's where you've been sneaking off to at night... to do a little sleuthing with Ivo. No wonder you're always falling asleep at work."

"Thanks, sis," quipped Jacob, pleased that his own suspicions regarding dark movements in the Society had been confirmed by his sister's covert operations.

"So have you and Ivo found out anything ...?"

"Not yet. The people who've been coming at night are good at covering their tracks - but we will eventually."

"So what now?" asked Kaira.

"We place the pamphlet in an area near the lady in white and the two of you come back tomorrow to see what it tells us."

"What about you?" inquired Guppy.

"I don't think I'll be let off work for two days which is why one of you needs to put it in the book we choose."

"Why?" asked Kaira.

"Because the person who plants the Blindman's Watch is the only person who can read what's inside when it's taken out: it only responds to that person's touch. So, do we use the Blindman's Watch to find out more?"

Kaira and Guppy nodded.

"Right. Let's go and see who the lady in white is."

They agreed the best place for the Blindman's Watch was close to the bookshelf the mystery lady in white had disappeared down somewhat furtively. They also agreed that Kaira should be the person to plant the pamphlet: it would be a safe introduction to the use of magical artefacts.

They decided on the M shelf on the adjacent side as it provided a good place to study her from: not quite spying, Jacob had argued. Appearing too close to her would arouse suspicion, particularly if she was linked in some way to the disappearance of the books and the strange sign which was now occupying much of their thoughts.

Thankfully, the M bookshelf was currently static, providing the necessary cover to place the magical pamphlet in. The book chosen was *Menphelin's Fables*, a standard Society volume in the Mythology section of The Pancithon. There was another reason for hiding it here, however: the number of books which had gone missing from the Mythology section of the Society library recently.

It was forbidden for a book to be taken out of the library so the very fact that this had occurred was the first sign of wrongdoing. Theodore Kusp selling Laudlum was the second and the rumours of Searings a much more signifi-cant omen of dark movements in the Society.

With the morphing pamphlet planted in *Menphelin's Fables*, they continued their discussion of recent Society events, the Worble charm continuing to provide protection from anyone paying secret attention to the three, young Society members huddled together by a bookshelf.

"If someone's using a sign that's worried your dad and

aunt, it's a known sign but probably only to senior members of the Society," explained Jacob. "Also, if it's not in *Symbols, Runes and Omens* it's not an official sign, suggesting it's been disbanded."

"Disbanded?" queried Guppy.

"Banned," clarified Kaira, beginning to follow Jacob's train of thought. "So you think that someone's using a banned sign as a statement?"

"Maybe."

"Of what?" asked Guppy.

"A rebellion, maybe or a protest. You say you definitely heard the word 'Searings', Kaira?"

"Yes."

Kaira then pointed a finger at nothing in particular: a gesture signifying a thought-process crystallising. "You said it might be a rebellion or protest?"

Jacob nodded.

"And that it's probably a banned sign or symbol?"

He nodded again.

"So maybe we're looking at it the wrong way round."

"Meaning?"

"Meaning, maybe we should find out about banned groups instead of symbols."

Guppy and Jacob glanced at her.

Kaira continued. "If we think it's a banned sign and Searings have started what no-one's talking about, it makes sense that the return of a banned sign links to the return of a banned group."

"Impressive," Guppy stated with a smile.

"I don't suppose there's a section here on banned groups?" Kaira added, her quick thinking and interest in Society mysteries a sign of Guppy's growing influence.

"Not on banned groups as such," Jacob mused "but the

Histories section should have something, particularly *Battles & Betrayals*."

"So do we go there now or later?"

"Later," replied Jacob just as the shelf they were taking refuge behind began to move onto the central walkway: "The lady in white's on the move."

They walked in the direction of the moving bookshelf until they were back on the central walkway, trying to glimpse sight of the tall, elegant lady in the buttoned, white coat as the letter M stopped spinning beneath their feet, a sign the bookshelf they had taken refuge behind was safely static for the time being.

With the Blindman's Watch in place, it was time to find out a little more about this mystery figure who, according to Jacob, was out-of-place in The Pancithon. She appeared over-dressed and over-anxious, grabbing book-after-book from the L section and flicking through each with no attention to the contents as if she were looking for something inside one of them.

The sudden movement of the bookshelf she was anxiously inspecting made her jump, and as Kaira watched the letter L begin to spin at blurring speed, Jacob and Guppy paid closer attention to the woman who strode nervously out of the L section and onto the walkway behind them. She caught sight of them watching her and seemed to make a move towards them before thinking better of it and turning back towards a door at the south end of The Pancithon.

"She was looking for something inside one of the books ... as if someone had put something in one of them for her to find," stated Jacob as the mysterious figure stepped through the exit and into darkness.

Guppy looked up at her brother. "What makes you say that?"

"The way she was dressed, how jumpy she was; her whole manner was wrong ... and the way she flicked through each book. She didn't use her first visit here to immerse herself in Society knowledge, let's say."

"Did you recognise her?" asked Kaira.

Jacob and Guppy both shook their heads.

"But the Blindman's Watch would have. Looks like we won't have to wait until tomorrow after all."

"Wouldn't it be better to leave it inside the book to see who else turns up looking for things?" suggested Guppy.

"That might be a risk."

"Why?"

"If she was looking for something planted in one of the books, it's possible someone might want to cover their tracks," replied Jacob.

"Meaning?"

"Meaning if someone saw us put the Blindman's Watch inside the book, they might use a restrictive charm to neutralise it."

"Stop it working, you mean?" questioned Kaira.

"Yes."

"Do you think she knew she was being watched?" asked Guppy, controlling her instincts to follow the woman in white through the exit and into the darkness of the Perium beyond.

"Maybe; she was jumpy as soon as she entered the building. Then again, if it really was her first visit here, maybe she was just freaked out by all the moving bookshelves and spinning letters."

"Or maybe she was worried the thing she was looking for would fall into the wrong hands," added Kaira.

"That's a lot of maybes," quipped Guppy, a rare sign of exasperation falling over her face.

"Let's get the Blindman's Watch and head back to The Cendryll before your dad and aunt start worrying," suggested Jacob. "The two of you can take a look when we get back and Guppy can update me at home later on."

"Is it easy to use?" asked Kaira.

"I'll explain how to use it on the way back," replied Jacob. "And just when you were beginning to think your first day had been wasted sitting on a roof, eating ice cream and running away from a Melackin."

Kaira smiled, appreciating Jacob's ability to make light of bizarre events, although it was safe to say that everything that had happened today was bizarre, although bizarre was way more fun than the uneventful existence she had lived before this morning.

She couldn't conceive of life without the Society now: without Guppy, Jacob or The Cendryll, The Pancithon or Periums, charms or Cympgus', magical artefacts and moving shelves or the beauty of the Quij. And above-ground people thought *phones* were the best invention in the world.

6. Ask and You will Find

ASK AND YOU WILL FIND

The Perium chosen to return to The Cendryll was situated underneath the grand clock at the north end of The Pancithon above the reading-room doors. Kaira was used to this procedure now: a hand placed on the brass door-handle before it was pulled outwards and turned anti-clockwise, the sudden sensation that everything was spinning now passing more quickly as elegant gold lettering appeared and faded above the door handle, representing names of Society buildings ... Orium, Leverin, Velynx ... until the brass door-handle was pushed back in as the desired faculty appeared.

They stepped through the oak door and back into the hum of The Cendryll, the familiar sight of the Quij floating above. Returning here provided a pleasant sense of comfort to Kaira, knowing that her dad and aunt were close after their brush with Prium Koll. Not one to hide her emotions, Kaira was concerned her dad and Aunt Phee would see something in her expression which suggested all had not gone to plan with Guppy and Jacob.

Excitement and intrigue, not fear, were the over-riding

emotions, however, as she spied Quandary Corner, keen to share Guppy's favourite place to find out what was hidden within the Blindman's Watch.

Perhaps it was her new friend's fearlessness or an acclimatisation to the extra-ordinary nature of the Society which meant a brush with a Melackin did not create a lasting fear; either way, she was more confident she could skirt around the more problematic aspects of their morning above ground without raising suspicion.

She scanned the large expanse of The Cendryll for her dad and aunt amongst the crowds discussing Society matters, along the numerous opening-and-closing doors acting as Periums within the Society Sphere and towards the vast, spiral staircase stretching to the upper floors. The lift gave no additional clues nor did a polite request regarding the whereabouts of Casper Renn to various people in The Seating Station.

"Here they come," whispered Jacob at the sight of his mother's all-blue attire at the top of the spiral staircase, her gaze fixed on her children. Kaira tried to judge her dad and aunt's expressions as they made their way down with Meyen Grayling: not much to go on, she decided.

There was no clear sense of annoyance or concern yet Kaira knew that *tone* was everything with her dad; Casper Renn's first words would signal any contained frustration or suspicion.

Meyen Grayling had the same aloof manner displayed earlier today as if every gesture to other Society members was resented. Kaira had taken an instant dislike to her, compounded by Jacob's comment regarding their mother's habit of neglecting them, and Guppy confiding the subtle criticisms her brother frequently received.

As Meyen Grayling made her way through the crowds

towards them, accompanied by Kaira's dad and aunt, Kaira wondered if The Society for the Preservation of Magical Artefacts had developed a remedy to make you nicer and, if so, where it could be found.

KAIRA, Guppy and Jacob waited at the periphery of The Seating Station, clear in their collective plan to mention nothing of Prium Koll, the lady in white or Guppy's secret acquisition of the Now-Then. What the adults didn't know wouldn't hurt them, was Guppy's general philosophy. She had quickly learnt that feigning ignorance provided the benefit of greater freedoms within the Society for errant children like herself.

After all, Guppy was neither of age nor of significant importance to Society members, therefore revealing nothing meant invisibility and it was amazing what you could achieve when people weren't paying attention.

As the adults drew closer to the busy Seating Station, Kaira studied Aunt Phee; aside from the dust on her black dress, an unusual oversight for someone so elegant, there was no outward sign of unease or annoyance. Her dad was more of an enigma to read ... a general intensity to his standard disposition, along with an imposing air which signified his authority in The Cendryll. It was Meyen Grayling who spoke first, however, her disdainful tone instantly irritating Kaira:

"Creative Charms will be missing your presence, Jacob," she stated in a manner more suited to addressing an employee than her son.

Jacob, to Kaira and Guppy's surprise, didn't move.

Guppy allowed herself the tiniest of smiles, thrilled to

see her brother stand up to their mother for once. Although it had gone unspoken, it was clear how much Casper Renn's wish for Jacob to guide Kaira above ground today had lifted his self-confidence, evident in his quick thinking in using the Blindman's Watch and how he took charge in The Pancithon. It was almost as if, beyond his mother's admonishments, he was free of uncertainty - a quiet strength taking its place.

"So, Kaira," interjected her dad. "How was the tour? I trust Guppy and Jacob did a good job as guides?"

Kaira nodded approvingly: "It was fun."

"So we can quiz you on your new Society knowledge when we get home this evening?" her dad added, the first traces of a smile appearing around his eyes.

Reference to home made Kaira think of Churchill, her beloved cat, and the memory of lying on her bed last night, wishing desperately to understand the 'work-speak' of her dad. Before Cribbe & Corrow and the green, velvet curtain hiding the endlessly long corridor; the tray of gemstones marked RENN presented by Morlan Corrow, her first experience of a Perium and the Fillywiss Aunt Phee had given her to quell the dizziness.

Home was inviting, she mused, but The Society for the Preservation of Magical Artefacts was endlessly exciting and as much as she wanted to fuss over Churchill, her itching need to learn how to use her first artefact, the Blindman's Watch, was all encompassing. This would reveal the identity of the mysterious lady in white and what she was looking for in The Pancithon which may also explain other goings on.

If Theodore Kusp, a respected Society member, was selling Laudlum to Melackin on the Society black market he must have had particular reason, knowing the risks. Kaira

wondered where Theodore Kusp was now and hoped
Guppy would be willing to use the Looksee later to find out.

"Any highlights?" asked Aunt Phee, now sitting on the
outer edge of The Seating Station, brushing the dust off her
black dress.

"Merrymopes," Kaira replied with a smile.

"Sounds like my children were the perfect companions,"
interjected Meyen Grayling in her usual, detached tone.

"They were," replied Kaira with a forced smile,
wondering how someone so unlikeable could have such
lovely children.

Casper Renn then joined his sister on the outer edge of
The Seating Station, nodding politely to a number of
elderly gentleman situated on the centre bench who
appeared to be discussing the empty pages of No News is
Good News.

He unbuttoned his grey waistcoat and undid the buttons
on the cuffs of his white shirt, before saying, "Well, as lovely
as Merrymopes is, I imagine you'd all benefit from a proper
meal; I doubt a Belly Blitz fills you up anymore, Jacob."

Jacob smiled in recognition of Casper Renn offering him
the warmth and consideration his mother had once again
neglected to.

Meyen Grayling, sensing she was being outmanoeuvred
in her attempts to exercise her authority, stepped alongside
Jacob. "Thank you, Casper but I think Jacob needs to head
back to Creative Charms before they wonder where he ..."

"I'm sure they'll survive without Jacob's abilities for a
few more hours, Meyen. A small token of our appreciation
for today. Hopefully you'll join us?"

Slightly taken aback by the offer, and the fact that her
son was not his usual compliant self, Meyen Grayling
fumbled for a response: "Must get on" came the forced reply

before she brushed past her children towards the lift: a puzzle of insolence and ill-will. They watched her enter the lift impatiently and ascend to the fifth floor, seemingly disinterested in her children below.

As an array of Quij floated above them, collecting discarded books, Aunt Phee stood and brushed the final remnants of dust from her dress and flawless, brown skin. Smiling at Kaira, Jacob and Guppy, she said: "Dinner?"

THEY TOOK the spiral staircase to the fourth floor where Casper Renn's quarters were located. Kaira wondered why they hadn't taken the lift which was both nearer and much less strenuous; however as they ascended, the reason quickly became apparent.

"The Floating Floor," Guppy whispered in Kaira's ear as she stopped on the edge of a striking optical illusion. The floor was formed of the same, intricate marble pattern as the one below, however this one seemed to be *under water* - water which neither spilled over the bannister down to the ground floor nor over their feet!

To deepen Kaira's confusion, a group of men and women made their way across The Floating Floor towards them, acting as if it was perfectly natural to walk on water - not a mark on their clothing.

"Mum says it's an optical illusion the Society founders created as a bit of fun, which proves they had a sense of humour."

Kaira was conscious of her dad and aunt studying her. She wondered if this was their way of introducing a Society feature in order to experience her sense of wonder. Never one to be purposefully unappreciative, she stepped onto

The Floating Floor, shocked as her feet made contact with it immediately as if the water floating above wasn't there at all! Guppy followed alongside her, kicking out at the illusory water as proof it was merely a trick of the eye. Kaira studied her feet, seemingly underwater, as they moved in a perfectly natural fashion before Guppy nudged her and whispered:

"We need to eat quickly and get back to Quandary Corner before we go home."

Kaira nodded in agreement.

Jacob was talking to her dad and aunt which meant he would have to slip the pamphlet to them before returning to work in Creative Charms. It had already occurred to Kaira that, like Guppy's black market dealings, Jacob's evening jaunts with Ivo Zucklewick in The Pancithon weren't common knowledge so the less the adults knew about it, the better.

"Notice how they turn a bottle-blue colour as they get closer to natural light," Jacob said, pointing upwards at the Quij floating near them, their delicate, luminous bodies indeed changing colour underneath the skylight.

The promised meal took her attention away from the Quij and towards the green double-doors, opening onto a dining table dressed in cutlery, plates and flute glasses. At the centre of the table stood the strange, glass object spied at her house yesterday ... the one Aunt Phee had brought to the secret meeting. It was filled with the same green-coloured liquid: Jysyn Juice, Kaira remembered.

"Ace!" whispered Guppy as they entered behind Casper Renn, Aunt Phee and Jacob. "Entry to the secretive fourth floor. What do you think goes on in here?"

"Cooking?" Kaira quipped with a smile as they both eyed the comfort of the sofa behind the dining table. She was looking forward to a momentary pause in events, enjoying her favourite stew with her new friends who her dad and aunt clearly approved of, hopefully improving the potential of getting their hands on some Jysyn Juice.

~

DINNER WAS THE RELAXED, warm event Kaira had hoped for, her dad and aunt paying adequate attention to Guppy and Jacob to make them feel at ease. Guppy was quieter than usual, mildly overawed to be in the rooms of a senior member of The Cendryll, so it was left up to Jacob to make polite conversation, discussing their day above ground and how he was settling in.

Jacob's natural humility made him a perfect dinner guest. Never one to dominate or interrupt, unlike his mother, he politely answered Casper Renn's questions regarding work in Creative Charms and Aunt Phee's interest in the route Kaira had been taken on today.

Jacob skilfully negotiated both, honouring the three's collective agreement to mention nothing of Prium Koll, the mysterious lady in white or the Now-Then Guppy had acquired from Tallis & Crake. It became clear to Kaira that Jacob, like Guppy, was aware of the distinction between the established members of the Society and their youthful exploits.

The dinner, to some extent, was a polite investigation into their behaviour above ground today and, as exciting as their day had been, they hadn't entirely followed Society protocol. Sensing a need to change direction away from their adventures, Jacob asked about the stew everyone had devoured.

"It's a Caribbean twist on a traditional English recipe," Casper Renn replied. "Goat curry and yam forming the

Caribbean elements: my father's invention. I've made extra just in case anybody wants more."

They all did.

The quarters occupied by Casper Renn were surprisingly underwhelming. With the exception of the long dining table and sofa situated under the narrow sash window, there was little other decoration in the main room. Two other rooms were accessible via similar double-doors: one clearly an office with nothing other than a desk and chair, the other the kitchen where the meal had been prepared.

"Not very magical up here, is it," Guppy whispered to Kaira through a mouthful of stew.

Guppy was right: it wasn't. However, they both knew appearances could be deceiving in the Society. For all they knew, the green double-doors acted as Periums and the kitchen doubled up as a laboratory to make remedies. With remedies in mind, Kaira eyed the Jysyn Juice, wondering how likely their chance of getting some was. Although she already knew it made you fearless, based on last night's secret meeting at her house, she thought feigning ignorance the best strategy:

"What is it?" she asked her aunt innocently.

"Jysyn Juice."

"What does it do?" Guppy asked, mildly annoyed that there were now two Society artefacts she hadn't come across before: the Blindman's Watch being the first.

"It makes you fearless."

"Guppy won't need much of that then," added Jacob, offering his sister a smile. "She's the most fearless person I know."

"Want to try some?" offered Casper Renn to their surprise. "Don't worry; it isn't alcoholic."

Guppy was the first to try, pulling a disgusted face as she did: "It tastes like washing-up liquid."

Casper Renn smiled: "I probably should have mentioned its bitter after taste."

"I think I'll stick to Fillywiss," Guppy said, repressing the desire to spit the Jysyn Juice back into the flute glass.

Jacob and Kaira suppressed a laugh as Guppy, conscious of her need to be polite, forced herself to swallow the green liquid, coughing whilst she did.

"It's not that bad," offered Jacob politely. "Tastes like liquorice to me."

As Guppy's performance reached its dramatic conclusion, Aunt Phee got up from the table.

"Perhaps a little ice cream would help, Guppy?" she suggested.

Guppy agreed it would.

QUANDARY CORNER and the Blindman's Watch were negotiated after Jacob finally admitted defeat faced with his third portion of ice cream. All three offered their thanks for the dinner before Jacob returned to work in the Creative Charms Department whilst the girls returned to Quandary Corner and the fading light of The Cendryll.

Released from adult supervision, they were free to return to the mysteries held in the magical pamphlet. They perched in the wooden alcove comprising Quandary Corner, studying the blank pamphlet in Kaira's hands. Happy they couldn't be seen or heard by members occupying The Seating Station, they went over Jacob's instructions on how to activate the magical artefact.

"So the pamphlet's got ten pages and you need to flick

through it, but pause on each page as you do," began Guppy. "If you miss a page, it won't work and we'll lose whatever's recorded in it."

Kaira nodded, looking at the blank pamphlet before adding: "Then I close it and say, 'Clear Sight'."

"Yep. Then whatever information's held in it should appear on the pages."

"And when we've finished, I say 'Blindman's Touch' to make the information vanish."

"Right," confirmed Guppy. "Remember to pause on each page as you're flicking through."

Kaira nodded again, a mixture of excitement and nervous energy, not wanting to fail in her first attempt to use an artefact.

"Ready?" asked Guppy, sweeping The Cendryll floor for prying eyes.

Kaira nodded.

"Okay, off you go."

Kaira opened the pamphlet, being careful to pause on each of the ten, blank pages as instructed. Once on the final page, she uttered 'Clear Sight' and they both leant closer as she opened the pamphlet, waiting for the information to appear on its pages - but it didn't.

Guppy pulled an annoyed face. "*Fumbunction,*" she uttered.

Kaira glanced at Guppy. "I must have done something wrong."

Guppy pulled her legs up and placed her chin on her knees. "You didn't. Someone's covering their tracks."

"A restrictive charm?"

"Got to be."

"What's a Fumbunction?"

Guppy pushed her brown hair away from her face. "It's something we say when an artefact doesn't work."

Kaira sat in silence for a few moments, listening to the lift ascend behind her, its humming noise reminding her of their visit to the third floor this morning: the Looksee and Theodore Kusp. She sensed Guppy wasn't in the mood to discuss the lady in white so, instead, enquired about the restrictive charm used to neutralise the Blindman's Watch.

"Probably 'Invisilis' ... commonly used to cover your tracks; perfect to stop a Blindman's Watch working."

"There goes our chance of finding out who the lady in white is."

"Not necessarily." Guppy lifted her chin off her knees as a sliver of a smile appeared - a sure sign she was planning something. She then affected a formal, adult voice: "One should never underestimate the influence of the Graylings."

Kaira frowned.

"Something my mum likes to say before she flaunts her power."

"Sorry, what?"

The smile returned before Guppy whispered 'Comeuppance', reaching into the Keepeasy stitched into the pocket of her jeans. Keeping her right hand closed into a fist, she gestured for Kaira to move closer. "I prefer the saying 'One should never underestimate the wonders of Tallis & Crake'," Guppy added before opening her hand to reveal a silver spinning top.

"A Now-Then?" guessed Kaira.

"Yep."

"What does it do?"

"Takes you back to a past event: an event you watch in the present."

Kaira began to follow. "So we could use it to go back in

time to The Pancithon - to find out what the lady in white was doing...?"

"Precisely."

"How does it work; the past and the present? I mean, how do you watch what happened in the past without being seen by whoever's there?"

"The past and present are two different time zones, completely separate from one another so although you're essentially in the same physical space, you're not in the same space at the same time."

"So the lady in white won't be able to see us although we'll be right where she is ... was?"

"Precisely," added Guppy again. "We can watch her every move from the comfort of the present."

"You're a genius, Guppy Grayling."

Guppy then affected an arrogant posture, sitting upright in Quandary Corner whilst pretending to straighten an imaginary tie. "I like to think so, Miss Renn. The only thing we'll have to be careful of is not being seen using the Now-Then in The Pancithon."

"Why?"

"Because children aren't supposed to use artefacts or charms ... tends to go down badly."

"So how do we avoid being seen?"

Guppy paused before regaining her confident poise: "No idea."

Both girls let out a laugh, causing a few stern looks from The Seating Station. At the sight of Meyen Grayling exiting the lift, Guppy added: "Home time. Meet here in the morning?"

Kaira nodded: "If I'm allowed back."

They exchanged a friendly hug before Guppy's mum spoke:

"Playtime over," came the familiar, emotionless utterance, the blonde hair as immaculate as the light-blue suit dress - neither adding any well-needed warmth to the cold personality. "Come along, Guppy" added her mum with a pinched smile partially resembling a sneer.

Kaira noticed how she made no eye contact with her daughter, her attention entirely focused on ensuring her immaculate appearance was maintained, and as she watched her friend step away from Quandary Corner, she became conscious of the fact that Meyen Grayling seemed utterly unable to express love.

The return home to 12 Spyndall Street was somewhat underwhelming as, of course, Kaira knew it would be. The house was quiet apart from of her dad and Aunt Phee's muffled voices in the kitchen downstairs and Churchill's contented purring.

The last light of the day drifted in through her bedroom window, casting an odd array of patterns on the floor. She could not have envisaged something so fantastical as The Society for the Preservation of Magical Artefacts this morning, nor that she would learn the real history of the market square she and her dad had frequented throughout her young years.

Indeed, the distance she felt between the girl who had lay on the bedroom landing last night and the one who sat on her bed now was distinct: a change which had occurred in less than twenty-four hours yet could not be adequately measured in time.

Her dad's reasons for allowing her entry into the Society had something to do with last night's meeting. The Sign of the Symean symbolised the rise of something: Kaira was certain of this. A rise that symbolised trouble for the Society, and her dad keeping her close was his way of protecting her, she imagined. She just hoped that part of this protection included being taught about charms, artefacts and creatures as opposed to being treated like a troublesome child.

As Kaira fussed over Churchill, she pondered this question a little more: How much would she be taught and how much would she have to secretly discover? At least she had Guppy to discover things with: Guppy who was fearless and hilarious with an utter disregard for boundaries, and Jacob who provided a calm balance to his sister's impulsive tendencies.

All-in-all, Kaira concluded, it had been a very successful first day in the Society for the Preservation of Magical Artefacts - and it could only get better.

THE MORNING BEGAN with bad news: The Cendryll was not the first destination for the Renn household; a trip to Follygrin's was necessary beforehand despite Kaira's remonstrations. Follygrin's would forever be known as the 'dusty, creaky shop' in the Renn household - termed so by a six-year-old Kaira who had since been utterly disinterested in the 'gems' it had to offer.

'Gems' to her dad and Aunt Phee meant old stuff which appeared to serve no purpose at all, and although she had gathered that Follygrin's was part of the Society as it was situated on Founders' Quad, Kaira could think of nothing in it that was 'gem' like.

She thought of Guppy and the Now-Then, their plan to return to The Pancithon and go back in time temporarily thwarted. The trip to Follygrin's would probably lead to other dusty, creaky shops yet resistance was useless.

She had already been told to 'get a move on' a number of

times and was conscious that annoying her dad could lead to her staying above ground today, so as the morning sun rose above Spyndall Street, Casper Renn closed the gate to Number 12 and marched ahead with Aunt Phee, keen to get his hands on the 'gems' that awaited.

FOLLYGRIN'S WAS SITUATED on Willisp Way on the west-end of Founders' Quad. A narrow, three-story Tudor building in desperate need of a lick of paint, it was somewhat outshone by the two other buildings occupying the street: Helping Hand and Pat's Caff.

Helping Hand was a grander building than Follygrin's, made of local limestone and standing a few feet taller, its most striking structure the enormous, ornamental hand situated above the shop window, opening-and-closing to symbolise the concept of generosity in the shop's name. It existed for those down-on-their-luck, providing clothing, food, guidance and a general dose of compassion much applauded by the townsfolk.

Situated between Helping Hand and Follygrin's was Pat's Caff, a roundhouse also made from local limestone with a thatched roof known for its flavoured hot beverages and colourful bottles of strangely-named syrups lining the walls. What the syrups contained no-one cared to know; all that mattered was the richness it added to your hot drink, making a hot-chocolate taste like nothing you'd had before.

Of course Kaira now understood, walking past Pat's Caff towards Follygrin's, that the syrups were Society concoctions. The sweet smell of the cafe emanated onto Willisp Way as a customer entered, creating a longing in Kaira for their famous hot chocolate and the luscious, purple syrup which tasted of marshmallows and cream and cherries ... but instead there was Follygrin's.

"I know this isn't your idea of fun," her dad said as they entered the empty, creaky shop, "but we'll be back in The Cendryll before you know it. Your aunt and I just need to collect something upstairs."

"We won't be long," Aunt Phee said reassuringly, conscious of Kaira's desire not to be there.

"Okay." Kaira was used to this routine, her dad and aunt disappearing upstairs whilst she killed time on the ground floor, wishing she was somewhere else. However, today could turn out to be different, she thought. Follygrin's was a Society shop, after all, and being left alone to look around downstairs may allow her to uncover its secret offerings.

As her dad and aunt made their way upstairs to the 'gems' on the upper floors, Kaira was left alone to peer into the glass display cabinets. She glanced at the pocket watches, pen knives and toy cars in one cabinet before her attention was drawn to the crowds of children outside Wimples on the opposite side of Founders' Quad.

The contrast in the two shops could not be greater - a fantastical, frenetic, colourful sweetshop and an empty, dusty antique shop - yet Follygrin's was sure to have its own wonders, Kaira mused, if only she knew what to look for.

"How can I be of service?"

The voice startled her, making her knock into a glass cabinet. She wasn't sure where the elderly, ashen-faced man had appeared from - certainly not from the stairs which she had a clear view of.

"Perhaps a little guidance would be of use? The young are often a little lost."

Kaira stood perfectly still, having no idea what to do or say.

"No need to be alarmed, Miss Renn. I am an old friend of your father's: Francis Follygrin."

The old, pale man then offered a bow similar to Morlan Corrow's gesture in Cribbe & Corrow yesterday morning.

Kaira wondered how certain Society members knew her name. She had never heard of Francis Follygrin but reference to his friendship with her dad put her at ease. "I was just looking around; I'm waiting for my dad who's collecting something from upstairs."

"Yes," Francis Follygrin concurred before brushing the dust off the glass cabinet closest to him. The holes in his grey cardigan were hard to ignore as was the thinness of his frame, a particular fragility making Kaira wonder how old he was. "Your father won't be long. My eldest is helping him locate a particular item ..."

"What is it?"

"Discretion in all Society matters, Miss Renn."

Kaira was struck by the old man's grey eyes which were alive with curiosity and wisdom - wisdom, perhaps, he was willing to share. "I was wondering about the things in the glass cabinets ... how they link to the Society, I mean."

Francis Follygrin nodded slightly before walking over to the cabinet Kaira had been peering into earlier. He took out a toy car before stating: "The wonder of uninviting things is their inconspicuous nature, Miss Renn. No-one really pays attention to them, you see."

Kaira frowned, staring at the toy car and wondering if the light in Francis Follygrin's eyes was not wisdom but madness. The shock of what happened next flooded through her as the old man flicked the toy car up into the air, smiling as it transformed into a mirror.

"Take a Vaspyl for example," he continued. "Better known as morphing steel. A wondrous invention because of its ability to be inconspicuous whilst being able to morph into any steel object within the space available to it." Francis Follygrin offered Kaira the mirror with another slight bow.

"Is this for me?"

"Potentially. Follygrin's provides the first Society artefact free of charge, Miss Renn."

"Really? I can keep it?"

"If you choose to, yes. Of course, there may be more useful artefacts."

"More useful than a Vaspyl?" Kaira couldn't think of *anything* more fantastic than morphing steel.

Francis Follygrin reached into the pocket of his well-worn cardigan and brought out a circular, leather-bound notebook with a glass, bevelled edge and brass clasp.

"A notebook?" uttered Kaira, failing to disguise her mild contempt.

"A Follygrin, Miss Renn."

"Named after you...?"

"After my grandfather. A particularly clever invention."

"Does it morph into stuff like the Vaspyl?"

"Unfortunately not."

"I'll take the Vaspyl then, please." Kaira said, conscious that her dad and aunt would appear any minute which would only lead to questions.

"Of course, Miss Renn, although you may be interested to know that the Follygrin can tell you something about everything in the Society..."

Kaira paused, her hand clenching the mirror ... a mirror which had been a toy car: a Vaspyl. Was a Follygrin better...? Would it tell her about the lady in white and what the Sign of the Symean was? But *morphing steel*! The sound of floorboards creaking upstairs signified her dad and aunt were on the move.

"Can you show me how it works?" she added quickly.

Francis Follygrin bowed and flicked open the brass clasp on the edge of the circular, leather-bound artefact. The cover was lifted gently before he flicked through the pages to reveal a letter on each: the letters of the alphabet.

He then returned to the first page lettered 'A' and rubbed his forefinger across the letter, causing the ink to bleed across the page before other letters appeared, forming five words: *Ask and You will Find*. Kaira looked up at the mysterious, old man, waiting to understand the Follygrin's power: it didn't take long.

"Caspor Renn," he uttered, and the pages began to turn, settling on the letter 'C' which quickly faded. A sketch then began to form ... an intricate sketch of the very shop they were in and the upstairs floor her dad and aunt were on. As she peered closer, she observed her dad pocket something wrapped in red velvet, shaking the hand of the man she assumed to be Francis Follygrin's son.

"Incredible," whispered Kaira, fixated by the ever-evolving illustration.

"Unfortunately, I must hurry you along, Miss Renn. Much to do ... much to do."

As mesmerising as both artefacts were, Kaira knew the Follygrin would help her more and that Guppy and Jacob would unquestionably agree: a Vaspyl couldn't uncover Society secrets.

"I think I like the Follygrin more, thanks."

"The Follygrin it is," stated Francis Follygrin before adding, 'Bequess' and handing the artefact to Kaira.

"It's really mine?" queried Kaira, her excitement overriding her need to know what the Bequess charm was.

"Indeed, Miss Renn, and I would advise you to keep it

out-of-sight whenever possible; above-ground people and some Society folk will express keen interest in it."

Kaira nodded, deciding her coat pocket to be the best place to hide it. Once safely stored away, she turned to thank the old man but he had vanished in the same manner as he appeared - timely in fact for her dad and Aunt Phee appeared on the stairs moments after, their own artefact secretly hidden away.

"The Cendryll?" suggested Aunt Phee.

The Cendryll it was.

7. The Lady in White

THE LADY IN WHITE

Kaira found Guppy waiting impatiently in Quandary Corner, discreetly studying the Now-Then acquired from Tallis & Crake.

"Where have you *been*?" she asked, placing the silver spinning top back into the Keepeasy in her jeans' pocket.

"Sorry," offered Kaira. "My dad and aunt made me go shopping with them."

Guppy pulled a disgusted face. "*Shopping*?"

"To Follygrin's, but look." Kaira reached into her coat pocket. "I got this."

Guppy's annoyance immediately changed to shock. "A *Follygrin*," she whispered in awe, reaching out to check it was real.

Kaira nodded, smiling in anticipation of using the magical artefact resting safely in her palm. "An old man appeared out of nowhere and offered me a Vaspyl or this; I chose this because I thought it would help us more. It tells you stuff about the Society. "

Guppy gestured to hold it, staring at it longingly. "It's so delicate and rare: *amazing*. And the old man offered you a Vaspyl or this?"

Kaira nodded.

"Did he introduce himself ... say who he was, I mean?"

"Francis Follygrin."

Guppy paused, offering Kaira a puzzled look: "Couldn't have been."

"Why?"

"Because," began Guppy, "Francis Follygrin is dead."

They sat in silence for some time, studying the Follygrin and the greater puzzle of the mysterious appearance of an old Society member presumed dead. The silence was finally broken by their sighting of Jacob, moving through the busy crowds on the main floor of The Cendryll. He avoided the gazes of a group dressed in green overcoats: the same group who had passed them on The Floating Floor yesterday.

"Who are they?" Kaira asked Guppy, nodding towards the group in green.

"They're from The Orium: the faculty who make the laws in the Society. Their appearance normally means someone's done something wrong."

"Theodore Kusp, you mean?"

Guppy nodded. "Must be. Mum won't say where he is although I doubt they've kept him locked away in that room all this time."

Kaira glanced past Jacob towards the group in green once more: three women and two men all of a similar age ... fifties at a guess ... stern, serious and secretive. Where was Theodore Kusp ... and Farraday and Smyck...? Kaira imagined the latter pair were on Society business but Farraday had been such a large part of her life it was odd not having him around. The doors lining the walls of The Cendryll continued to open-and-close as people entered and exited rooms which doubled as Society offices and Periums ... a collection of figures both distinct, such as the group-in-green, and indistinct yet all fascinating to Kaira.

"Hey, Kaira. Feel a little more at home now?"

"Better than home," Kaira smiled, thankful Jacob had arrived to interrupt her many thoughts, including the whereabouts of Theodore Kusp, the stern group-in-green, the lady in white and the ongoing mystery of the Sign of the Symean.

"So, sis; what's the plan. I've only got an hour today so back to The Pancithon to use the Now-Then?"

Guppy waved her brother closer before showing him the Follygrin, aware that under-age members were not allowed to have artefacts in their possession.

Jacob's shock was evident: "You got that from Tallis & Crake?"

Guppy shook her head: "Kaira got it from Follygrin's." Jacob gestured to look more closely at the circular, leather-bound notebook with the bevelled, glass edge. "Blimey, Kaira; you're one lucky girl. Do you know how *rare* these are?"

"The old man showed me a Vaspyl first, which was brilliant, but I thought the Follygrin would help us more."

"Good choice," Jacob said with a smile.

"Francis Follygrin gave it to her," added Guppy.

Jacob looked from Guppy to Kaira before whispering the expected reply: "Francis Follygrin's *dead*."

"Obviously not," added Guppy. "Looks like we've uncovered another secret."

"Will the Follygrin tell us more about him?" asked Kaira.

Jacob nodded. "Although we've got more pressing matters and limited time so I say Kaira keeps the Follygrin hidden away, we go to The Pancithon and use the Now-

Then to find out more about the lady in white - then we can put the Follygrin to use later. Agreed?"

"Agreed."

"Okay. Let's go."

~

THE PERIUM CHOSEN WAS on the ground floor, the brass plaque identifying it as Fimiations. Kaira chose not to enquire about the meaning of Fimiations nor why each of the doors lining the walls of The Cendryll were all different sizes and colours: the focus for now were the glances from the Society members working in the room they had entered.

The room itself was a marvel of smoke and sparks of light. Fimiations, Kaira gathered from the labels on cluttered desks and various jars of powders, was part of the Creative Charms department and the smoke, and the sparks of light were part of the testing process as she witnessed no charm being successfully used.

The long, wooden tables stretched the length of the room which, like all rooms in the Society, appeared much greater than the exterior structure suggested was possible. Silver objects cluttered one table whilst brass decorated another, the purple powder covering the floor and hanging in the air the other striking image.

Kaira did as instructed and ignored the angry stares and muffled queries regarding their presence in the room, leaving Jacob to the apologies and appeasements. The muffled comments, however, turned to angry yells as Kaira, startled by a strange, yellow creature, jumped and knocked over a jar of purple powder, sending glass shattering across the floor.

"Sorry!" she yelled before feeling the familiar dizziness

return and her arm being pulled through a door into darkness.

THE SIGHT of the moving bookshelves, low-hanging lamps and grand clock on the north wall established they had reached their destination. The Pancithon seemed distinctly emptier than yesterday with only a few figures seated under the clock - the reading room doors lacking the to-and-fro activity of yesterday. Nor were there many members scanning the moving bookshelves, the ever-wondrous Quij far outnumbering those they served.

The plan was simple: return to the L section the lady in white had been scanning yesterday and find out what she was looking for. The only part of the plan concerning Jacob (less so Guppy) was being caught using the Now-Then.

It had been agreed, after some heated debate, that Guppy and Kaira would use the artefact to go back in time and Jacob would keep watch, being less likely to lose concentration or get distracted. Sensing his hour already passing, Jacob grudgingly agreed.

"We haven't got long so let's get started. And remember, Guppy, if I tap the bookshelf, you stop *straight away*. Being caught using an artefact will get us all banned if not kicked out all together and imagine how that would go down with mum."

Kaira felt a tinge of anxiety at Jacob's comment; she could clearly imagine how getting caught and kicked out would go down with her *dad,* already picturing the contained fury in his face: an expression which never failed to fuel a flame of fear within her.

"Kaira, remember to step away from Guppy when she

spins the Now-Then. If you break the sphere of light, you break the link to the past but if I knock the bookshelf and Guppy carries on, I *want* you to break it by stepping into it. Okay?"

Kaira nodded, already dizzy with the thought of seeing the past emerge before her very eyes.

The gold letter L began to spin near their feet - a sign the bookshelf in question was about to move outwards towards the central walkway.

"Even better," commented Guppy as she reached inside her jeans' pocket. "Gives us better cover now. It's just the bookshelves on the other side and the doors behind us to keep an eye on."

"I've got that covered," replied Jacob with a clear sense of urgency. "Come on; let's find out who the lady in white is," he stated as he reached up to signal for the Quij, his hand held out to welcome the beautiful, luminous insects. A simple whisper sent them on their way to the bookshelf containing Jacob's request: *Mantzils and More*. Looking back towards Guppy and Kaira would arouse suspicion, however standing on the end of the L bookshelf waiting for the Quij to deliver his book wouldn't and it gave him a perfect view of the Pancithon. So far, so good.

GUPPY AND KAIRA found a covert spot at the far end of the bookshelf, a few inches from the wall. From here, only Jacob could see them. Guppy uttered 'Comeuppance' and took the silver spinning-top out of her jeans' pocket.

"So," she began. "The Now-Then has to be spun clockwise; this represents the present. It will spin for about ten seconds then slow down and start spinning anti-clockwise.

As soon as it slows down, and before it starts spinning anti-clockwise, we need to step away from it. You'll see a faint sphere of light appear which will rise as high as the tallest person or object within the past event."

"The lady in white."

Guppy nodded. "Or one of the shelves above us, if she reached to look for a book there yesterday."

"And then?" queried Kaira.

"Then we sit and watch, making sure we stay outside the sphere of light."

"And the lady in white can't see us?"

"It's different time zones, remember."

"And what if she moves towards us?"

"We move when the sphere of light moves and stop the Now-Then when it gets too close to the end of the book-shelf - or if the bookshelf moves back towards the wall. Ready?"

Kaira nodded, aware of Jacob's increasing agitation.

Guppy kneeled and placed the silver spinning top on the floor; she spun the Now-Then clockwise. "Okay, step back," she instructed as the silver spinning-top paused and wobbled before beginning to spin anti-clockwise. The sphere of light formed slowly like tiny flecks of dust caught in bright sunlight, and there she was: the lady in white - faint at first then increasingly distinct as the magical artefact continued to spin.

"Are you sure she can't see us?" whispered Kaira, now choosing to stand rather than kneel, anticipating the need to move at any moment.

Guppy waved the question away impatiently as she studied the mysterious figure's movements, moving around the sphere of light to get a closer look. "Nothing," she stated as she continued to circle, careful not to step too close. "I don't recognise her at all; she must be from another faculty but what's she *searching* for...?"

They watched her every move, circling the sphere of light to see what books she picked from the shelves and piled on the floor. She was clearly looking for something ... something she expected to be hidden in one of them.

Jacob took a few steps back into the bookshelf and turned to gesture a need to hurry: they had aroused suspicion in The Pancithon and someone was heading their way.

"*There*," pointed Guppy as the lady in white froze at the sight of a small square of paper attached to the pages of the book with sealing wax.

"The wax vanishes once the paper is removed from the book," explained Guppy. "One of the oldest artefacts in the Society: a gynst."

Kaira moved closer to the sphere of light, fixated on the tiny piece of paper in the lady in white's hands – hands which were clearly shaking. She could also see Jacob gesturing for her to step into the sphere and break the connection to the past.

"Guppy, we're going to *get caught*," she uttered, remembering their agreement to cease if Jacob gave the sign to stop.

Guppy, transfixed by the piece of paper in the lady in white's hands, barely heard her ... watching, waiting and whispering, "*Come on*" until the paper was finally unfolded to reveal five words written in a scrawling hand: 'The Rise of The Ameedis.'

At the sound of footsteps approaching, Kaira stepped into the sphere of light and ordered Guppy to pick up the Now-Then who did so immediately, sensing the danger. She placed the silver spinning-top back into her jeans' pocket, whispering 'Keepeasy' seconds before four figures appeared at the end of the bookshelf, their intimidating presence immediately evident as they surrounded Jacob.

"Who are they?" whispered Kaira as she looked at the group dressed in grey, buttoned coats with a gold insignia stitched onto the collar.

"Bullies," said Guppy as she strode towards Jacob, glaring at the four adults surrounding him.

Kaira followed, wishing her dad was here now to fend off the group who were trying to search Jacob.

Guppy stood between Jacob and The Sinister Four - Ulyn Pavel, Tunula Creswell, Sylan Ryll and Aneesha Khan - returning their venomous stares. The insignia on their coats symbolised their arrogance and preoccupation with power: a power they often wielded cruelly creating fear in other Pancithon members, but Guppy feared no-one.

Sylan Ryll was the ringleader; a lithe, pale specimen with fire-red hair and speckled skin, his penchant stone decorating his silver walking-stick: a Vaspyl no doubt which could morph into any number of viscous weapons. The other man standing by his side, Ulyn Pavel, was much broader and taller with jet-black hair, caramel skin and elegant features which belied the cruelty beneath. Tunula Creswell was the most sinister, though; a cretin of a human being with closely cropped black hair, pallid, almost translucent complexion dominated by bug-like eyes.

It was Tunula who had attacked Jacob in his first week in the Society when he had entered a private reading room by accident. In their role as Implementers, The Sinister Four took it upon themselves to teach Jacob a lesson, agreeing that Tunula Creswell should draw blood as a punishment.

It was utterly excessive and unnecessarily cruel, however the Society elders turned a blind eye and so did Meyen

Grayling. Guppy, on the other hand, wasn't going to allow anyone to harm her brother: even Implementers.

"How *dare* you stand between us, child!" spat Sylan Ryll, his lithe figure and sunken cheekbones as ugly as his yellowing fingernails which reached for Guppy's arm until they suddenly froze at the sound of another voice: older and more authoritative:

"Lay one hand on her and your position won't be the only thing you lose, Sylan."

Sylan Ryll stepped away from Guppy and Jacob immediately, turning to face Farraday and Smyck: two people Kaira was *very* happy to see.

The aura of intimidation and venom shrank from Sylan Ryll's face as Farraday gave him a taste of his own medicine.

"Do you know who this is, Sylan?" Farraday asked, pointing to Kaira whilst ensuring his close proximity to the Implementer caused maximum unease.

"They've been up to no good, Farraday. This is the second day they've visited, hiding in bookshelves and following members around as if it were a playground."

"Following who around?" interjected Smyck who had stepped into the path of the other three Implementers as they attempted to distance themselves from their counterpart.

"Cialene..." offered Aneesha Khan as Smyck stepped closer, insisting on an answer.

Farraday then raised his hand and ran it down Sylan Ryll's grey coat collar, dishing out his own slice of intimidation. "And why would your old friend Cialene Koll be spending time in The Pancithon?"

"I ... I ..." Sylan Ryll's fear made Kaira wonder what *exactly* Farraday's role in the Society was, although she was enjoying watching this bully squirm.

"She ... she often comes in to browse," added Aneesha Khan, her forced smile as authentic as her answer - the lie compounded by her dark, curved eyebrows which danced across her forehead.

"Aneesha, you've *really* got to work on your *lies*," Smyck mocked in evident disdain. "Cialene is a common thief and her trade is above ground so she must have been up to something."

The four Implementers looked shocked that Society matters had been uttered in front of children but none had the courage to voice their disapproval; this would be left for another time when they had the advantage - when Casper Renn's influence in the Society was eroding and the likes of Farraday and Smyck were pets at their command.

Shadows were moving again ... beyond the Society Sphere and on its margins ... shadows with a different vision and a growing allegiance. They had already guessed that the young girl with Guppy Grayling was Kaira Renn: under age children were rare events in the Society and only someone with Casper Renn's power and influence could negotiate the induction of his daughter at the age of twelve.

Therefore, hollow apologies and pleasantries would be offered and they would return to their facade of loyalty until the time was right to strike against a Society which believed that the 'preservation' of magical artefacts was an adequate representation of its history.

"Back to my original question, Sylan. Do you know who this young lady is?"

Nothing was offered.

"Well, let me introduce you. This is Kaira Renn."

Apologies were duly offered to avoid any suspicion of a direct disregard for Casper Renn's authority, initiated by Aneesha Khan:

"Miss Renn, my sincere apologies. We were just ..."

"You were just throwing your weight around," Guppy interjected. "Trying to scare my brother again. I know who you are: The Sinister Four. Implementers. *Bullies*. Well, I'm not scared of you with your *silly* coats and collars."

"Okay, Guppy," said Jacob, worrying this may escalate out of control.

Guppy clearly couldn't care less. "So, no apology for me and my brother? Or do you just apologise when you're *scared*?"

"Our sincere apologies to you and Master Grayling," uttered Ulyn Pavel through gritted teeth, his eyes burning with fury at this humiliation. "I hope we meet again."

Guppy smiled before replying, "You've *really* got to work on your *threats*, Ulyn; aren't Implementers supposed to be scary...?"

"Well, off you scuttle," instructed Farraday, waving the four away as if they were irritating insects. "And it would be wise to heed this fact - wherever Kaira and her friends are, Smyck and I will always be close by."

Sylan Ryll, Aneesha Khan, Ulyn Pavel and Tunula Creswell wasted no time in leaving, their frames bowed in defeat as they drifted away towards the north wall under the grand clock, not daring to glance back.

With The Sinister Four gone, Kaira expressed her relief and joy at seeing Farraday with a quick hug, gaining the briefest of laughs from the burly figure in his familiar garb of black leather jacket, brown waistcoat and black jeans. Smyck shook Jacob and Guppy's hands and asked them if they were okay. After reassurances they all were, conversation returned to more serious business:

"So what are you really doing here?" asked Farraday. "I

imagine there are more interesting pursuits than a library for the young?"

Kaira, Guppy and Jacob looked to one another, unsure if revealing their true plan would get them into trouble.

"Don't worry," began Smyck. "We were kids once; mischief is part of the fun."

"We were trying to find out who the lady was we saw yesterday and what she was up to," Jacob said.

"Why?" queried Farraday.

Jacob paused, before adding, "Because we've seen and heard a few things recently ... things we think are linked."

"To what?" enquired Smyck.

"To something that's happening in the Society: something bad."

Farraday and Smyck exchanged a glance.

"And you think Cialene Koll is involved ... the lady you saw?"

Jacob, Guppy and Kaira nodded in unison.

"She was rushing around yesterday, scouring bookshelves, looking for something so we came back today to find out what it was."

"And what did you find out?" asked Smyck.

"She found a piece of paper hidden in a book with a message on it ... written in a scrawling hand."

"What was the message?"

"The Rise of The Ameedis," added Kaira. "Does it mean anything to you?"

Smyck nodded, rubbing his bald head. "It means Cialene Koll is in danger."

"What are the Ameedis?"

"Slow death," replied Farraday with a distracted expression.

"That's cheerful," uttered Guppy.

"We need to find Cialene Koll before the Ameedis do."

"I think we just have," uttered Jacob, nodding towards the grand clock on the north wall and the figure who had just appeared out of one of the reading rooms, dressed in the same clothes as yesterday, dishevelled, distant and on edge.

Farraday ushered them all behind the bookshelf before saying, "Certainly not her usual immaculate attire."

"She looks scared and her hair and makeup is a mess," stated Kaira, stepping back behind the bookshelf for cover which, thankfully, was not currently moving.

"Looks like she's been hiding here since finding the message," conjectured Farraday. "We don't want to trigger any panic. Cialene is the nervous sort. If she sees us all standing in the very spot she was in yesterday, she'll suspect we're on to something so you three stay out of sight for a while."

"Too late," said Jacob peering around the bookshelf. "She's spotted us; she's on the move. Is she using a Cympgus to leave...?"

It was only when Cialene Koll had produced the tiny ball of light to create the Cympgus that Guppy suddenly appeared close behind her. No-one had noticed Guppy tip-toe to the back of the bookshelf and squeeze in-between the end of the long, oak structure and perimeter wall, navigating her way to the north end whilst staying out-of-sight of the others. She then darted for the Cympgus Cialene Koll was escaping through, determined to follow.

"What's the kid *doing*?" spat Smyck in disbelief. "Cialene's using the Cympgus because she's desperate. Does she want to get herself *killed*!?"

Kaira didn't wait to answer the question, instead chasing

Guppy to quell her mad plan with Jacob trailing close behind.

"Kaira!" uttered Farraday in alarm as she and Jacob sprinted past puzzled members appearing from behind the bookshelves. The panic rose in him as he watched Guppy vanish through the Cympgus to follow Cialene Koll - the light-based Perium vanishing as The Sinister Four approached it.

As figures spilled out of the reading rooms to vent their frustration at the disturbance, the gestures of alarm rose at the realisation of the place Guppy had unknowingly followed Cialene Koll to: Dyil's Ditch ... No Man's Land ... a place beyond Society Square crawling with danger.

"It's a trap!" Smyck shouted to Kaira and Jacob, waving them back before forming his own Cympgus in order to find Guppy before it was too late. "A kid's got no chance in Dyil's Ditch so we better find her before something else does."

Kaira and Jacob were pushed through the door-shaped Cympgus without explanation, the footsteps of Farraday and Smyck close behind. The experience of walking on an invisible surface in utter darkness came far more naturally to Kaira this time as her thoughts were dominated by the fear on the older members' faces as they uttered the words 'Dyil's Ditch'. 'No Man's Land' and 'Mudlands' were the other names used, and Kaira knew for certain that Guppy had made a terrible mistake.

∽

"WATCH YOUR STEP," instructed Smyck as they continued walking on invisible steps in the pitch black of the Cympgus.

Kaira felt something moving beneath her feet and

grabbed behind her for support, holding onto to what felt like Jacob's arm whilst tapping her coat pocket to make sure the Follygrin was still securely hidden.

"It's okay," uttered Jacob behind her. "When you feel things moving beneath your feet it means we're coming up to a drop; it will feel like you're going down a massive slide."

"A *drop*!?"

"Don't worry. You can't fall off so just go with it."

Go with it, thought Kaira. Of course, what could be more relaxing than the anticipation of slipping and falling onto a slide in total darkness with no sense of safety or what you might smash into? Let alone the fact that they were using the Cympgus to find Guppy in *Dyil's Ditch* - a place older Society members had shuddered at the sound of.

"Okay, get ready for the drop," uttered Jacob. "After a few seconds, you'll see the faint outline of a slide and what's ahead which will help you to relax. Oh, and everyone screams the first time they fall, so feel free."

Jacob's attempt at humour didn't have the desired effect as the sudden drop onto the invisible slide released the expected scream. Wriggling his arm free to save it from injury, he smiled as Kaira saw the faint outline of the enormous, moving slide appear, tilting one way then the other, covering the entire width of the dark space they were in. Jacob was right: there was no possibility of falling. They continued to be propelled down the slide at incredible speed, Kaira's screams now a mixture of fear and enjoyment until the steep angle of the slide began to level out, signalling the end to their journey.

"Quickly," instructed Smyck from somewhere ahead. "Jacob, stay close to me; Kaira, stick to Farraday's side. The smell will hit you straight away and your feet will sink into the mud but where the mud ends, No Man's Land begins where one wrong step can be your last."

Kaira reached for Farraday who found her hand and led her out of the darkness into the terrible smell Smyck had warned them of. They had reached Dyil's Ditch: the land of mud and moving monsters.

THE SMELL WAS sudden and violent as if entering was considered an offence. There was no sight of Guppy or Cialene Koll across the large expanse of mudlands, their vision largely restricted by a curtain of fog hanging ominously, distorting what lay ahead. Silhouette shapes of buildings rose and fell in the dim light, some crashing through the mud and others rising out of it like an army of monsters: the screaming buildings as they were known in the Society. The glow of the fire-orange sky could be glimpsed through the fog along with a strange cracking sound; the sound of lightning although there was no evidence of lighting in the sky.

"This way," instructed Smyck, studying the mudlands below as he took each step. "Stay on this track," he added, pointed to a well-trodden outline which represented more solid ground than the surrounding marshland which gulped and belched - the guttural rhythms a symbol of how quickly it swallowed those who mistakenly strayed into it.

"Why can't we see Guppy?" asked Jacob, brushing insects away from his face whilst remaining focused on the path beneath his feet.

"The fog has a particular texture," Farraday replied as he picked up his pace. "It only allows you to see a few feet ahead but this is one of two safe paths and if I'm right, Cialene Koll is heading west."

"What's west?" asked Kaira.

"A place where you make dark bargains: The Spitting Tree. The sound of lighting you can hear is coming from a tree up ahead: it spits lightning into the sky ... an unknown type of Gorrah that acts as a barrier to the underworld beneath it."

"There she is!" Smyck pointed to the figure of Guppy, appearing in the fog up ahead, moving hesitantly and in some discomfort.

"She's hurt," exclaimed Kaira whose attempt to run was curtailed by Farraday's firm grasp.

"Do *not* do that!" he barked. "Do exactly as I say so we all get out of this *alive*."

"She must have got caught in the marshland before she found the path," said Smyck. "She's okay - a few pulled muscles maybe."

Farraday then stepped forward into the fog ahead of them and uttered 'Fixilia' before disappearing into the fog.

"Wait for Farraday's signal," instructed Smyck as the fog rolled over them, muting the fire-orange sky and the silhouette of the timber buildings rising and crashing through the mudlands. "The Fixilia charm will restrict Guppy's movements," explained Smyck as he waited for Farraday's all-clear, "but we need to know it's worked and that there's no danger ahead before we carry on."

A faint whistle signalled the all-clear and they stepped forward into the fog, brushing insects from their eyes to see the sight of Guppy desperately trying to move her feet without success. Farraday was a few yards behind, still checking for danger as the rhythmic sounds of the screaming buildings echoed through Dyil's Ditch.

A second sound then became apparent .... higher in pitch ... a squealing, manic chorus somewhere above them in the fog. Smyck's reaction to this new chorus of noise made it evident they were in danger. He pulled Jacob and Kaira closer before making an arc with his arms and uttering 'Velinis'. The fog around them turned a pale green, encompassing the space they were in. Kaira watched as Farraday reached Guppy and carried out the same gesture as Smyck had done, forming the defensive charm as the primitive squealing, now reaching a crescendo, descended closer to them. Jacob shouted first, quickly followed by Kaira as Cialene Koll appeared out of the fog ahead and threw out her right arm, yelling 'SEARAIES' causing a shard of light to fly towards Guppy and Farraday.

Jacob was held back by Smyck as he attempted to rush forward to protect his sister until the spurge of blood from Cialene Koll's neck and her collapse into the marshland caused him to freeze in fear. Guppy and Farraday were unharmed, washed by the protective green aura of the Velinis charm, yet the sign from both men to stay down as they looked above was a clear sign the danger was not over.

An explosion of sound followed as an army of small, black, winged creatures descended through the fog and smashed into the protective shield around both groups, their blood-red eyes and vampiric teeth causing Kaira to scream in terror until she realised they could not penetrate the green aura of the Velinis charm. Jacob and Smyck were both in position to retaliate - an instinct perhaps - until the small, vampiric creatures suddenly smelt blood and turned to the body of Cialene Koll, her white coat and dress covered in-blood as she slowly sank into the mudlands, crying out for help.

The Ameedis swarmed down onto her, the agents of

death quickly stifling her screams. Kaira closed her eyes as the Ameedis sunk their vampiric teeth into Cialene Koll's body, feeding on her blood. She only opened them again when she was certain Farraday's Disira charm had transported them to safety and the familiar surroundings of Founders' Quad.

8. An Unexplained Absence

AN UNEXPLAINED ABSENCE

The building Farraday had successfully transported them to wasn't immediately familiar to Kaira although a quick glance out of the window told them they were on the top floor of Helping Hand. She studied the enormous ornamental hand opening and closing towards the crowded lanes, symbolising the shop's principle of support and generosity, before moving her focus to the welcome sight of excited children outside Wimples on the opposite side of the quad and Cribbe & Corrow on the adjacent corner.

The crackling fire and smell of Farraday's 'battle brew' (tea with a splash of Jysyn Juice) offered small comfort as did the blanket provided by Smyck; her hands and legs were still shaking and she couldn't rid herself of a chill which ran through her body.

As she studied the fire's flames, the image of the fire-orange sky and the piercing shrill of the Ameedis swarmed her mind. The traumatic experience of the vampiric creatures exploding out the fog towards them before attacking the sinking body of Cialene Koll wouldn't leave her - the blood-covered clothes of the lady in white proving fatal as the Ameedis descended.

The strange quiet which hung over the upstairs room of 'Helping Hand' was due to Farraday's fury, unleashed on Guppy the moment they arrived via the Disira charm. Kaira had initially put her hands over her ears as Farraday roared at Guppy, incessantly attacking her "childish stupidity" and how it had almost cost them their lives.

"We could have saved her. Smyck and I could have got to Cialene and protected her from the attack but instead *you* follow her to one of the most *dangerous* places in our world as if we're playing some sort of *game*! And look ... look at your brother's eyes: how terrified he is ... and Kaira who can't stop shaking. For what!? Your *selfish, childish stupidity*!"

The tears in Guppy's eyes finally spilled down her cheeks, causing Farraday to pause and regain some perspective. His anger was only scaring the children more, and they had other things to worry about: news had reached him that Weyen Lyell and Philomeena Renn were on their way.

Weyen Lyell - senior member of The Orium who, word had it, had arrived at The Cendryll moments after news of Guppy's illegal use of the Perium to enter Dyil's Ditch. Visits from The Orium elders invariably meant punishment for disregarding the policies they had created to protect Society members, and Farraday knew it was going to take all of his guile and Philomeena's charm to stop Guppy's permanent exile from the Society.

Smyck continued to pace the room, repeatedly checking for danger outside in the busy mid-day streets of Founders' Quad. There was no obvious sign of Melackin appearing on the margins of the quad or amongst the busy crowds but it was only a matter of time.

Word would spread that the Grayling girl had chased

Cialene Koll to Dyil's Ditch and fact would turn to hearsay: that Guppy Grayling had used a Recindia charm to force the Searing to rebound onto Cialene Koll instead of the simple Velinis charm Farraday and Smyck had used to neutralise the danger.

The Kolls, once a noble family, had descended into criminality with violent retribution part of their repertoire: retribution which would unquestionably follow. As the excitable sounds from Wimples reached the upstairs floor of Helping Hand, Smyck stepped towards the sink to wash the oily substance from his hands and forearms - Dyil's Slime - and wondered what was truly out there.

Why the screeching buildings in No Man's Land were rising and falling more frenetically...? What Cialene Koll had done to jeopardise her life...? Who had sent the Ameedis and, critically, who was behind this sudden wave of darkness...? A darkness which would soon become rumour in No News is Good News: rumour of war.

Jacob sat on the battered green, leather sofa situated at a right-angle to the blazing fire, his vacant expression a sign he was still in shock. His left leg bobbed up and down incessantly as he tried to warm his hands on the cup of 'battle brew' Farraday had handed to him, the Jysyn Juice yet to kick in.

Smyck studied Jacob from the window, concerned that his shock signified a deeper level of trauma: an Ameedis attack was, after all, a particularly hideous experience. More Jysyn Juice was needed, Smyck decided, dutifully walking over and emptying the small, glass bottle of green liquid into Jacob's cup.

Guppy lay, curled up on the adjacent sofa, her face turned away to hide her tears. She was certain her moment of madness would lead to her expulsion from the Society, and perhaps her brother's too. What had she been *thinking* following Cialene Koll to Dyil's Ditch?

She remembered darting between the bookshelves in The Pancithon, voices and figures becoming a blur as her only focus was the Perium the lady in white had exited through. It was as if she was running on auto-pilot, not a moment's hesitation as she stepped through the Cympgus and into the fog of Dyil's Ditch.

Although Guppy wasn't one to easily give in to fear, it was clear from the moment her eyes adjusted to the fog that she was out of her depth. The fog seemed impenetrable at first, attempts at brushing it away to gain greater visibility causing it to engulf you further, weighing on you ... and the smell; a stench that made you want to vomit.

It was the screaming buildings, though, that made her jump in alarm and lose her footing on the path she had been following Cialene Koll along ... a narrow, curved ridge-like structure leading towards The Spitting Tree.

She felt the pain in her legs the moment she lost her footing and slipped into the mudlands, as if there were an army of hands hidden beneath its depths, yanking at her ankles and pulling her down. It was only her quick thinking that saved her, first trying the Undilum charm with no effect before uttering 'Spintz', a creative charm which formed a shower of light - light which brought the path back into view, allowing Guppy to grab on and pull herself out.

This transgression was different; Guppy knew this for certain. This was different to 'acquiring' her mum's artefacts, different to trading those artefacts in Tallis & Crake and different to sneaking into out-of-bounds rooms in The Cendryll to listen in on secret meetings with the Looksee. No ... this fit of blind impulsiveness had put everyone's life at risk and cost a life. Guppy knew the punishment would be severe, and the tears continued to fall.

The pattering of rain on the window changed the rhythmic sounds of the room, adding a backdrop to the crackling of the fire. Rain typically meant an increase in custom for the shops on Founders' Quad, evident in the sound of increased footfalls entering Helping Hand below. Although Kaira had only entered the shop a few times in her life, she remembered its structure, wooden cubicles lining each wall numbered 1-21 - empty cubicles with nothing but coat hooks and benches to sit on.

Legend had it that you wrote your 'need' on a piece of paper and discreetly passed it to the person behind the counter before entering your allotted cubicle. Once safely seated on the wooden bench, you reached up to a coat hook and yanked firmly, holding on as the floor of the cubicle descended suddenly into an entirely different space dominated by a large, hexagonal counter with numerous workers waiting to attend your every need.

As she studied Jacob and Guppy, both in various states of trauma, Kaira wondered if Helping Hand had a cubicle to help their current situation; an 'erase bad choices' cubicle, perhaps? Her second thought followed soon after. How long would it take for her dad and aunt to arrive? And what were the chances that her second day in the Society was to be her last...?

THE SMELL of hot chocolate woke Kaira who found herself curled up in an armchair by the dying fire, wrapped up in the blanket Farraday had produced earlier. She was surprised to see the room dimly lit by wall lamps and the curtains drawn - not, it turned out, because evening had fallen but rather as a precautionary measure ordered by Weyen Lyell: an elegant, well-groomed black man with a shock of afro hair, currently standing by the fire.

Kaira's passing thought regarding Weyen Lyell, beyond noticing his green overcoat worn by members of The Orium Circle and the rainbow-coloured quartz penchant stone of his ring, was how much he reminded her of her grandfather, Isiah Renn, who had 'turned bad'.

Beyond this, she was far more concerned with discovering if the maker of the hot chocolate was who she hoped - Aunt Phee - because in this particular moment she wanted to be held and told everything was going to be all right. Childish, she knew, but her world had been spinning from the moment she had stepped foot into The Cendryll.

Any naive thoughts that The Society for the Preservation of Magical Artefacts was a fairy tale of spells and charms within the safe confines of charming buildings had been obliterated. This world, for all its fascination and wonder, was dark and unquestionably dangerous.

Smyck and Farraday took turns to stand by the drawn curtains and peer down onto the busy streets, checking for any sign of danger amongst the crowds on Founders' Quad whilst Jacob, Guppy and Kaira remained stationary and silent in their various states of shock.

It was the combination of Aunt Phee's hot chocolate and her suggestion that Jacob show Kaira and Guppy around the other upper floors of Helping Hand that got the three communicating again.

Their conversation was uneasy at first, stilted and forced, until a particular creative charm put them at ease, allowing them to rediscover their bond of trust and acceptance. The charm was Gamas, a popular creative charm primarily because it allowed you to create any game you could imagine: simple or intricate, single or multi-player, formed in streaks of light and energy.

They settled in a makeshift study furnished with a large, red sofa surrounding an open fire which Jacob lit. Two single beds rested under the eaves in the far corners of the room and four armchairs decorated a table hosting an unrecognisable board game. Kaira and Guppy sat in the middle of the sofa whilst Jacob chose the floor as the magic of the Gamas charm brought relief and laughter to the room.

Jacob began by explaining the creative charm to Kaira whilst Guppy adopted the rare role of quiet observer, her long, brown hair falling over her face and her legs tucked up in their familiar position under her chin.

"So," began Jacob. "You've probably worked out that the name of the charm is the first thing you say, so 'Gamas'."

Kaira followed along, uttering the word.

"You then feel a vibration from your penchant so the ring on my finger and from your bracelet."

Kaira nodded, a smile of appreciation touching her face: she was finally being taught how to use charms.

"You've then got about twenty seconds to imagine a game before you have to start again; the charm works by projecting what you imagine into light and energy. Want to give it a try?"

"Okay." Kaira glanced at Guppy for support in the hope this would reinstate their bond although her friend was still clearly musing on her reckless behaviour. "Can I imagine anything...? An existing game or a made up one...?"

"Whatever you like."

"Okay, ummm .... I'm not sure."

"I can start if you like," offered Jacob in support.

Kaira then heard Guppy whisper "Skittles" in her ear just in time for her to imagine the game and for it to appear in vivid, aurora-blue light behind the sofa much to her delight. It was certainly a wonder to hold a ball of blue light in your hand and throw it towards shimmering, blue skittles which silently evaporated when struck, quickly reforming in their original position ... and the laughter came as Jacob attempted a cricket manoeuvre, bowling the ball of light towards the skittles only for it to bounce noiselessly and disappear into smoke through the window.

It was agreed that the winner would choose the following game and day turned to dusk as draughts, snooker, noughts-and-crosses and darts were played, Jacob being cajoled into skipping before drawing the line at hop-scotch, the trio falling onto the sofa in fits of laughter.

Jacob's idea of the Gamas charm had been the ideal anti-dote to the morning's events - a much-needed distraction as Farraday, Smyck, Philomeena Renn and Weyen Lyell continued to confer in the room next door. Kaira hadn't enquired about her dad's absence nor had Guppy or Jacob mentioned their mum, a sign of relief that punishment had been temporarily averted.

All would become clear once events next door were complete, conversation and debate not going particularly well based on the tone of Farraday's voice contrasted with the measured, authoritative statements of Weyen Lyell.

"I'm sorry."

Kaira and Jacob turned to Guppy who was studying the fire's dying flames, a cloud of guilt hovering over her once more.

"It's okay, Guppy. You're safe; we're all safe." Jacob shuffled closer to his sister as she leant in for a hug, a symbol of the extent to which her brother acted as sibling and guardian.

"It was so *stupid* of me to follow her. We're all going to be in trouble now and it's *typical* mum isn't here to help."

"Aunt Phee and Farraday will stick up for us," added Kaira as she poked the fire to keep it alive. "And Smyck, probably. After all, he did help us get to Dyil's Ditch so we could find you."

"Maybe for you, Kaira but I've messed up badly. Weyen Lyell being here is proof of that; senior Orium members only arrive with judgements when someone's broken their precious laws."

"You're only thirteen, Guppy," Jacob said reassuringly. "How hard can they be on you?"

"They can kick me out; ban me from ever stepping foot into the Society again."

"But you *have* to be here, with us, with mum..." "Who is so distraught she isn't even here."

"Maybe she's discussing things at The Cendryll," Kaira offered. "My dad's not here either so they're probably trying to smooth things over."

"No offence, Kaira, but my mum and your dad don't exactly see eye-to-eye."

"But we're all involved in this. It doesn't matter that you followed Cialene Koll through a Perium to Dyil's Ditch ... We followed too and I'm underage so my dad's going to have to defend me. He also asked Jacob to look out for us so he's going to have to defend us all."

"Kaira's right; we're all in this together. If we weren't, we wouldn't have gone with Farraday and Smyck to find you before you got yourself killed."

There was a pause before the morose cloud surrounding Guppy lifted - her self-indulgent pity replaced by a more familiar inquisitiveness. "I just wanted to know where she was going and what she was so scared of. When I heard the older Pancithon members whisper 'Dyil's Ditch' it felt like it was impossible to stop ... as if that place was another part of the puzzle."

"Except 'that place' has mudlands that literally *swallows* people," Jacob interjected.

"Not to mention vampire birds who sink their teeth into you at first sight," added Kaira, picking up on Jacob's humorous teasing of Guppy now they had partially appeased her guilt and worry.

"Or the screaming buildings that take you to-and-from an underworld of monsters, and let's not forget The Spitting Tree; the one that spits lightning into the sky because of some Gorrah curse on it..."

Guppy offered a sarcastic smile to them both. "Well, at least we know one thing."

"Which is...?" queried Kaira.

"Cialene Koll was headed for The Spitting Tree when she got attacked."

"So?"

"So why would someone who was trying to escape danger run straight towards it?"

"Farraday said The Spitting Tree is a place where you make dark bargains."

"So she was going there to bargain for her life," conjectured Jacob.

"But with who?" questioned Guppy. "Who has the power to make such bargains...? And are they the same people behind the Searings, the note that scared Cialene Koll, the Ameedis attack ...?"

The knock on the door postponed their discussion regarding the mysteries of Dyil's Ditch. It was Aunt Phee informing them that dinner was ready and to prepare for Farraday's cooking. Her smile signified reassurance, Kaira thought: a symbol that this wasn't the end for them in the Society after all.

Aunt Phee's warning regarding Farraday's cooking turned out to be a welcome one as Kaira, Guppy and Jacob joined the adults in the kitchen of the upstairs quarters of Helping Hand. They used the sink to double-check they had washed the Dyil's slime off their hands and forearms before joining the table filled with pots of mashed potato, carrots, peas and enormous slabs of ham.

How the adults had come by the food was not obvious although conjuring things from thin air seemed to be a particular quality of this world, Kaira realised. Weyen Lyell and Aunt Phee occupied the respective ends of the table with Farraday and Smyck on opposite sides, leaving four chairs for Kaira, Guppy and Jacob to choose from.

Weyen Lyell was the indeterminate presence in the room for although it was commonly known that Orium members arrived to deliver bad news, there seemed to be no sign of unease between the adults. Kaira could feel Guppy fidgeting on her chair, her legs swinging back and forth - a clear sign of her anxiety - although it wasn't long before Weyen Lyell offered his judgement.

Once again musing on how much he reminded Kaira of her grandfather, Isiah Renn, she watched as he politely declined the food bowls being handed round, his shock of afro hair and enormous rainbow-coloured penchant stone glittering in the room.

If there was a phrase to accurately describe Weyen Lyell, unassuming power may have sufficed; here was a man at ease with the authority bestowed on him. His green overcoat had been removed to reveal a three-piece mauve suit, a pocket-watch chain evident. The senior member of The Orium was, undoubtedly, a man of style.

"I think it's fair to say your niece and her friends have had quite a busy day, Philomeena," began Weyen Lyell, politely declining Smyck's offer of Jysyn Juice.

"Jacob and Guppy have done a wonderful job of keeping Kaira company over the last two days," replied Aunt Phee in defence of the three, her smooth, brown skin complimented by the white, floral dress. "As you know, Casper and I have been taken up with recent events in The Cendryll."

"Indeed," concurred Weyen Lyell.

Kaira wondered if this speech had been rehearsed - a ruse adults sometimes played to build fear in a child to make their point. Jacob, however, saw something else: a familiarity between Weyen Lyell and Philomeena Renn: intimate.

"Of course, you are all familiar with The Orium's role in the Society. We make and uphold all laws, including reforming those felt to be out-of-date or prejudicial. We are seen by some as a symbol of stability and authority, and others as sticklers for rules: 'fuddy-duddies' and other such terms."

Kaira, Guppy and Jacob were doing their best to chew Farraday's huge slices of ham as Weyen Lyell's elaborate speech continued. It was always better to know your punishment straight away, thought Kaira, instead of having to listen to adults' elongated explanation of why you were being punished as if this was supposed to make you feel better. As Guppy's legs swung more frenetically under the dining-table, Weyen Lyell continued:

"The Orium Circle agreed that this matter needed to be dealt with swiftly and appropriately. After all, children entering a dangerous, out-of-bounds territory and putting their lives, and the lives of others at risk, is a serious offence."

Jacob put his fork down and Kaira and Guppy paused their chewing of Farraday's impenetrable ham.

"The question at hand is whether your impulsive act was one of protection or endangerment of Society members..."

"Protection," blurted Guppy through a mouthful of rubber ham, putting her hand over her mouth at the sight of Weyen Lyell's cutting glance.

"We were trying to protect Guppy who was trying to find out why Cialene Koll was so scared," interjected Kaira in support of Guppy's impulsive response.

Aunt Phee glanced over with a 'not now' look but Kaira continued anyway. If they were going to be banned from the Society, it wasn't going to be because they didn't defend each other.

"We found a note, you see. A note in a book in The Pancithon on the bookshelf Cialene Koll was searching through. You could tell she was scared when she found it."

"And Guppy chased Cialene through the Cympgus, having no idea where it would lead, out of protection and not childlike curiosity...?" queried Weyen Lyell.

"Both," added Jacob before Aunt Phee and Farraday tried to interject; an attempt blocked by Weyen Lyell's raised hand.

"Go on," he instructed, holding Jacob's gaze.

"Guppy chased Cialene Koll out of curiosity and a knowledge that she was in danger, and we chased Guppy when we knew where the Cympgus was taking her. If we hadn't, Guppy would probably be dead as well."

"An act of bravery rather than stupidity, one could say," continued Weyen Lyell with a small smile. "Which is why I came here to let you know, that after conferring with The

Orium Circle, we have agreed that a change to laws regarding under-age members is in order.

There are no longer to be any restrictions on what can be studied, taught or learnt nor are there to be any restrictions on movements within Society Square. As Philomeena, Farraday and Smyck have eloquently argued, if we are to let underage members into the Society, then we need to ensure they are fully equipped to deal with all eventualities like today's event, for example."

Kaira, Guppy and Jacob looked at each other in shock, their mouths open to reveal the uneaten ham they had been politely chewing for Farraday's benefit: a comic sight for the adults.

"However," concluded Weyen Lyell. "I must warn you of the severe consequences of going outside Society boundaries without adequate permission, supervision or reason in the future: certain expulsion will follow."

The hand placed on Weyen Lyell's shoulder by Philomeena Renn as she stood to fill cups with Jysyn Juice confirmed Jacob's initial reading that their bond, whatever it may be, was a significant factor in their reprieve.

"I'm sure Kaira, Guppy and Jacob would like to thank you, Weyen," she added as a prompt for the three to remember their manners.

"Thank you, Mr. Lyell," they said in unison, their profound sense of relief evident in the pause of Guppy's swinging legs and their successful attempts at chewing through Farraday's ham.

"Do you think Farraday calls this 'battle ham' because, you know, you've got to battle through it," whispered Guppy, causing the three to snigger.

"I hope you're not disrespecting my cooking," snapped Farraday, keenly aware the ham was inedible.

"Cooking?" Smyck said, keen to join in on the joke. "This fork wasn't bent when I got it."

The room erupted into laughter as Farraday finally conceded he had almost choked on the ham earlier but thought no-one else had noticed.

"I think we need more Jysyn Juice to wash this down," suggested Smyck, his bald head reddening as the laughter grew in the room.

"Do the new rules apply to remedies as well?" Guppy enquired craftily.

"Now now, young lady," Aunt Phee said, holding the jug out of Guppy's reach. "I think you've had enough excitement for one day."

"Just a little, Philomeena," Weyen Lyell encouraged, the intimate tone evident again. "After all, we have something to celebrate."

"Yes, we do," Aunt Phee agreed, and walked over to hug Kaira, whispering "We'll talk later; your dad's been caught up but he's fine."

Kaira returned the hug before Aunt Phee embraced Guppy and Jacob. Kaira looked on, happy she was forming an established group of friends, something she hadn't had for a long time. As the Jysyn Juice flowed amongst the adults and laughter replaced relief amongst the younger Society members, Kaira's thoughts turned to her dad.

Being 'caught up' meant being away for a period of time, and as much as she loved the sense of belonging Aunt Phee and now Guppy and Jacob provided, she was conscious that her dad's increasing absence reminded her of the void left by her mother's death.

Fragments of memories were all that were left of her mother, based on treasured photographs in her bedroom, but 12 Spyndall Street was feeling less like home as her rapid introduction to The Society for the Preservation of Magical Artefacts continued.

Home would be the Society soon: its buildings, people and mysteries ... yet as her Society family grew, Kaira knew how critical it was to have the anchors of her Spyndall Street one: her dad, Aunt Phee, Farraday, the memory of her mum and Churchill - her beloved cat - who would soon be feeling abandoned.

GUPPY FELL ASLEEP FIRST, carried to one of beds in the makeshift study by Jacob who did his best to stay up with the others until he also gave way on the red sofa ... his tall, slight frame occupying most of the generous seating space. The adults occupied the four seats surrounding an unknown game on the wooden table Kaira had seen earlier, each taking turns to keep watch from behind the curtains. Kaira had already gathered that the building was protected by numerous protective charms, including the Sensiril charm; a charm which sensed danger, rendering unconscious anyone posing a threat.

"Like being stung by a really big wasp" was how Smyck had described it.

So it was fair to say Kaira felt safe, allowing her to study the strange board game Farraday and Smyck were about to play. The game was called Rucklz, a game formed of lines of black dots which, when touched, hovered above the board. Once a dot was touched it became 'active' in the game at which point each player had to make a shape to attack or defend their opponent's moves.

Once a shape was destroyed, a line of dots disappeared from that side of the board. The aim of the game was to destroy your opponent's defences until all their dots had gone, making them unable to make shapes to attack and defend with.

"A game of skill and wit," was Smyck's description of it as he and Farraday prepared to play.

Kaira watched in earnest, keen to learn enough to play the winner and aware that Aunt Phee and Weyen Lyell wanted some space. Like Jacob, she wondered about the nature of the relationship between the member of The Orium Circle and her aunt, picking up on the sense of intimacy surrounding them.

Aunt Phee, to Kaira's knowledge, had never had a significant other, although what she did when she wasn't spending time with Kaira and her dad was anybody's guess. It would be nice to think of her aunt with someone, thought Kaira whimsically before returning her attention to the game of Rucklz now under way.

"Game on," stated Farraday, rubbing his hands with glee.

"Hope you've been practising after your last beating," Smyck teased as he cupped his hands around his hovering dot, forming what looked like a wrecking ball which quickly rolled towards Farraday's end of the board. Farraday's response was immediate, stretching his hands apart and then upwards to create a vertical barrier which easily accommodated Smyck's wrecking ball which made its way up the barrier before rolling back down towards Smyck's end of the board.

Kaira watched in amusement as the two grown men became increasingly animated, Smyck activating his second dot, making an elasticated barrier which rebounded the wrecking ball back towards Farraday whose impatient response produced a hammer to smash it, realising too late that it was made out of mithium - an indestructible metal disguised as glass. Farraday cursed under his breath as he watched a row of dots vanish on his side of the board.

Sensing that this game would last some time, Kaira checked on Guppy and Jacob who were both fast asleep, humorously adopting a similar position: flat on their back with an arm covering their eyes. She tried to give new life to the open fire, holding a discarded newspaper over it before Aunt Phee came over and asked her to step aside. Philomeena Renn threw some yellow powder over the fire, creating a spurge of flames.

"There's a trick for everything," her aunt commented with a smile, "Yoomph powder, for example, and now you're an official member there's no need to keep things hidden anymore. Oh, and your dad's been informed about the change in the law for under-age members."

"Is he okay with it?" queried Kaira, certain her dad wouldn't be.

"He understands it. Your dad has spent much of his life forging peace in the Society, including what lay beyond the Society Sphere."

"Society Sphere?"

Aunt Phee sat on the edge of the red sofa, careful not to disturb Jacob's sleeping figure, and patted for Kaira to join her. "The Society Sphere is a large expanse of space within which all Society faculties, buildings and land exists protected by powerful, indestructible charms. As long as you are inside the Sphere, your penchant acts as your protection."

"What's outside the Sphere?" asked Kaira.

"Wild places."

"Magical?"

"Yes, but darker magic."

"Dangerous?"

"Very."

"And penchants don't work outside the Sphere?"

"That's right, so you are entirely unprotected and surrounded by danger in the form of the land itself, the creatures who inhabit it and the people who exist within it."

"Is Dyil's Ditch outside the Sphere? Is that why Farraday was so angry with Guppy?"

"No, Dyil's Ditch is within the Society Sphere but outside Society Square."

Kaira frowned, "I don't understand. If Dyil's Ditch is within the Sphere, why is it so dangerous?"

"Because Dyil's Ditch is a moving monster. Take the mudlands, for example, the way the marshland pulls you down or suddenly vanishes, leaving a sheer drop; The Spitting Tree whose shards of lightning kill anyone touched by it and the screaming buildings, of course."

"And The Ameedis?"

"The Ameedis almost never stray from The Wenlands unless an attack is ordered which is very rare indeed."

"The Wenlands...?"

"A place outside the Society Sphere where a group called the Quliy live: known as 'shadow people' because of the way they manipulate time and their surroundings to remain undetectable."

A mild pressure began to form at the back of Kaira's head as the wealth of information fought for space in her already overcrowded memory.

"Don't worry," said her aunt, rubbing Kaira's shoulder reassuringly. "There's plenty of time to learn. The first thing we'll do tomorrow is get you some items: things which will come in handy as you spend more time moving between the Society and above ground."

"Can I get a Keepeasy?" asked Kaira, hoping that her

aunt didn't enquire into why this artefact was of particular interest. She hadn't mentioned the Follygrin to anyone but Guppy and Jacob and felt a little guilty that she was keeping her aunt in the dark, but for now it seemed the best way to avoid further questions.

"Yes, a Keepeasy is essential to keep artefacts, books and remedies hidden above ground. That can be easily acquired."

"And I just sew it into my coat?"

"It's self-sewing," added Aunt Phee with a smile. "We're surrounded by magic, after all."

They then shared some time discussing her dad's absence - traditionally off-limits - Aunt Phee's memory of her mother, Kaira's worry that her beloved cat, Churchill, was being neglected and what to expect now she and Guppy had been officially accepted into the Society.

KAIRA WOKE FROM DEEP SLEEP, finding herself tucked up in the bed adjacent to Guppy's in the makeshift study which had become their hideout in Helping Hand. She rubbed her eyes before turning towards the red sofa by the fire, checking on the whereabouts of Aunt Phee and Jacob. The gentle sound of her aunt's voice carried to her from what sounded like the small kitchen, and the sight of Jacob's leg hanging over the armrest of the red sofa signified that he was still fast asleep.

The sound of Weyen Lyell's voice was the spur to rise out of bed. Arriving to inform Kaira and Guppy of the conse-quences of their actions was one thing, mused Kaira, however staying all night was quite another, confirming her earlier belief that he and Aunt Phee were conducting a secret, romantic relationship.

Not that Kaira minded, of course; she loved a mystery and to think her aunt was the centre of this one was heart-warming. Her imagination began to construct their secret rendezvous, meeting in out-of-the-way establishments in Society Square or travelling through Periums and Cympgus' to get away from prying eyes ... although what she heard next prompted her to focus more on the present and the very reason they were hiding away in Helping Hand.

"So Cialene stole it unaware of its potential importance?" came Aunt Phee's voice from what turned out to be the window at the far end of the room. She and Weyen Lyell had taken two of the armchairs over to the window to provide some distance from the sleeping figures, a faint fountain of light hovering in front of the curtain: the Spintz charm Guppy had used to re-discover the path in Dyil's Ditch.

Kaira was careful not to be seen, tucked behind the wall at the edge of Guppy's bed, aware that this conversation may begin to unravel the mysterious goings on in the Society.

"Yes," came Weyen Lyell's rhythmic tone. "It seems that Cialene had been in a relationship with Soral Blin who wore it on a necklace, usually keeping it hidden. However, over time, she must have seen it, recognised its rareness and black market value. Cialene was a common thief, after all. She obviously started to panic when news of Soral Blin's murder reached her, trying to rid herself of the arte-fact on the black market as quickly and discreetly as possible."

"Why the Imdyllis curse...?" Aunt Phee added. "Why now? Curses haven't been used in the Society for years."

"Of course his murder remains very much under wraps

at the moment," Weyen Lyell stated. "We wouldn't want panic to spread."

Kaira knew enough to know that an Imdyllis curse was Gorrah: dark magic. Searings, murders, curses, an Ameedis attack. If this wasn't proof The Sign of the Symean was a bad omen, she pondered, what was?

She was drawn back to the rhythmic tones of Weyen Lyell's voice. "The use of such an extreme curse suggests revenge, and a possible link between Soral Blin and the death of Pavor Koll three years ago. The Koll family is a Nordic family heavily steeped in myth and legend, as you know. There had been rumours for many years that the Kolls believed in a particular legend: The Legend of the Terrecet.

They searched for it ... became obsessed with it to the point of destruction. Rumour has it that a fragment of the dark artefact was finally discovered, causing the family to fracture between respectability and criminality. A battle then ensued between the desire to protect the fragment alongside a plot to exercise its dark power."

"Rumours abound in the Society, Weyen," suggested Aunt Phee, "and the existence of a Terrecet is a particularly far-fetched one."

"Certainly, except for the nature of Soral Blin's brutal murder. The Imdyllis curse rips the body slowly, ensuring excruciating pain. It was a punishment, in my opinion. A punishment for Soral Blin's crime: killing Pavor Koll for the fragment three years ago."

"Also a rumour. Isn't it better to focus on what we know, Weyen? After all, rumours spread which become hearsay, forming into myth then legend and, finally fact."

"Stated as eloquently as always, Philomeena," concurred the senior member of The Orium. "Regarding what we know, we know that Cialene was acting very strangely days before her death yesterday at the hands of the Ameedis - something we all wish the children hadn't seen."

"Very much so," added Philomeena Renn.

"We know that Cialene had moved between the black market establishments: Tallis & Crake, The Hideout, finally selling it in 'The Blind Horsemen' to Alice Aradel and her mob. We also know that, by then, rumour of Soral Blin's murder began to travel through black market channels and owning the artefact - fragment of the Terrecet or otherwise - was viewed as an omen of danger."

"We have evidence that Pavor Koll owned the artefact Soral Blin was murdered for...? That Soral murdered Pavor for it...?"

"Unfortunately only eyewitness accounts, most of whom are dead now. Despite this, we would be foolish to ignore a possible relationship between the murders of Soral Blin, Pavor Koll and, now, Cialene Koll. If Cialene and Soral both stole something and were murdered for it, this forms the possibility that what they stole is precious and sought after."

"The instrument of the underworld," came Aunt Phee's voice again.

"Yes. The legend describes an instrument of dark power, allowing communication and manipulation of all dark elements: creatures, landscape, even Gorrah ... which would explain Cialene's panic in The Pancithon..."

"Realising she had stolen something people were willing to kill for," uttered Philomeena Renn, the gravity of the use of curses and sudden attacks weighing heavily on her. "The note Kaira, Guppy and Jacob said Cialene found in the book, The Rise of the Ameedis, was a threat on her life. Which raises the question: If a Terrecet does truly exist and

Soral and Cialene were murdered for it, who put the note in the book and are they behind the killings?"

"Which is where the trail ends and pure guesswork begins, although a number of informed guesses can be made. Erent Koll, for example; the nephew of Pavor Koll. It is conceivable that he used the Imdyllis curse on Soral Blin out of revenge. We all know Erent Koll chose criminality over respectability many years ago, using Gorrah as a weapon of fear before being expelled from the Society. His last confirmed sighting was Dyil's Ditch near The Spitting Tree, forging a dark bargain with the underworld beneath, no doubt."

Kaira turned at the sound of Guppy mumbling in her sleep, hoping it wouldn't suggest to Aunt Phee and Weyen Lyell that their conversation should be paused. Thankfully, the two adults felt comfortable enough to continue:

"And a fragment of a Terrecet would be something he would certainly kill for. After all, the Koll family imploded in their obsessional search for the dark artefact, Erent Koll leading current generations towards deviance and criminality. Prium, Cialene ... the list goes on." The Spintz charm continued to add a colourful presence to the room, adding light to an increasingly dark mood.

"If Cialene sold the fragment to Alice Aradel, we should be able to confirm its existence over time. More importantly, it must be stored temporarily in The Phiadal until its magical properties can be determined. The Velynx will, of course, be its home if the myth is proven to be true," stated Aunt Phee.

Kaira's interest was piqued at reference to The Phiadal. This wasn't a faculty she had heard anyone mention; a place where unknown artefacts were stored until their magical properties were determined. Guppy would know, she concluded, and continued to listen in.

"The added complication is that Alice Aradel sold the artefact to Blaze Flint the following day as rumour spread of the murderous pursuit of a legendary artefact."

"The Blackmarket Rat," uttered Philomeena Renn. "A barely alive rat, at the moment: Voxum Vexa curse."

"The asphyxiation curse."

"He was purple when we found him ... currently being administered Srynx Serum. He should be as right as rain in a few days."

"And Blaze Flint no longer has it?"

"So he says. We searched his premises thoroughly but to no avail. Flint has few morals, money being the only thing he remains loyal to. Alice Aradel knew he would buy the artefact once aware of its potential rarity and value. Unfortunately, Society history is of little interest to him, therefore not realising he had put a price on his life by purchasing it."

"So we have no idea who attacked Blaze Flint or the current whereabouts of the artefact?" queried Philomeena Renn, a clear tone of concern evident.

"No, unfortunately only guesswork."

"And what are The Orium Circle going to do to investigate further?"

"The necessary surveillance of likely suspects, however those we suspect move in the shadows and margins of the Society Sphere. An exercise in chasing ghosts."

"Casper was right," reflected Aunt Phee. "The darkness is returning. Isiah has been spotted in The Sylent and Erent Koll is potentially carrying out attacks again. Guppy and Kaira's presence in Dyil's Ditch when Cialene was attacked may also lead to problems."

"Casper will organise the necessary protections."

"But at what cost to him...? He's already paid too high a price defending the Society."

The senior Orium member then stood, adjusting his tie. "Does Kaira know of her grandfather's history in the Society...? That he married a Koll and 'lost his way', shall we say...?"

Kaira froze, the idea of being associated with murderers, Melackins and common criminals detestable. Her grandfather marrying into a *criminal family*...? Which meant she had Koll blood!

"She knows enough for now. What she needs to learn is how to protect herself and who to trust ... and she needs to learn fast."

"I'm sure you'll see to that," he replied as Aunt Phee stood and stepped towards his open arms.

Kaira peered from behind the wall, hoping Guppy's mild wheezing would stop. The Spintz charm's light fountain faded as Philomeena Renn rested her head on Weyen Lyell's chest, uttering,

"Do you think we are on the verge of another battle?"

"Possibly."

"After all the work we have done, focusing on preservation and not destruction."

"Some will always want to destroy ... will always crave power ... will always want to render others powerless."

"So we prepare to fight; to defend the Society?"

"Yes. To the death, if necessary."

9. Penchants, Charms & Revelations

PENCHANTS, CHARMS & REMEDIES

The return to The Cendryll the following morning was a welcome relief from the intensity of yesterday's events in Helping Hand. As much as Kaira had learnt yesterday, including the Gamas charm, the rules of Rucklz and Aunt Phee's secret romance with Weyen Lyell, the Ameedis attack on Cialene Koll still dominated. An attack which had brought a new visitor to Helping Hand, Weyen Lyell, who had discussed murders with Aunt Phee and the pursuit of a mythical, dark artefact that controlled the underworld.

The Cendryll was the only place Kaira could divulge what she had overheard last night but Guppy and Jacob were not with her now. They had left Helping Hand with Smyck and Weyen Lyell before Kaira. Aunt Phee wouldn't say if they had returned home or to The Cendryll, and Farraday was equally non-committal, only saying that Guppy and Jacob had "things to sort out".

There was no return home to 12 Spyndall Street this time; that would have to wait - as would the new school term. Aunt Phee explained that, in the current climate, being unprotected above ground was not a good idea and since no twelve-year-old wanted to be walked to school, the Society would provide her with the necessary education and protection.

Kaira had conflicting emotions about not returning to school. On the one hand, it was fantastic news because she never felt a sense of belonging there like she did in the Society with Guppy and Jacob. However, she was concerned that, without her two friends, she may end up feeling just as lonely in the Society as she had at school.

As she entered The Cendryll with Aunt Phee, Kaira glanced over to find Quandary Corner, the empty space solidifying Guppy's absence. Her guess was that their brush with danger in Dyil's Ditch and Weyen Lyell's appearance had led to a morning meeting with Meyen Grayling.

Kaira also guessed that Guppy and Jacob's mum wasn't going to respond well to news of their illegal journey to Dyil's Ditch let alone the fact that they now had greater freedoms in the Society. Kaira tried once more to glean information from her aunt.

"Guppy is going to be spending the day with her mother so it's just me and you," came Aunt Phee's reply. "Jacob will be along to teach you creative charms this morning, at my request."

"Is Guppy working with her mum now?" asked Kaira. "Meyen is understandably angry at the moment. I'm sure you'll see Guppy soon. For now, we'll use your father's rooms as a base to learn charms and remedies: charms with Jacob in the morning and remedies with me in the afternoon."

Aunt Phee's unusually abrupt tone represented her own anger with Kaira for putting her life in danger in Dyil's Ditch. Philomeena Renn's anger was, however, like her brother's, a quiet fury and Kaira knew only too well the consequences of further disobedience. Realising no further information was forthcoming regarding Guppy's current whereabouts, she tapped the Follygrin in her coat pocket, formulating a plan to find her best friend.

"Oh, and your lessons may require visits to The Pancithon for further reading, but more of that later," her aunt added.

Kaira nodded, returning to her idea of using the Follygrin. She was also tempted to use it to find out her dad's whereabouts but also concerned it would reveal aspects of his job she wasn't ready to learn. Surely, if he was in danger her aunt would tell her?

"Kaira," came Aunt Phee's voice as they approached the spiral staircase, leading up to the Floating Floor.

She looked up at her aunt's gentle face, the dark curls falling over the open-necked navy shirt with matching blazer.

"Obviously, I'm disappointed that you put yourself in danger yesterday. Your father, although he isn't currently here, shares that disappointment. I hope you realise that Weyen did us all a favour yesterday in persuading The Orium Circle to change the law for under-age members."

Kaira nodded. "Yes, Aunt Phee. I'm really sorry."

"You also put Smyck and Farraday in a very difficult position. Imagine how they would have felt if something had happened to you, Guppy or Jacob in Dyil's Ditch. The Ameedis are vicious creatures; thank goodness Farraday and Smyck used the Velinis charm in time. They risked their lives to save you yesterday."

Kaira bowed her head guiltily, knowing that her aunt's disappointment was always followed by an explanation of the consequences to follow.

"However, I'm also impressed with your bravery and loyalty: not many twelve-year-olds would put themselves in danger to save a friend."

Kaira looked up at her aunt, trying to work out if this meant she would be allowed to see Guppy in the future or not. Adults were confusing sometimes, she concluded.

THEY REACHED The Floating Floor via the large, spiral staircase. Kaira stood at the edge of the striking optical illusion once more, studying the water which neither rippled nor spilled over the bannister. She navigated The Floating Floor with greater ease this time, understanding that her feet would make contact with it whilst the illusion of walking on water continued.

She kicked out at the illusory water as Guppy had done yesterday and studied the Quij floating near the bannister, their luminous wings flitting silently as they continued to collect and organise The Cendryll's book collection.

Jacob was looking behind the sofa as they entered Casper Renn's quarters on the fourth floor, a mild look of frustration on his face.

"Oh. Hi, Kaira. Mrs. Renn."

"Philomeena, Jacob. I'm sure we're beyond Society formalities now."

"Oh, sorry. Okay."

Aunt Phee placed her handbag on the dining room table, studying Jacob with a touch of amusement. "You seem a little on edge, Jacob. Something the matter?"

"Well, it was supposed to be a surprise …"

"A surprise?" asked Kaira, looking a little puzzled as

Jacob got on his hands-and-knees, peering under the sofa. "Have you lost something?"

Jacob looked up. "I really hope not."

"Well, can we help you look?" added Kaira, recognising the anxiety building in him.

"I suppose," he replied as Aunt Phee wandered through the double doors into Casper Renn's spartan office.

"So," said Kaira. "What are we looking for?"

"This, perhaps," came Aunt Phee's voice as she stepped back into the main room, holding Kaira's beloved cat.

"Churchill!" exclaimed Kaira, rushing over to stroke the large, tabby cat curled up in her aunt's arms. "How did you get him in? Is dad here as well?"

"You can thank Farraday for that, and the rucksack of clothes he has brought for you from home. Your dad will be back very soon."

"Can I hold him?" asked Kaira, taking Churchill and lying on the sofa, giving him some overdue fuss.

"A little time with Churchill then charms lessons," stated Aunt Phee as she turned towards the kitchen, musing on her brother's continued absence, the danger he was putting himself in and how long she could maintain the ruse that Casper Renn was perfectly safe.

LESSONS BEGAN after Aunt Phee left them for the morning, attending to her role as head of the Restrictive Charms department. They decided the long dining table was the best place to sit, leaving Churchill the luxury of the sofa under the bay window. Deciding she would discuss last night's revelations when Guppy was with them, Kaira immediately asked about her friend.

Jacob, understanding the importance of Kaira and Guppy's relationship, gave in: "Guppy's with mum whose pretty angry with her at the moment - and me. I'm surprised she didn't stop me coming here to help you this morning. I don't think I've ever seen her so red in the face."

"Why is she angry with you?"

"Because I'm the one who was supposed to keep an eye on you both. I didn't even see Guppy disappear behind the bookshelves to follow Cialene Koll."

"It's not your fault, Jacob. I didn't see her vanish, either."

"Older brothers tend to get the blame," Jacob added with a weary smile, rubbing his face and shaking the dark hair out of his eyes.

"Do you think your mum blames me?"

Jacob looked across the dining table in surprise. "What for? Guppy's madcap idea to follow a Koll to Dyil's Ditch? Not at all, Kaira. As much as I love my little sister, she can be pretty maddening sometimes. I know you've become close but don't worry, Guppy's missing you too. Unfortunately for now, though, she's shackled to mum."

"Maybe the Follygrin can help?"

"Great idea, but let's do some work on charms otherwise I'll be in trouble with your aunt as well. The faster you learn charms, the faster we can get to Guppy."

Not wanting to get either of them into any more trouble, Kaira re-focused on her first lesson on creative charms. She started by asking where she could find a paper and pencil.

"Note-taking is generally discouraged," Jacob explained.

"Why?"

"Probably because we learn charms to eventually use them: in certain situations, I mean."

"Dangerous situations...?"

"Sometimes, but there are different charms for different

things. So, for example, the Gamas charm I showed you yesterday is a creative charm used for entertainment and relaxation."

"So there are fun charms and serious ones...?"

"Right."

"Is there a lot to learn?"

"Loads," replied Jacob with a wry smile. "But don't worry, you're a Renn. You'll pick it up quickly."

Kaira reached for the buttered toast Aunt Phee had placed on the table, wondering why 'being a Renn' would benefit her.

And as the lessons on charms began in her dad's quarters on the fourth floor, the day-to-day business of The Cendryll continued below. The Quij illuminated the building with their elegant rhythms whilst a variety of groups in different coloured garbs conferred on recent, troubling events in the Society - events so rare they slowly appeared in *No News is Good News*: the Society pamphlet which had remained blank for over thirty years.

KAIRA'S LESSONS were exciting and, sometimes, hilarious as she battled to commit Jacob's teachings to memory. Jacob was, in many ways, a natural teacher: patient, clear and aware when his instructions were misinterpreted.

His empathetic qualities also allowed him to remember the struggles he'd had when being taught charms by his far-less patient mother. They began with the Canvia charm which allowed you to write or draw on any solid surface, using it as a canvas for ideas and imagination.

Jacob used the dining table to demonstrate the charm, first touching the table and uttering 'Canvia' then using his finger to write the names of each creative charm on its surface. Kaira watched as words appeared on the polished oak: Acousi, Amora, Bildin, Flori, Gamas, Magneia, Pictal, Pryal, Raeya, Spintz, Trinca, Ventril.

"Take your pick," said Jacob as Kaira peered closer to the words, pronouncing them in her mind whilst trying to guess their purpose.

She pointed at the word Flori in the centre of the dining table. "Maybe this one."

"Okay," said Jacob, maintaining his sitting position at the table. "Your cat might get a little jumpy, by the way ... when he starts seeing strange things appear out of thin air."

"Oh, right. Should we move him into my dad's office?"

"He seems to be asleep now although it might provide him with some entertainment if he wakes up."

"Maybe we can leave him until he wakes up?"

"Sure. Okay, ready?"

Kaira was, and the Flori charm began a morning of wonder, magic and laughter. The charm allowed you to produce any flower imaginable in the palm of your hand. Kaira watched in utter fascination as, after several attempts, she finally mastered the charm and a daisy grew from her hand ... small and bowed at first before the stalk grew stronger and the flower lifted towards the light in the room.

The smile on Kaira's face grew when a daffodil, carnation, tulip and, finally, a rose formed in the palm of her hand. Each formed a memory of her dad sitting at her bedside whenever she was ill or feeling sad about her mum, performing magic tricks - her favourite one his 'flower trick' - only now she knew the magic was *real*.

The thought of her dad triggered a longing to see him, a feeling recurring more frequently as time passed without his return. She didn't want to imagine a life without both parents and though she knew this was an over-reaction to his absence, it was still a possibility.

The Ameedis attack on Cialene Koll had brought home the danger in the Society, as had the screaming buildings and The Spitting Tree in Dyil's Ditch - not to mention the murders of Society members for the fragment of an artefact which controlled the underworld: the Terrecet.

She closed her hand, whispering 'Undilum' to undo the magic spell and moved over to stroke Churchill.

Sensing the Flori charm had triggered powerful memories for Kaira, Jacob suggested a break and reached for the remaining pieces of buttered toast on the table. "We can do more later. Pretty impressive for the first lesson, though."

"Thanks," replied Kaira as she curled up with Churchill on the sofa, comforted by two things: having a friend and teacher as considerate as Jacob and owning a rare artefact such as a Follygrin. It was the Follygrin which would act as her compass to her dad and Guppy - two emotional anchors she needed in her life.

After a short conversation about their plans to use the Follygrin, and three cups of tea later, Kaira and Jacob returned to their creative charms lessons. Kaira was conscious that Aunt Phee wanted her to learn quickly and had placed that responsibility onto Jacob, neither of whom she wanted to let down.

Jacob's gift of bringing laughter to a room was once again evident through his choice of the Acousi charm: a creative charm which allowed you to create your noise of choice.

"Can it mimic other people's voices?" asked Kaira excitedly, her mood lifting.

"Yep," replied Jacob, sharing in the fun. "It can create any sound as long as, like all other creative charms, you clearly imagine it."

"Okay," Kaira said as a challenge. "Do my voice."

"Easy," replied Jacob with confidence. He started by clearing his throat and shaking his head as if he were about to enter an important game - humorous dramatics that brought laughter - laughter which grew into howls of joy as he uttered words in an exact representation of Kaira's voice.

"Hello, I'm *Kaira*; *pleasure* to meet you," Jacob began comically. "I'm looking for my Aunt Phee. I don't know *where* she's gone and I'm very *worried*."

"Keep going!" encouraged Kaira now curled up on the sofa in fits of laughter, causing Churchill to flee to the safety of Casper Renn's spartan office.

"I'm *new* here, you see, and I don't *really believe* in magic but I'm surrounded by all these *strange people* and I just want to go home to my *duvet* and *slippers* ... but now my cat's here and I don't know how he got in or how to get him out!"

Kaira's laughter continued until it was her turn to try the Acousi charm. She decided on a helicopter, believing this would highlight the extent of her improvement after the initial struggles with the Flori charm.

"A piece of advice," suggested Jacob as Kaira gained control of her giggles. "A helicopter's quite hard; focus on the rhythm of the propellers and their increasing speed."

"Okay." After one unsuccessful attempt, Kaira successfully produced the sound of a helicopter - so loud it caused some alarm outside the room on the fourth-floor corridors.

"Tone it down in there!" came a loud voice from the fourth-floor corridor, the frustrated figure not quite brave enough to enter the room of a senior Society member.

Kaira and Jacob paused their entertainment, conscious

that the noise was causing some alarm to Churchill who was still hiding in her dad's office.

"Well, a pretty successful first day, I think," stated Jacob with an expression of satisfaction. "You've definitely got the 'Renn rub'."

"The what?"

"The 'Renn rub'; it means you've got your family's gift for magic. Anyway, let's use the Follygrin to find Guppy then we can arrange a regular place to meet until she's unshackled from mum."

Kaira grabbed the Follygrin from her coat pocket and brought it over to the long, dining table.

"Do you know how to use it?" asked Jacob.

"Francis Follygrin showed me."

"The old man back from the dead," quipped Jacob, receiving a forced smile in return.

Kaira was clearly focused on locating Guppy - the identity of the old man who provided the Follygrin less of a concern for now. "Okay, here we go," she said and flicked open the brass clasp and watched the cover lift gently to reveal the first page lettered 'A'.

She remembered Francis Follygrin's actions and rubbed her forefinger across the letter 'A', causing the ink to bleed into five familiar words: Ask and You will Find. "Guppy Grayling," uttered Kaira and the pages of the Follygrin turned, settling on 'G' just as it had in Follygrin's.

The letter faded, replaced by an intricate sketch of a room unrecognisable to Kaira. Guppy was sat, alone, filling a row of bottles, her long, brown hair covering her face although Kaira and Jacob could still glimpse the sad expression.

"Do you recognise the room?" she asked, an anger rising

in her. What was wrong with Meyen Grayling; a mother who seemed to enjoy punishing others?

"She's in Liabilities on the third floor."

"What's that?"

"It's a room for unstable creative charms; charms that do different things each time you use them. Remember the room we used to get to The Pancithon yesterday?"

Kaira nodded.

"That was Fimiations where unstable creative charms are tested to see if the cause of the inconsistency can be found. All the smoke, smashed glass and yelling was because of the unexpected reactions and small explosions. Remember the yellow creature that made you jump and knock the glass container over."

Kaira nodded.

"It's called a Williynx; it's there to test each charm to see if it's safe."

"That's cruel," declared Kaira.

"They're never hurt. If they flap their wings and fall asleep when the coloured powder is placed near them, it's a fail. If they flap their wings and squawk, it's a thumbs up."

Kaira frowned at the idea of any creature being used to test charms despite Jacob's insistence that no harm was done. Added to this, she wasn't quite sure how it linked to them helping Guppy.

As if he had read Kaira's mind, Jacob continued, "I suppose you're wondering why I'm babbling on about creatures who fall asleep. So, the room Guppy's in is where the powders go that the Williynx test: the powders in unstable creative charms. Liabilities is where we bottle the powders. They're stored and labelled available for future use."

"Guppy's been made to fill bottles full of *dangerous powder*?"

"The powder isn't dangerous - just when it's used to form a creative charm."

"So," said Kaira, stunned at Meyen Grayling's lack of compassion for her children, "how can we get her out of there?"

"We need to communicate with her first."

"Can't we just pay her a visit? Pick up some of the powder from Fimiations and deliver it to her?"

"That won't work. Mum would have already given specific instructions to monitor people connected to Guppy: i.e. you and me."

"But she's being treated like some sort of *slave*." Kaira stood from the dining table to stop herself saying something about Guppy and Jacob's mother that she would regret. When she gathered herself and sat back down, Jacob was squinting at the illustration of Guppy in Liabilities, his nose almost touching the Follygrin. He was also running his forefinger along the bevelled, glass edge. Kaira watched as the intricate drawing changed as he did so.

"I think I've found a way of communicating with Guppy," he uttered, pointing at a small, silver box on the desk behind his sister. "See that box; it's a Scribberal - the artefact we use to communicate with other members: letters, notes, memos, that sort of thing."

"How are you doing that?" queried Kaira as she watched the intricate illustration revolve and magnify.

"This," gestured Jacob as he continued to move his forefinger along the glass, bevelled edge. "You run your finger along the edge to rotate the picture. See, now we see Guppy's face instead of her back. You rub the sides of the edge to magnify and reduce it."

"She looks miserable."

"She does. We just need to find your dad's Scribberal ... should be in his office somewhere."

Kaira paused. "What if my aunt comes back and catches us? We're already in enough trouble."

Jacob stood, closed the brass clasp of the Follygrin and handed it to Kaira, saying, "It's our only way of helping Guppy and, let's face it, if we can get away with going to Dyil's Ditch, I don't think using a Scribberal's going to get us into much trouble."

"And what if someone walks into Liabilities while Guppy's using it?"

"I'll take the blame," said Jacob, already on his way into Casper Renn's sparse office. "My mum already thinks I'm useless so I'll just say I was sending a message to say the charms lessons were going well."

"Will she believe you?"

"Probably not, but if it keeps Guppy out of trouble and gets her out of that room, it's worth it. So what do you think: Scribberal or no Scribberal?"

The Scribberal it was.

10. Scribberals & Secret Meetings

SCRIBBERALS & SECRET MEETINGS

S tepping into her dad's office filled Kaira with curiosity and unease as, despite Jacob's suggestion that using the Scribberal was a mild indiscretion, using artefacts belonging to her dad still felt unnatural. Kaira had already prepared a modified version of the truth if Aunt Phee returned unexpectedly; they were sending a message to Guppy to see how she was. Her aunt was supposed to be gone the whole morning so, if this remained the case, they were safe.

Jacob searched Casper Renn's desk drawers for the Scribberal whilst Kaira looked behind a black curtain covering a row of shelves. She found it tucked away on the top shelf: a small, metal box with a lever protruding from the front and the S. P. M. A. logo engraved on the lid.

"Is this it?" she queried.

It was. They used her dad's desk to write the note.

"So," Jacob began. "We write the note, put Guppy's name on the front and put it in. We then move this handle up to lock it and across to send it. The Scribberal does the rest."

"How will Guppy know when it's arrived?"

"Scribberals rattle when a message is received." Jacob then proceeded to write a quick note, showing it to Kaira.

HEY, Sis

Need a bit of advice on creative charms /// teaching Kaira at the moment \\\ J

"SHOULDN'T we add something about meeting up?" she queried.

Jacob pointed to the three diagonal lines on either side of the message. "We have. We can't be too obvious in case the note is seen. The first three lines mean 'Are you okay' and the next three mean 'need to meet'. It's our secret code from when we were young to get around our mum's punishments."

"Okay. What now?" asked Kaira.

"We send it and wait for Guppy's reply. She'll just need to find some paper and a pen."

Jacob lifted the lid of the Scribberal and placed the note inside. He then moved the small, metal lever upwards and across, causing the Scribberal to wobble a little.

"Okay, message sent."

Kaira lifted the lid and, sure enough, the note had vanished.

"Right, I'm starving," added Jacob and moved out of Casper Renn's office towards the kitchen.

～

JACOB'S NEED TO satisfy his hunger outweighed any thoughts of continuing Kaira's charms lessons. He was, after all, touching six foot and a little on the thin side. They found eggs, bacon and beans in the kitchen and the remainder of the bread on the chopping board. It was during the cooking of what amounted to a mid-day breakfast that they reflected on the last two days' events.

They discussed the drawing known as The Sign of the Symean, Meyen Grayling's role in The Cendryll, the terror of the Ameedis attack on Cialene Koll, hypothesised on the possible whereabouts of Kaira's dad and, of course, how long it would take for Guppy to reply.

Kaira didn't mention that she had Koll blood - according to Weyen Lyell - a consequence of her grandfather marrying into the Koll family. This would be left for a better time, when she knew more about the dark deeds of Isiah Renn and the extent to which he was involved in the unsettling events infiltrating the Society.

The rattling sound from the office signalled Guppy's reply and they immediately left their food to inspect the contents of the Scribberal.

Hey,

Glad lessons are going well. These powders really make you sneeze. Missing you both. Trying to create a charm which makes parents disappear but no luck yet!

P.S. Try Zucklewick's for help with charms. Ask for a copy of *Penchants, Charms & Remedies.* G x — 3C

"Anything about meeting up?" asked Kaira impatiently.

"Yes, now. In Calamaties on the third floor."

"Where does it say that?"

"Look ... the '3C' at the end with the dash. '3' means third floor, 'C' is for Calamaties and the dash means now."

"Okay, let's go."

"I'm taking the bacon with me."

THEY LEFT Casper Renn's rooms on the fourth floor, ensuring to return the Scribberal to the bookshelf behind the black curtain. Kaira was bursting to tell them about the conversation between Aunt Phee and Weyen Lyell.

There were so many aspects to discuss: murders, her family's link to the Kolls, sightings of her grandfather - Isiah Renn - who had gone bad, the trading of dark artefacts in The Blind Horsemen, Erent Koll potentially ordering the attack on his own cousin, fragments of a Terrecet and the attack on Blaze Flint to retrieve the dark artefact.

Was there really a Terrecet - the instrument of the underworld? If so, it would undoubtedly be connected to the appearance of The Sign of the Symean: the sign Theodore Kusp drew and saw branded on Prium Koll's neck? And where was Theodore Kusp...? There had been no sight of him since Kaira and Guppy had used the Looksee.

As they made their way into the lift, judging it to be more discreet than using the spiral staircase, they mulled over what to say if Aunt Phee or Meyen Grayling saw them. If they were seen, Jacob suggested whilst stuffing the bacon into his mouth, they were going down to the ground floor to collect a copy of *Penchants, Charms & Remedies*. This shouldn't arouse suspicion as it linked to the charms lessons he had been instructed to deliver.

Despite being legitimate members of The Society for the Preservation of Magical Artefacts now, recent events had created anger amongst some senior members so they had to tread carefully. They merely had to follow the amended Society rule on under-age practices as stated by Weyen Lyell: their actions would require supervision, permission or reason.

Recognising that supervision meant adults trailing along with them, and permission something Guppy was not likely to seek, they settled on the 'reason' part of the law. The reason, they would contend when explaining future brushes with danger, was a desire to protect and preserve the Society - and what more noble reason could there be?

KAIRA THOUGHT about checking the Follygrin to see if Guppy had reached Calamities but thought better of it. The Cendryll was buzzing with activity and she remembered Francis Follygrin's advice to keep it hidden.

"The Entrinius charm will do the trick if Guppy isn't there," Jacob assured Kaira.

"And we use the Pryal charm to check the room's empty?" Kaira checked.

Jacob nodded along, still chewing on the bacon.

They exited the lift and made their way along the third floor which formed the circular perimeter of The Cendryll. A small group entered a room further along the corridor, thankfully not glancing back at the pair hovering outside Calamaties. With a mouth still full of bacon, Jacob put his ear to the door and whispered 'Pryal', jumping back when it creaked open, the smiling face of Guppy peering out.

Kaira and Guppy hugged as she ushered them into the room and locked the door.

"Did mum tell you where I was?" Guppy asked.

"No, the Follygrin," Kaira said, tapping her pocket.

"Of course. Well, I don't know how long we've got; I think mum's got some of her spies to check up on me. I'll just say I had to rush to the toilet - bad case of the runs."

"Charming," added Jacob.

"Anyway, you said you needed to meet. We're not really here to talk about charms, are we?"

"No," replied Kaira, glancing at the cabinets lined with artefacts and the empty Parasil on a table by the door. "We wanted to make sure you were okay, but I've also got something to tell you both."

Jacob paused: "Is your dad back...?"

"No."

"Sorry, Kaira; I thought you meant..."

"It's fine, honestly. I wish he was but it's something else - something I heard last night at Helping Hand when you were both asleep..."

"About all the crazy things going on in the Society?" Guppy conjectured, sitting in one of the leather chairs.

"Yes, about that."

"Have you heard *No News is Good News* is live again? The Society pamphlet's been blank for over thirty years: a sure sign something's going on."

"What did you hear, Kaira?" prompted Jacob who had taken up a position by the door, listening for movement outside. He would use a Cympgus to get them out if they were in danger of being caught. Philomeena Renn would be in Restrictive Charms for another half-an-hour, giving them enough time to discuss things before returning to their respective rooms.

"Okay," began Kaira, standing by the cabinet closest to the door. "It's about Cialene Koll ... why she was attacked."

"Go on," Guppy prompted, suddenly immersed in the deepening mystery.

"Okay, well my aunt and Weyen Lyell were sitting by the window talking last night. They obviously thought we were all asleep but I woke up and heard their voices."

Guppy gestured to get to the point quickly.

"Sorry. They said that Cialene Koll was attacked by the Ameedis because she unknowingly stole something that was valuable: *really* valuable."

"Did they say what it was?" asked Guppy.

"A fragment of a Terrecet."

Jacob turned his attention away from the door momentarily: "Instrument of the underworld."

"Stole it from who?" asked Guppy.

"Soral Blin who, apparently, murdered Pavor Koll for it, maybe knowing what it was. Apparently the Koll family were obsessed with finding it, believing it was real."

"Wow," remarked Jacob. "So Cialene Koll was attacked by the Ameedis because she stole an underworld artefact."

"Okay, take it easy, big brother," interjected Guppy. "The Terrecet is more a fairy tale than reality. What else, Kaira?"

"Well, they mentioned someone called Soral Blin. Apparently, he was killed by the Imdyllis curse a few weeks ago. *Very* top secret."

"What!?" cried Jacob before putting his hand over his mouth to regain control. He lowered his voice before saying, "*No-one* uses the Imdyllis curse anymore."

"It gets worse," continued Kaira. "The last person to buy it was Blaze Flint. The Blackmarket Rat, they called him, and someone used the Voxum Vexa curse on him: he's barely alive."

Guppy's expression darkened momentarily - as if she were battling her fear. "Like Jacob said, Gorrah hasn't been used for years ever since the Society banned anyone expressing even an interest in it. So who's got the artefact now: this fragment...?"

"No-one knows. Looks like Blaze Flint doesn't know who attacked him or won't say."

"Well," began Guppy. "We should find out more about the Terrecet ... look into the legend in more detail. There might be something in it that provides clues: how it was created, the family who originally owned it, how it was used and if it was destroyed. Two days ago, we thought The Sign of the Symean might be a symbol of a banned group based on the fact Theodore Kusp saw it branded on Prium Koll's neck, but if a fragment of a Terrecet really has been found then maybe it's bigger than we thought."

"You mean the sign could link to the Terrecet in some way?" suggested Jacob.

"Yes, perhaps," replied Guppy before uttering 'Comeuppance' and digging into the pocket of her jeans. She pulled out the small book Kaira had first seen during their first meeting in Quandary Corner: *Symbols, Runes and Omens.* "I remember saying that there's no reference to the sign in here," she said, motioning towards the battered book. "Now, with what we know about the Terrecet and how it controls the underworld, including creatures, maybe we've been looking in the wrong place."

"You think the Symean still might be a creature?" queried Kaira.

"It would make sense, wouldn't it? Whoever's desperate to get their hands on the fragment wants to control the underworld..."

"And all underworld creatures," added Kaira. "So the Symean could be a powerful underworld creature that would be controlled by a Terrecet."

"And the branding on Prium Koll's neck isn't necessarily the sign of a banned group or a new one, but the mark of someone who believes in the existence of the Terrecet and is hunting for it ... which would also explain why he was secretly buying Laudlum from Theodore Kusp because it's the remedy that lengthens the life of people who've used Gorrah."

"If people are looking for the same thing, I'd say that made them a group," stated Jacob.

"Not if they're willing to kill each other for it," countered Guppy, brooding on the plan formulating in her ever-inquisitive mind.

"So if it does exist...?" asked Kaira.

"If it does, a race has begun to find the other fragments. Black market rats like Blaze Flint and thieves like Cialene Koll who would trade anything to the highest bidder. Gorrah's bad, Kaira ... turns people bad quickly, taking away their guilt and kindness. You've only got to look at the Melackin to see how easily people can go bad in the Society, misusing magic for greed or power. Revenance Remedy stops Melackin from getting worse but there will always be evil out there: ex-Society members outside the Sphere, getting sucked into the darkness."

"Like Erent Koll," Kaira said. "They think he might have killed Soral Blin who killed Pavor Koll for the fragment years ago. They also think he might be behind the attack on Cialene Koll, maybe thinking she still had the fragment."

"His *own cousin*...?" uttered Jacob in shock.

"We need to find out more about the Terrecet," stated Guppy.

The conversation paused momentarily as each considered the information at hand and Guppy's plan to dig deeper. It was Jacob who voiced his concerns regarding his sister's plan:

"Do you really think it's a good idea for us to go snooping around, Guppy? If these attacks are connected and people are starting to use Gorrah again, I say we focus on staying underground. Also, Kaira needs to learn protective and defensive charms before we put ourselves in anymore danger."

"Well, I wasn't suggesting going back to Dyil's Ditch," quipped Guppy a little sternly. "Do you think you can handle a visit to the *library*...? "

Jacob eyed his sister with mild disdain, not appreciating his courage being called into question.

Guppy continued: "If we can make the link between the Terrecet, the Koll family's pursuit of it and confirm the Symean is a creature, we'll know if the fragment is potentially real. If it turns out it might actually exist, I'll bet anything the branding on Prium Koll's neck is a symbol used by those hunting the Terrecet."

"But how do we get to The Pancithon without being seen?" Kaira questioned. "My aunt's got me doing lessons in the mornings and afternoons."

"And I'm stuck in a room filling bottles with powder, so we need a plan. What about a midnight trip?"

"A *what*?" Jacob's increasingly pale complexion and wide-eyed expression was mildly comical to his sister who rarely experienced profound fear.

Kaira was less frightened than concerned that this was going to lead them to another wild wasteland. "Shouldn't we just wait until things calm down with your mum?"

Guppy looked at them both, before conjecturing, "Do you think that's likely to happen anytime soon? Look, we can do one of two things, I suppose. We can sit on our hands and do as we're told, waiting for other attacks to happen, or we can try to help our parents sort out what's going on. Isn't that why The Orium Circle changed the rules for under-age members ... because they need as much help as possible?"

"And if we get caught?" queried Jacob.

"We'll say we had *reason* to believe we could prove the existence of The Terrecet," interjected Kaira, subtly reminding Jacob of their earlier discussion on how to bend the new rule regarding under-age members.

Jacob sighed, realising he was losing this battle. "You think this is a good idea, Kaira?"

"I think it's a *terrible* idea," she replied with a fleeting smile. "But I want to find out more about the Terrecet because I think my dad's trying to stop whatever's going on too."

"And we either help or hide," added Guppy. "No-one's going to be checking on us at midnight. We head to The Pancithon, cram through *Maud's Manual of Mythological Creatures* then *Mantzils & More* and head back. In the meantime, I'll try to use the Looksee to find out what mum's up to. She couldn't wait to get rid of me this morning which isn't unusual, but it was more her shifty behaviour - as if she had some secret."

"You think mum knows what's going on?" questioned Jacob. "Knows more than Kaira heard, I mean?"

"Maybe," replied Guppy. "Oh, which reminds me, Theodore Kusp is back in Restrictive Charms. I think Kaira's aunt pulled a few strings to let 'the Laudlum incident' pass, as mum likes to call it."

"One more thing," Kaira declared. "My aunt mentioned a place I haven't heard of before ... where they would store a potential Terrecet fragment to assess its magical properties: The Phiadal."

"Where bovies are stored," uttered Jacob.

"Bovies?"

"Artefacts with complex magical properties."

"Where is it ... The Phiadal?" Kaira asked.

"Another mystery," Jacob added. "Most people pretend it doesn't exist. Mum won't tell us, and you just get glared at if you ask."

They all turned towards the door at the sound of footsteps.

"Tell me that's not mum's voice," Guppy said, jolting out of the chair.

Jacob rushed to the door, peering through the key hole. "It's *her*," he whispered, "with The Sinister Four. They're *coming in!*"

Guppy was already two steps ahead of Jacob, uttering 'Cympgus' and then 'Whereabouts', watching as the small ball of light from her penchant stone formed an emergency exit. The light-based Perium took the shape of a curtain this time, all three vanishing safely behind it before the door opened.

Meyen Grayling entered with Ulyn Pavel, Tunula Creswell, Sylan Ryll and Aneesha Khan. Each studied the room momentarily, Aneesha Khan sniffing at something invisible:

"Can anyone else smell bacon?"

THE CYMPGUS TRANSPORTED them back to Casper Renn's quarters which were still, thankfully, absent of Philomeena Renn's presence. Sensing that the morning had passed and her aunt would be here any minute, Kaira urged Guppy to return to the third floor before she was seen. Guppy thought of using the Perium in Casper Renn's office but decided against it. After all, appearing in a room with the risk of others present didn't exactly remove suspicion.

The lift was the safest and most natural option, they finally agreed, and if she was seen and questioned, Guppy would say she was missing her brother and replying to his request for help on creative charms - the note Jacob had written to her proof of this. For now, though, it was time for Kaira to learn remedies with her aunt, Jacob to return to his role in Creative Charms and Guppy to the powders which made her sneeze.

Before they went their separate ways, they planned their midnight jaunt to The Pancithon. Since none of them had returned home last night after their brush with danger in Dyil's Ditch, it was unlikely they would return this evening, suggested Kaira. Guppy and Kaira could ask to share the spare bedroom in Aunt Phee's quarters and Jacob would go for one of his evening trips to visit Ivo Zucklewick - something he had been doing recently so nothing out-of-the-ordinary.

Meyen Grayling had little authority over her son, who was now eighteen, and Kaira was confident she could work her charm on Aunt Phee, saying she was missing her dad (which she was) and needed company, so the emotion would be genuine.

Finally, they agreed that, if caught at any point, they would each take the blame, saying they had given each other the idea. The less the adults suspected collective plotting of new intrigue and adventure, the more lenient the punishment would be.

"So, midnight at The Seating Station," Guppy clarified, hugging them both before returning to the lift and the bottling of strange powders on the third floor.

As Guppy left for the lift and Philomeena Renn prepared her return to the fourth floor, Meyen Grayling locked the door of the room her daughter and son had just been in. She gestured for Ulyn Pavel, Tunula Creswell, Sylan Ryll and Aneesha Khan to occupy the four leather chairs surrounding the circular wooden table.

She tapped the empty Parasil three times, watching as a sea-blue liquid appeared within it – a remedy used to ensure honesty: Telynin. Once consumed, the speaker could not lie nor deviate from the truth. Meyen Grayling, it seemed, knew The Sinister Four well.

Dressed in her favourite colour of light blue, she had used the ruse of inviting The Sinister Four to The Cendryll to follow up on yesterday's events in The Pancithon. She was adopting the facade of concerned mother, something she struggled to pull off at the best of times.

The real reason she had invited the four Implementers was somewhat darker: to collect the fragment of the Terrecet retrieved from Blaze Flint. There were many questions to ask and points to clarify, and the Telynin would ensure absolute truth ... for no-one could know of this dark trade nor where the fragment would be secretly stored.

Each party knew that Calamaties was a room rarely used and that its name implied its general function - discussions regarding disastrous events. It was safe to say that yesterday's events in The Pancithon and Dyil's Ditch fit adequately into this category.

Also, the DO NOT DISTURB sign on the door formed using the Canvia charm would ensure privacy or, at least, a polite knock to inform them of an emergency. The final layer of secrecy was added by the Worble charm which would distort their voices, stopping any attempt to listen in, and once the Telynin remedy had been handed out, Meyen Grayling's need for secrecy and control would be complete.

"I take it you have it?" she began, gesturing for The Sinister Four to drink the Telynin which they did without complaint. Each kept their grey, overcoats buttoned, the gold insignia stitched onto their coat collars a reminder of their roles as Implementers in The Pancithon.

Tunula Creswell nodded, her pallid, translucent skin a stark contrast to her bulging eyes, "Safely stored away."

"Away?" queried Meyen Grayling, her face flushing with anger.

"Now now, Meyen," Tunula Creswell teased. "Merely a mild attempt at humour; it's safely stored among us. We simply need to confirm you have kept *your* side of the bargain?"

The mother of Jacob and Guppy Grayling tapped her handbag: "Of course. I gave my word."

Sylan Ryll then spoke, the penchant stone on the handle of his silver walking-stick glimmering in the light. "Perhaps we should prove we each have what was promised...?"

"Agreed," declared Aneesha Khan coldly, her wide smile at odds with her total lack of warmth.

"There," stated Meyen Grayling as she took out a black pouch jingling with the familiar sound of Kyals. "10,000, as agreed."

Tunula Creswell's cold, green eyes glistened. "You've been industrious, Meyen."

Dismissing the sarcasm, Meyen Grayling crossed her arms and legs, waiting in silence.

Ulyn Pavel then stood slowly, his broad frame mildly restricted within the grey overcoat. He brushed his jet-black hair into place before glancing at his reflection in the glass cabinets lined with artefacts. "The Legend of the Terrecet," he whispered dramatically, taking a leather pouch out of his pocket and placing it onto the circular table.

The Sinister Four each stood and retreated a little as the pouch began to move on the table as if its contents were a creature struggling to escape. The movement became increasingly frenetic, the sound of metal knocking on the wood mildly alarming to everyone present.

"They say it reacts to each act of Gorrah," Sylan Ryll offered as explanation. "The darker the Gorrah, the greater the reaction ..."

"As if it's communicating with the underworld," added Tunula Creswell in wonder.

"Like a fish out of water, isn't it," uttered Aneesha Khan, the smile having now vanished, "trying to wriggle its way back to the darkness. Imagine if it really *is* what many are suggesting..."

"The very reason it must be contained," stated Meyen Grayling as she stepped gently towards it, uncertain whether it was safe to pick up. "And regarding Blaze Flint; you did as instructed ...?"

"Exactly as instructed," replied Sylan Ryll. "The Removilis charm was used to ensure he has no memory of our visit or the artefact being taken. The Voxum Vexa curse was used by whoever got to him after we had gone, clearly furious they had missed out on acquiring the artefact."

"Rumour is Erent Koll delivered the curse."

"Perhaps ... Erent, Prium, Isiah Renn. There are a number who seek it ... have sought it for many years."

"And you weren't seen?"

"Of course not. This is our speciality, after all."

"Except for the mess with Cialene. The instruction was

to keep her under close guard until we could learn more; instead she ends up dead..."

"Clearly not *our* doing. Everything was in place but then *your children* and the Renn girl started meddling ... turning up in The Pancithon, acting suspiciously and spying on Cialene."

Meyen Grayling frowned in mild contempt: "So, two girls and an adolescent boy scared her into escaping to Dyil's Ditch...?"

"No," interjected Ulyn Pavel. "We're saying that we have fulfilled *our* part of the bargain. A Scribberal was used to send an anonymous message to Cialene regarding her theft of the fragment and the consequences – to be found hidden in a book in The Pancithon. The 'Rise of the Ameedis' note was placed in the allocated book in the L section, as planned, followed by our offer of shelter and protection once she had found it.

Everything was going to plan; we had created the necessary fear to make her scared of going above ground. She was kept under close guard and we had planned to interrogate her regarding Soral Blin and what he'd learnt about the fragment before killing Pavor Koll for it ... but then *your son and daughter*, and Kaira Renn re-appeared, going to the very shelf we had placed the note in. When we went to check what they were up to, Farraday and Smyck appeared. Cialene must have seen all this and, in her paranoid state, assumed she was going to be arrested so decided to make a run for it."

The atmosphere changed in the room as The Sinister Four, mildly affronted by the suggestion of incompetence, withdrew into a silent stand off.

"Of course," Meyen Grayling said, sensing the deal was on the verge of collapse. "My apologies. Your skills are well-known; I shouldn't have questioned your execution of the plan."

A collection of delicate movements followed as Aneesha Khan stood to count the 10,000 Kyals and Meyen Grayling, in turn, nervously picked up the leather pouch, placing it gently into her light-blue handbag.

"Well, I think our business here is done," uttered Guppy and Jacob's mother. "And before we go, I don't think I need to remind you of the consequences of uttering a single word about our transaction: immediate expulsion and all traces of your interaction with this object removed from memory."

"You have our word," Tunula Creswell declared with an insincere bow of honour and loyalty, qualities none of The Sinister Four possessed.

"And should you think you 'have one over me', as some like to say, I will simply deny it and ensure everyone connected to you loses everything and is banished beyond the Society Sphere to The Wenlands: land of the shadow-people who, I'm told, are *vicious* and *without mercy*."

This final point was not lost on the four whose general demeanour of arrogance and detachment changed momentarily to fear. With her authority re-established, Meyen Grayling gestured it was time to leave, uttering 'Undilum' to undo the Worble charm now the secret deal was done. The group made their way down to the ground floor of The Cendryll via the spiral staircase, returning to inconspicuous Society chatter, the effervescent Quij illuminating the way.

Once certain the four had returned to The Pancithon via a ground-floor Perium, Meyen Grayling made her way back to her quarters in the farthest reaches of the fifth floor. She entered and locked the blue double-doors, closing the curtains before sitting at her large desk. The plan to reclaim the fragment from Blaze Flint via dubious means broke numerous Society laws and would lead to her immediate expulsion were it ever to become known. It was, in her mind at least, a risk worth taking.

As her handbag jerked across her desk, signifying the increasingly violent movements of the artefact inside, Meyen Grayling was convinced that what Soral Blin and Cialene Koll had stolen and died for was a fragment of an age-old legend: the instrument of the underworld. A Terrecet which must be hidden, camouflaged, wrapped in layers of Taulyn to neutralise its violent powers until the moment came to decide its destiny...

11. Midnight Maraudings

MIDNIGHT MARAUDINGS

Midnight came and Kaira and Guppy sat on the edge of their beds in Aunt Phee's quarters, listening for any sound of movement from the room next door. Philomeena Renn appeared to be fast asleep, based on the rhythmic sounds of her breathing so, with Churchill curled up on Kaira's bed, they prepared for their midnight jaunt to The Pancithon.

Conscious that they would be making their way to the ground floor in total darkness, Guppy produced another wonder from her Keepeasy: a small vial of clear liquid which she promptly opened and squirted into her eyes.

"Here," she said, offering the bottle to Kaira. "Crilliun ... eye drops to help you see in the dark."

Kaira took the vial and copied Guppy, having learnt to trust rather than constantly question her friend. The eye drops initially worsened her vision before a turquoise hue fell over the room, bringing everything into clearer focus.

"Okay?" checked Guppy as Kaira wiped her eyes.

She finally nodded and they tip-toed to the door, opening it and peering along the fourth-floor corridor. The

Cendryll was silent, without movement or the illumination of the Quij who lost all light and colour during sleep. Confident the coast was clear, they stepped out, closing the door quietly behind them.

Now it was simply a matter of making their way to The Seating Station on the ground floor without being seen, the chances of which were good as few members used The Cendryll as a full-time dwelling, and those that did were fast asleep or occupied with Society matters.

Kaira had also formulated a convincing excuse should they be seen: her beloved cat Churchill had escaped and, being away from home, would be confused and scared. Churchill was fast asleep on her bed, of course - a fact they would circumnavigate should they need to.

Thankfully, their journey was without event, their bare feet muting their footsteps and the star-filled skylight providing further illumination as they descended the spiral staircase and made their way across The Floating Floor. There was no sign of Jacob at The Seating Station, and Quandary Corner was equally empty so Kaira and Guppy agreed to wait some minutes then continue without him.

Their secret trip to The Pancithon was already rife with risk and each minute that passed only added to the chance of Philomeena Renn or Meyen Grayling waking to find empty beds. Kaira sat on the wooden benches of The Seating Station whilst Guppy paced, her impatience growing. The sudden sound of the lift descending made them rush for cover until Jacob's voice appeased their fear.

"Guppy, Kaira ..."

"Why did you take the lift?" whispered Guppy.

Jacob shrugged: "It was quicker."

"It's *louder* as well."

"Relax. Mum's snoring and no-one patrols the corridors at night."

"Crilliun?" offered Guppy.

"Got some. Let's go."

THEY USED the same door Kaira had entered through on her first day - to the right of The Seating Station, slightly lower and narrower than the others. She glanced at the S.P.M.A. letters engraved on the brass door knob before deciding it was time to try using a Perium herself. Placing her hand on the door handle, Kaira pulled it towards her and turned it anti-clockwise.

The familiar spinning sensation returned as the names of Society buildings appeared above the brass doorknob. Now familiar with each faculty, Kaira turned the handle quickly until *Pancithon* appeared in elegant writing. She pushed the door handle back into place and, within seconds, they found themselves in the Society library once more.

The depth of darkness was greater here, lacking the skylight of The Cendryll and the colourful illumination of the Quij who slept in circular formations on the top of the bookshelves. The purple hue of the Crilliun provided them with adequate night vision, however, incorporating the moving bookshelves and the grand-clock on the north wall.

"We might not be alone," Jacob whispered. "Ivo says night-time visits are getting more common so turning on the lights will be a giveaway to anyone up to no good."

Kaira nodded and looked ahead, listening for echoes of footsteps or voices ... but the only sound was the rhythmic motion of the moving shelves which, like the spinning, gold letters, seemed to never sleep. Guppy led the way towards the M section, pausing to ensure the space between each bookshelf was unoccupied. For now, at least, they were alone.

"So," she whispered as they reached the currently static bookshelf in the M section, "I think we should split up to get through the books faster. Jacob, if you look through *Mantzils & More: Creatures Past and Present*, Kaira and I will check *Maud's Manual of Mythological Creatures*."

"Okay. Remind me what we're looking for again."

"Any reference to the word 'Symean'. If it's a creature, it should be in one of them. If we find it, it should say if it's an underworld creature or not and then, hopefully, there's some reference to the Terrecet and how it controls underworld creatures."

"So, if we find something it's more likely the Symean and Terrecet exist...?" queried Kaira, not at all convinced that myths proved anything - even in a magical society.

"No," Guppy replied, "but it *will* confirm the possibility that people believe in the myth, and that the fragment that's appeared and vanished has strengthened their belief."

"Which would explain why books on mythology have been going missing and curses are being used for the first time in years," added Jacob. "Ivo doesn't remember anything like it. Apparently, sales of mythology books have shot up in Zucklewick's too."

"Right, come on," instructed Guppy. "I say we need to be out of here before the grand clock strikes one."

The search was on. The books resided on adjacent sides of the M section, Jacob's on the left-hand side and Kaira and Guppy's on the right. It took some time for Kaira's eyes to adjust to the text in *Maud's Manual of Mythological Creatures* - partly because it was faded and also due to the fact that the Crilliun seemed more effective over distance than close up.

Jacob seemed to be having no such trouble, sitting cross-legged on the floor as he scanned the pages of *Mantzils & More: Creatures Past and Present*. Guppy's research methods were somewhat different, running her forefinger vertically then diagonally down each page before flicking to the next.

"Got something," whispered Jacob, waving Kaira and Guppy across.

They waited for the gold letter M to stop spinning before following the moving bookshelf onto the central walkway and over to him.

"Look," he said, pointing to an illustration of a black, winged creature looking as if it were about to fly off the page.

Kaira read the description beneath: "The Ghulix is a creature of The Wenlands; a descendant of the Viadek and Symean (see *Menphelin's Fables*). A dynamic and destructive creature, the Ghulix is vulture-like in its pursuit of prey and unaffected by extreme changes in the weather. One swipe of the creature's armed wings is enough to sever a person entirely in two."

"Sounds friendly," quipped Jacob as Kaira read on. Guppy, in the meantime, was busy scanning the shelves for a copy of *Menphelin's Fables*, kicking herself that she hadn't thought of this earlier: the very book they had placed the Blindman's Watch in! A book containing the most well-known fables, legends and fairy tales in the society.

"Here," whispered Guppy, holding a small blue volume with a damaged spine and cover. As Jacob and Kaira peered closer, she flicked to the contents page but found no reference to the Symean. Her frustration rising, she scanned each fable until she finally spotted the word on page fifty-nine ... in a fable called *The Curse of the Saralin Sands*.

They all began to read the fable before Jacob suggested it would be a good idea if one person read aloud and the other two listened and kept a look-out through the gaps in the shelves. Kaira, being the one holding the book, offered to read. She began in a whisper, the sound of her voice accompanied by the rhythmic motions of the spinning gold letters and moving bookshelves.

LONG AGO IN *the days when magic was feared and those who possessed it hunted, there existed a land of spinning moons and stars: a place forever in darkness beyond the magical kingdom of Moralev: The Saralin Sands. Many had heard of the land yet it remained a myth; a bedtime story for young children who dreamed of adventuring to the fantastical land ... until one did.*

Elias Reepe, a young boy of ten with no particular magical ability, crept out of his village one night and into the mountains of Moralev in search of the mythical sands. Laughed at by the other village children because of his strange appearance and even stranger dreams, the boy spent many a day alone in the mountains until the fated day when he glimpsed a shimmering light far in the distance.

The journey to the land of spinning moons and stars was long and arduous, the wind whipping and the rain lashing down onto the boy, forcing him to find shelter in the mountain caves. On he walked, searching for the mythical land and the strange creatures who guarded its powerful magic, offering entry to those willing to pay a price.

After seven days and nights, the boy reached the land of spinning moons and stars, and the oldest creature of The Saralin

Sands - the Symean - rose out of the golden sand. Towering over the boy and made entirely of sand, the creature offered a bargain: safe entry for stolen time. Seven steps for seven grains of golden sand.

'I must trade years of my life for grains of golden sand?' Elias Reepe queried.

'Yes,' replied the Symean, 'for the sand has the power to defeat death, beckon the creatures of Saralin and bend the will of men. It is the very sand that spins the moons and stars.'

Bend the will of men, the boy thought as he stood in the shadow of the guardian of The Saralin Sands, and he imagined what it would feel like to never be laughed at again. Seven steps. I will still be a boy: just seventeen, he thought to himself. So he took the bargain and the Symean rose up into the air and out of the sand, allowing him entry to the land.

As he took his first step, the glimmering sand rose and encircled him, spinning in the air as he suddenly grew a foot taller. More sand rose and circled above as he took his second step, a shadow of a beard appearing speckled with grey. Having no reflection to look into and entranced by the Symean and the land of spinning moons and stars, Elias Reepe continued until he had made his seventh step: an old, grey man bent in pain.

'Seven steps for seven grains of sand,' he reminded the Symean in a rattling voice. On uttering these words, the guardian of The Saralin Sands bowed in honour of the agreement and collected seven grains of golden sand, placing them in the hands of the old man: once a boy.

'Now I can defeat death,' the old man (once a boy) uttered, greed swimming in his eyes. 'Control the creatures of the Saralin and bend the will of men.'

'You must first form an object from the grains of sand which, once made, cannot be damaged or destroyed.'

The old man imagined a band of connected triangles made of

indestructible metal worn around his forearm, one of the seven fragments shielding his hand. As he spoke, the grains of golden sand transformed into the shape he desired before morphing into mithium - an indestructible metal. Before long, the inter-connected triangles were complete, each humming across The Saralin Sands.

'Why does it hum?' asked the old man (once a boy) as the vibrating object was passed to him.

'It carries the power of our land ... the magic within the golden grains of sand and the many creatures beneath. Use it well and beware its power.'

'But I will die before long,' the old man uttered.

'You cannot die,' the creature replied. 'This is your bargain; to defeat death, beckon all creatures, bend the will of men.'

'I will never die? I will live forever as an old man!?'

'Seven steps for seven grains of golden sand.'

'You have cheated me!' hissed the old man - moments ago a boy - raising the object towards the Symean who cowered, uttering a warning but it was too late. The object spun, humming louder until it exploded with lightning, ripping through the creature who evaporated into the sand it was formed from.

The lightning then poured out of the object, terrifying sparks ripping into the sky and destroying the spinning moons and stars. When the last star was extinguished, the old, greying figure - moments ago a boy full of wonder and innocence - looked at the smoke and sparks emitting from the object. He had learnt too late that the fairy tale of his childhood was, indeed, a curse ... a curse all men knew only too well: The Curse of the Saralin Sands.

Now, with the object smoking on his arm and hand, the boy inside the frail, old body cried and vowed to put a curse on the world in revenge.

Wiping his tears, he turned back towards the mountains, unaware of the rising shadows in the distance who watched the *frail figure vanish into darkness, holding the instrument of the underworld ... and The Legend of the Terrecet was born.*

Guppy closed the volume, blinking as the purple hue of Crilliun began to wear off.

"Here," said Jacob, holding out the small vial of clear liquid.

Guppy duly added more eye-drops and handed the vial to Kaira.

"Well," prompted Guppy, blinking and wiping her eyes.

"Well, it's a pretty good fable," Jacob remarked. "One I've never heard of."

"But is it more than a fable?" questioned Kaira. "Are there fables and legends which are actually true?"

"Well, there's the Mantzils fable," Jacob replied without further elaboration, "and there are some creatures in fables that exist, like the Jaqus."

"So fables are a mixture of fairy tales and historical events?"

"Basically, yes," Guppy replied as the grand clock on the north wall struck twelve-thirty. "Maybe there's more in here ... in another fable, I mean. It just seems a little incomplete; they normally end by saying what happened to the character."

"And we can't take the book with us?" asked Kaira, becoming increasingly conscious of the risks of being found out of bed the longer they stayed.

"No," replied Jacob. "Too much risk of it getting into the wrong hands above ground. No second chances if you're found trading Society books on the black market."

"Can't we hide it in Guppy's Keepeasy along with her copy of *Symbols, Runes and Omens*?"

"I 'borrowed' mum's copy which lives in The Cendryll," explained Guppy. "Not an option, Kaira. We need to carry on checking so we know what to listen out for when we bump into Blaze Flint."

"*Bump into...?* The black market rat isn't someone I want to bump into, thanks very much," Jacob remarked.

"I was thinking more along the lines of paying a visit to The Blind Horsemen ... pretend we're looking for mum. A perfect place to pick up on black market gossip about the fragment and its current whereabouts."

Jacob's annoyance reappeared, the frown rising as he held his sister's gaze. "And none of the adults are going to question why two under-age girls are in a pub?"

"Who said anything about going in?" said Guppy with a smile. "I was thinking more along the lines of passing by. A Pryal charm should work as long as it's not too noisy outside."

The grand clock's chimes fell silent, echoing through the building - an echo replaced by the more violent sound of a door slamming.

"*Down*," whispered Kaira as the lights in The Pancithon came on and the Quij blossomed into life, fluttering upwards.

They crouched in the far corner of the M section, peering between the shelves towards the north wall. Only two figures could be made out in the distance, the purple hue of Crilliun picking up an insignia on the coat collar of each person: one male, one female. Implementers.

"Sylan Ryll," whispered Jacob, a wave of anxiety passing over him. "I'd recognise that creep anywhere."

"And Aneesha Khan," added Guppy, glimpsing the sinister grin and dangerously long fingernails, sharpened to maximise pain. It was a puzzle to Guppy to see a faction of The Sinister Four; they always operated in their infamous quartet - monitoring, questioning and generally intimidating other members of The Pancithon. Tonight, however, it was just the two of them, striding down the central walkway in tense tones of disagreement.

"We've gone over this, Sylan. There is *no trail*; however continually removing books may lead to suspicion."

"The mess with Cialene has started rumours," replied Sylan Koll, his fiery red hair swept back from his feral face. "Why did *those three* have to turn up...? Children prying in Society matters..."

Aneesha Khan suddenly stopped and put her finger to her lips: "Wait. There's someone else here..." The venomous stare turned towards the hiding place of the three individuals they most sought revenge on - their sneaking around causing the mess with Cialene Koll and their humiliation at the hands of Farraday and Smyck. Children had no place in the Society and this would be a perfect statement to prove just that.

As the two Implementers moved cautiously towards the M section, Jacob nudged Guppy and whispered, "I need something sharp."

Realising there was no time to question this request, Guppy uttered 'Comeuppance' and took a silver pen-knife out of her pocket. She handed it to her brother and watched as he cut the palm of his hand before pressing them together and closing his eyes tightly.

"What's he doing?" whispered an increasingly anxious Kaira.

Guppy put a finger to her lips and pointed above with the other - towards the sight of an army of Quij - their luminous bodies now blood-red, floating towards Aneesha Khan and Sylan Rill.

Kaira glanced at Jacob, his bloodied hands pressed together and his eyes still closed, and she suddenly remembered their first meeting when he had looked up at the Quij and opened the palm of his hand, almost calling them to him ... and he was calling them now. She crouched lower as Aneesha Khan and Sylan Ryll drew ever closer, the Implementers peering between the bookshelves, sensing their prey were trapped.

The gold letter M began to spin as Sylan Ryll's boot made contact with it, and as the bookshelf began to slide onto the central walkway, the army of blood-red Quij attacked at ferocious speed, buzzing and swarming towards The Sinister Two.

Sylan Ryll and Aneesha Khan, preoccupied with their own plan of attack, realised the counter move too late, looking up moments before the blood-red army descended on them, the insects burning and scratching as they made contact. Ryll swished pointlessly at the air with his silver cane ... a Vaspyl which he morphed into a sword to no avail.

The Quij were far too fast and imaginative for his meek defences and swarmed over his face and body, burning and scratching until he scampered backwards along the central walkway, bloodied and desperate, his flailing arms offering little resistance against the violent attack.

Aneesha Khan wasn't so lucky; her shock of immaculate black hair was an ideal target for the Quij to tear and attach themselves to. "Sylan!" she yelled in terror and disgust as her associate abandoned her, scampering to the safety of the reading rooms.

Khan's long, sharpened nails - like Sylan Ryll's steel walking stick - were no match for the ferocity of this co-ordinated attack, her body and face covered with the fire-red insects, burning, swarming and scratching as they tore at her hair.

"Jacob, stop!" insisted Guppy, pulling at her brother's arm to shake him out of the trance he appeared to be in.

"SYLAAAAN!" Aneesha Khan screamed in terror, sobbing as she crawled into a ball on the central walkway.

"Jacob! *Stop*! They're really *hurting* her." Kaira joined forces with Guppy to shake and prod Jacob until he finally opened his eyes and unclasped his hands. The Quij retreated the moment he did, floating upwards towards the dark eaves of The Pancithon - their luminous, multi-coloured forms returning as the ferocious buzzing died away.

"What the *hell* was that!?" demanded Guppy as she continued to prod his arm. "Why didn't you stop?"

Jacob gave no reply, handing the pen-knife back to his sister and kneeling to peer through the bookshelves. He studied the strewn body of Aneesha Khan on the central walkway, slowly getting to her feet, bloodied and disoriented. Her face and hands were scratched with clumps of black hair strewn across the wooden floor.

At the sound of a reading-room door slamming, muting Aneesha Khan's sobs, Kaira said, "Come on, before they re-appear" and they headed towards the door on the south wall.

Back in the safety of The Cendryll, the three sat at The Seating Station, the star-filled skylight aiding the purple hue of the Crilliun. Jacob had suddenly become distant, looking towards the silhouette of Quandary Corner.

"They drew blood," he began in way of explanation. "On my first week here ... just because I entered a silent reading room by accident. They *drew blood* in front of *everyone*, including mum and *no-one* told them to stop or tried to help. They're *bullies* who deserved a taste of their own medicine."

"You were behaving just like them," countered Guppy, troubled by her brother's tone of violence and vindication. "You've always said you hate how they abuse their power; well didn't you just abuse yours...?"

Jacob turned to face his sister, the distant expression fading. "What do you mean?"

"You wouldn't stop. You didn't seem able to."

"I just wanted to scare them and make them realise people can fight back."

"But the Quij went *crazy*," interjected Kaira in defence of Guppy's remarks. "Scratching, burning and drawing blood. I don't know how you did it, but they seemed to be carrying out your instructions."

Jacob seemed genuinely shocked by this knowledge. "I obviously didn't mean to hurt anyone," he conceded, pushing the dark hair away from his face. "The plan was just to scare them. I just snapped. It felt like all the anger and resentment came flooding out of me. I'll take the blame if Aneesha or Sylan link the attack to us."

"How can they?" replied Guppy. "They've got no proof we were there."

"They could use a Now-Then."

"And so could we," added Kaira. "To prove their involvement in Cialene Koll's death. Anyway, we were just looking for a book and they were the ones about to attack us. You were only doing what you were instructed to: protect us."

"What about the Quij?" queried Guppy. "Won't they get hurt now by The Sinister Four?"

Jacob shook his head. "The Quij are treated like an endangered species in the Society; no harm will be done to them. Anyway, I'm fairly sure Aneesha and Sylan will be wary of them from now on."

"So we say nothing," instructed Guppy in unconditional support of her brother. "And if we're questioned about the attack, we play dumb."

"Lie, you mean," stated Kaira, wondering how another mistruth would go down with her aunt and increasingly absent father.

"Unless you think it's a good idea to tell your aunt and our mum about tonight after yesterday's dice with death in Dyil's Ditch...?"

Realising Guppy was right and sensing it was time to change the subject and improve Jacob's dark mood, Kaira added, "Well, at least we know that the Symean and Terrecet are linked. One's a talking creature made of sand and the other's an object that kills everything: not much of a fairy tale, is it?"

It was possibly Kaira's comical puzzlement at the darkness of the fairy tale or the tension easing between Jacob and Guppy that caused a ripple of laughter between them - each looking up at the star-filled skylight before standing and making their way to the spiral staircase.

The Crilliun's purple hue provided adequate illumination to navigate the spiral staircase, leading to Aunt Phee's quarters and Meyen Grayling's fifth-floor dwelling. They walked in silence, tired from their midnight marauding and another brush with danger.

There was more to find out about the missing fragment which had caused a swell of violence in the Society, Kaira ruminated. Dark allegiances were becoming ever apparent as if there was a shadow society forming, secretly spinning and weaving its plots. Their job was to uncover these allegiances and find the current whereabouts of the fragment recently thought to exist only in a fairy tale.

Aneesha Khan and Sylan Ryll also played on Kaira's mind, as did Jacob's momentary loss of control. It was in the moment of Jacob's trance, when he was communicating with the Quij, that Kaira drew a parallel with the boy in the fairy tale. Both were hypnotised by the power at their command, using it to enact retribution, and her understanding of the Society's focus on preserving magic became more evident - for its misuse could lead to catastrophe.

12. Presents & Revelations

PRESENTS & REVELATIONS

Morning arrived quickly, the autumnal sunlight falling onto Kaira and Guppy's tired eyes. Aunt Phee had already tried to wake them without success, assuming their sleepy state was due to the burgeoning of adolescence. The harsh sunlight had no such sympathy, however, continuing to pierce through the curtains until each gave in, finally opening their eyes. Remnants of Crilliun remained from last night's escapade, adding a mild, purple haze to their peripheral vision.

A lot had been learnt, Kaira and Guppy agreed as they crept back into bed last night. They had another part of the jigsaw now pertaining to the link between The Sign of the Symean and the fragment which people had killed for - a link leading to Blaze Flint: the black market rat. Now all they had to do was find a way of bumping into him whilst keeping an eye out for The Sinister Four who, no doubt, would be keeping an eye out for them.

Aunt Phee's second call to wake them was less a request than a command so they shook off the desire to go back to sleep and proceeded to wash and dress before facing another eventful day in The Society for the Preservation of Magical Artefacts.

They found Kaira's aunt sitting at the small, circular table occupying the central space of her quarters, separating the bedrooms on either side - the table they had crept past last night to return from their midnight adventure. Two other doors rested awkwardly in their frames on the other two walls, leading to spaces as yet unexplored.

The most striking feature of the room was, without question, the open-plan kitchen stretching an impossible distance to the very top of The Cendryll, although how that could be, neither girl knew. The topic of the kitchen's impressive structure seemed an ideal opening to check if Aunt Phee had woken to find empty beds last night:

"Magic has its benefits," Philomeena Renn replied as she poured tea for them and returned to the kitchen for toast, marmalade and honey. Like Kaira, her long, brown curls fell over her shoulders, complimenting her caramel-coloured skin.

Kaira sometimes wondered if she would gain her aunt's elegance over time - the quiet dignity and undeniable beauty - although there were other times when this was of no concern at all ... like today as plans to investigate the deepening mysteries within the Society dominated her every thought.

"So, the kitchen *does* stretch to the top of The Cendryll?" asked Guppy as she chomped through her toast.

Philomeena Renn reached for the honey whilst glancing towards the walls which ran forever upwards. "I'm sure you've noticed, Guppy, that space, like all other things, can be manipulated in the Society."

"Like the long corridor in Cribbe & Corrow where I got

my penchant," added Kaira who slurped her tea to the mild irritation of her aunt.

"Have you been to all the faculties in the Society, Miss Renn?" asked Guppy, hoping to discover which ones offered the most intrigue.

Philomeena Renn smiled at Guppy's overt attempt at politeness. "Now you're a member of the Society, Guppy, I'm sure we can dispense with formalities. Also, 'Miss Renn' makes me feel old and stuffy."

"I don't think you're old and stuffy. I think you're ace."

"So Philomeena it is then," Aunt Phee stated as she bit into her honey-covered toast before picking up a spoon and clinking the edge of her tea-cup, causing the door closest to the kitchen to creak open.

Startled by the door opening of its own accord, Kaira's mouthful of tea spilt back into her cup whilst Guppy stopped biting into her toast, keen to learn the charm Philomeena Renn had used to get the door to open without leaving her chair. Although it was mid-morning, a darkness hung over the room with only outlines of furniture and objects visible, and before either could enquire into the function of the room, Philomeena Renn stood and said:

"Time for a little surprise."

The room they stepped into was at once uniform and elaborate; hundreds of small, square boxes lined two of the walls, each with a brass number-plate and key hole. Kaira counted two hundred before her attention was drawn to Guppy moving towards the window at the far end, and the faint images occupying each window-pane similar to the window in Cribbe & Corrow.

Aside from the numerous numbered boxes and the illus-trated window, a large mirror sat above the fireplace next to which stood a tall chair with a wooden box on it: number two-hundred-and-twenty-two.

Whilst Guppy continued to study the moving images on each window-pane, Aunt Phee picked up the box and reached for a key from her small handbag, uttering 'Comeuppance' as she did so. Placing the key in the lock of the wooden box, she turned and opened it to reveal a patch of silver fabric. Kaira looked at her aunt to gain some clue to what it was.

"Reach in," instructed Aunt Phee with her hand on the back of the tall chair.

Kaira did as she was told. "What is it?"

"What you asked for: a Keepeasy. Of course, your dad and I wouldn't only give you a Keepeasy for a welcome present. You need something to put in it otherwise it spoils the fun."

"There's something in it...?"

"I'm sure you know how to activate it," added Aunt Phee before watching her niece utter 'Comeuppance' followed by the shock on her face as the silver fabric ballooned inside the box.

"What's inside?" came Guppy's voice from behind them, and she watched as Kaira took out the Keepeasy and reached in to feel cold steel, remembering the first artefact Francis Follygrin had shown her.

"A Vaspyl," she uttered, drawing out the small, steel object currently in the shape of a key.

"Well, *try it*, Kaira," demanded Guppy excitedly. "Think of something and throw it in the air."

Kaira remembered the toy car Francis Follygrin had taken out of the cabinet - the one he had thrown in the air which magically morphed into a mirror. She thought of this as she threw the silver key into the air, watching it transform into the toy car of her imagination.

"*No way,*" cried Guppy excitedly. "Let me have a go!"

"No need," replied Aunt Phee as she reached up to another box, number two hundred-and-twenty-two, opened it with the same key and handed it to Guppy. "We wouldn't want to leave you out now, would we?"

Guppy took the box cautiously, clearly surprised by this act of generosity which symbolised a care and attention she rarely received.

"Go on, then," Kaira encouraged, pleased her friend had been included. "Let's see."

"No way!" Guppy uttered again, her hand shaking as she held a pocket watch in it ... an object she knew to be a Vaspyl. She threw it into the air and watched it morph into a candle-holder.

"Welcome to the Society, young ladies," declared Aunt Phee with a quiet laugh, and watched as Kaira and Guppy continued to throw their Vaspyls into the air, sighs of awe and wonder as they morphed into more intricate objects. When they finally tired of the Vaspyl's wonders, Guppy asked about the images on the window.

"They are images of each faculty in the Society," explained Aunt Phee "It gives us an overview of general activity and mood."

"Like spying," suggested Guppy, already loving the idea of having access to such a window.

"More observation than spying, although it does help us to keep an eye on things."

Kaira rubbed the silver fabric of her Keepeasy, wondering why her aunt had such a window and why, more importantly, there had been no mention of her dad. Where was he? He had never been gone from her life for more than a day and this thought alone concerned her; however, something stopped her bringing this up now.

"Okay, girls," said Aunt Phee as she returned the two boxes to their place on the walls. "Unfortunately, I've got a little work to do so I'm going to have to leave you for a while. Also, Jacob is needed back in the Creative Charms department so no charms lessons today, Kaira. We can do a little more on remedies later. Busy day today and we'll need to go above ground for a meeting in Society Square early this evening."

"I'd better go back to Liabilities before my mum finds out I'm slacking off," said Guppy - a mild tone of resentment evident in her voice.

"You can stay with Kaira, Guppy," stated Kaira's aunt. "Your mother will be caught up with Society matters all day and since you're already here, I'm sure she won't mind you keeping Kaira company."

"Really? Okay, thanks," replied Guppy with a smile before throwing the Vaspyl into the air one more time, watching it morph into a harmonica. She blew a few notes, feigning an expression of deep pain as if she were playing a sad ballad, drawing a giggle from Kaira.

"Just one thing, Guppy," added Philomeena Renn as she ushered the girls out of the room of secret boxes and keys. "You'll need to show Kaira how to attach the Keepeasy."

"Sure."

"And, Kaira, I've left a new coat for you on the door peg. Your other one is too small for you now and this one will grow with you, let's say. Okay, girls. I'll see you in a few hours. I'm sure I can trust you to keep out of mischief until then..."

∾

"I COULD TEACH YOU SOME CHARMS," offered Guppy as Aunt Phee left.

They stood by the small, circular table occupying the centre of Philomeena Renn's quarters, eyeing the kitchen which stretched ever upwards.

"Do you think that's a good idea?" questioned Kaira, knowing that Guppy wouldn't be interested in teaching creative charms - a sure way of getting into more trouble.

"Okay, what then?"

"Teach me about Society stuff," suggested Kaira.

"Okay, like what?"

"Like answering all the questions I've got, the way you promised we would on our first day above ground."

"Then we talk about how we get to Blaze Flint," Guppy countered, always with one eye on adventure.

"And use my Follygrin to find out where my dad is."

"Deal," declared Guppy, comically offering a handshake.

"Well, Miss Renn, what would you like to learn about our magical world...?"

"My dad seems important here. What's his role in the Society?"

"He runs The Cendryll."

"Runs it...?"

"Yep. You know, the boss."

"And my aunt?"

"Your aunt's sort of second in charge with my mum although mum likes to think she's the deputy. She wants to be the boss, of course, which is why we never see her."

"My dad and your mum don't seem to get on."

"Mum doesn't get on with anyone; she's just interested in power and who she can use to get it."

"Okay, what about Farraday and Smyck...? I've known

Farraday all my life; Smyck just appeared the other night at my house but seems to know my dad and aunt."

"They work closely with your dad and aunt, keeping an eye on what goes on above ground and reporting any suspicious activity. Their job is to maintain the Society's anonymity above ground and deal with those who bring unwanted attention to it."

"Like Theodore Kusp selling Laudlum on the black market?"

"Yes, like Theodore although that was an exception. It's usually Melackin like Prium Koll or black market rats like Blaze Flint who create waves. Theodore is a senior member of The Cendryll which is what made his actions so unusual but, like your dad said when we listened in with the Looksee, his wife has recently died and he wasn't in his right frame of mind: Melackin prey on weakness."

"I overheard Weyen Lyell say my grandfather married a Koll which means I've got Koll blood."

"Everyone's a mix, Kaira."

"Yes, but Kolls are Melackins which means that's maybe why my grandfather went bad ... because he married into Melackin blood."

Recognising the sensitivity of this point, Guppy put her Vaspyl away in the Keepeasy of her jeans' pocket and sat at the circular table. "Not all Kolls are Melackins, Kaira; it doesn't work like that."

"But Prium Koll is a Melackin, and Erent Koll..."

Guppy shook her head and gestured for Kaira to join her at the table, sensing a need for further clarification to appease her friend. "Okay, look. The Kolls were once an important family in the Society, largely responsible for recording ancient Society knowledge, including charms, remedies and legends. It started to go wrong with Erent Koll who was the first in the family to secretly study and practice Gorrah..."

"Dark magic," added Kaira.

"Right. Also, the Koll ancestors were obsessed with myths and legends and knew the power of magic in the wrong hands. They were one of the first families to suggest the Society focus on preservation of magic rather than its practice.

Too many problems between faculties were forming and battles threatened to destroy the peace the Society had maintained ... until it did. A great battle, years ago. Once the 'malevs' - as they're called in the history books - were defeated, the Society formally changed its name to The Society for the Preservation of Magical Artefacts."

Kaira spun her Vaspyl on the table's wooden surface, trying to process Guppy's information. "Okay, but that doesn't explain how the Kolls aren't all Melackin, and how having Melackin blood won't make me go bad."

"Right. So, Melackin is a term for someone who's gone down the wrong path but has been stopped: rehabilitated."

"How are they stopped?"

"Revenance Remedy; it removes all negative thoughts and feelings. Once their criminal act is discovered, they're given Revenance Remedy and then they are known as Melackin: Society members gone wrong but caught and mended before it was too late."

"Okay. What about Erent Koll: he's not a Melackin...?"

"No," replied Guppy, reaching for some cold toast.

"Erent Koll has gone *way* beyond petty crime. Rumour has it he's killed more than once - maybe for the fragment Cialene Koll stole and died for; the one everyone thinks is part of a Terrecet."

"And my grandfather...?"

Guppy bit into the cold toast and shrugged. "I don't know much about Isiah Renn except for the fact that he was supposed to have 'gone bad' with Erent Koll and was expelled from the Society a long time ago."

"So being a Koll doesn't make you a Melackin?" Kaira asked once more for purposes of clarification.

"No. Your actions make you a Melackin. There are plenty of Kolls that are good. The easiest way to tell how bad someone's gone is the colour of their penchant."

"How do you mean?"

"Each family has a penchant stone, right?"

Kaira nodded, remembering Morlan Corrow telling her this.

"The Grayling's penchant stone is topaz and the Renn's amethyst. Well, when you go bad, the colour in your penchant stone fades: the less colour it has, the more you're betraying the principles of the Society. If you do criminal stuff, the penchant stone starts to grey: black if you use Gorrah."

"You don't lose your penchant if you go bad...?"

Guppy shook her head, reaching for the marmalade. "No need. Once you've used a curse or, worse, killed someone, your penchant loses its powers. You're unable to access any faculty via Periums and it no longer offers protection. A security measure, I suppose, as well as a punishment."

Kaira continued to spin her Vaspyl on the surface of the table, thinking about her grandfather, Isiah Renn, the imposing Jamaican of her childhood memory with the loud laugh and deep voice. What had he done and why had he become an unmentionable in the Renn household? This thought led her to muse on her dad's whereabouts again ... an increasing preoccupation the longer he remained absent.

"Anything else?" asked Guppy, chomping on the final slice of cold toast.

Kaira pondered, remembering the Follygrin was still tucked away in her coat pocket.

"The Keepeasy; can you show me how to attach it?"

"Sure," said Guppy, standing from the table.

"Thanks," said Kaira. "Then let's use the Follygrin to find out where my dad is."

THE SPARE BEDROOM was decided on as the safest place to use the Follygrin; it provided a degree of secrecy in anticipation of Aunt Phee's sudden return. Before using the Follygrin, Kaira decided the best place for her Keepeasy would be the pocket of her jeans, following Guppy's advice.

Guppy explained that Keepeasies could be removed and re-attached with ease and were not damaged when clothes were washed so when Kaira changed trousers, it was simply a matter of transferring the Keepeasy to a new pocket.

With the Keepeasy in place, the girls sat on Kaira's bed in the spare room of Philomeena Renn's quarters and opened the Follygrin. Kaira rubbed the letter 'A' and watched it fade into the now familiar phrase: Ask and You Will Find.

"Casper Renn," uttered Kaira and they watched as the pages flicked to the letter 'C'. The ink faded into smoke before reforming into an intricate illustration of a figure walking alone in an unfamiliar, barren landscape, the wind and dust clearly troubling him as he lifted his overcoat over his head for protection: the figure of Casper Renn.

Kaira, her heart racing, peered closer, trying to locate

anything which would provide a clue to her dad's whereabouts.

"Do you recognise the place?" she asked Guppy who shook her head.

Kaira peered closer, squinting at the sight of a flickering shadow in the distance between the trees, mountains and dust clouds ... clouds created by the whipping wind as her dad continued his journey towards an unknown destination in an unknown territory.

Guppy watched the continuously changing illustration, managing feelings of guilt for she *did* recognise the place, but the last thing her best friend needed was to hear that her dad was travelling alone in The Wenlands. Shadow-lands. Land of the Quliy ... 'shadow walkers' who could manipulate time, allowing them to cover ground at light-ning speed, making them impossible to see or track.

"It looks dangerous," uttered Kaira, trying to contain a swell of emotion.

Guppy fidgeted with the Vaspyl, conscious that The Wenlands was outside the Society Sphere where penchants lost their power, providing no protection against curses: skill and wit were your only chance of survival.

"What's he doing there? Why is he alone?"

Guppy, not sure if Kaira was addressing her or internal-ising her thoughts, gambled on an answer:

"Whatever your dad's doing, Kaira, it's to protect us: to protect the Society."

Kaira watched the ever-evolving illustration but, more importantly, the hunched figure of her father battling with the wind and dust clouds, walking towards the army of trees and distant mountains. What she uttered next, Guppy had no answer for: "That's great but who's protecting *him*?"

They both watched the figure of Casper Renn continuing to battle the elements as the flickering shadows appeared in the distant trees, Guppy careful not to display any sign of recognition to protect Kaira from further upset. The image of her dad wrestling with elements beyond his control troubled Kaira, feeling angry that he had been left to wander a wilderness alone under Society orders or, perhaps, out of his own sense of duty.

The central root of her anger, however, was that no-one deemed it important enough to explain her dad's absence to her ... that he was risking his life for a Society which seemed unconcerned with his sacrifice, sending no-one to travel with him. What was magic without honour, she wondered...?

"Let's try out the Vaspyls," Guppy suggested, attempting a diversion from the Follygrin and the growing anxiety in her friend.

Kaira was reluctant at first but after another period of time studying the Follygrin, realised that the moving illustration of her dad only provided more questions - deepened an ever-evolving puzzle which increasingly immersed them all.

Finally, she gave in to Guppy's suggestion and they each explored the wonders of their respective Vaspyls, conjuring numerous shapes both miniature and magnificent, functional and fantastical, marvellous and malevolent.

The morning passed in this experimental fashion, laughter replacing worry as the magical, morphing steel tested their imaginative capabilities. It was only Philomeena Renn's return that paused the creative conjurings. It was time to learn more about remedies.

"Okay, let's introduce you to the properties of remedies," Philomeena Renn said to Kaira as she entered her quarters on the fourth floor of The Cendryll. Kaira's aunt seemed preoccupied, her unusually detached tone a sign something was on her mind. "I probably should have explained why some members have their own quarters," she added. "Each room in The Cendryll is dedicated to a specific aspect of charms.

There are five types of charms: creative, investigative, restrictive, protective and defensive. There are also many other aspects of charms, like cataloguing, testing and discovering new ones. Quarters like these, however, allow access to particular rooms in other faculties: rooms which will allow me to teach you more about remedies."

Kaira's aunt removed a hairband from her wrist and tied her brown locks back before picking up a silver candle-holder on the mantelpiece and tapping it three times. On the third tap, the most neglected door in the room - the only door that had not been explored by Kaira and Guppy - rattled before scraping open to reveal a space bursting with light, colour and a sweet smell reminiscent of strawberries.

Never one for indecision, Guppy stepped towards the open door, blinking as the light stung her eyes.

"Be careful of Mivrilyn," Philomeena Renn warned. "The oldest Williynx in the Society ... not the friendliest to strangers."

Finally deciding it was time to prompt Aunt Phee out of her state of distraction, Kaira took her hand and said, "Just in case the Williynx isn't friendly."

The touching gesture of attention and solace drew her aunt out of her internal reverie, prompting her to lead the way into the light-filled room:

"Welcome to another world of wonders, Kaira," declared Aunt Phee, squeezing her niece's hand in appreciation.

"Where are we?" asked Kaira, shielding her eyes from the intense light emanating from the room.

"The Feleecian," replied her aunt. "The faculty for remedies."

Mivrilyn, the oldest Williynx in the Society, lived up to her unfriendly reputation, squawking and hissing at Guppy's gentle attempts at introduction.

"It's probably a good idea to keep your distance for a while," Philomeena Renn suggested, gesturing for Guppy to move away from the table the Williynx was perched on, her yellow-feathered body arched in a stance of aggression.

Kaira let go of her aunt's hand as her eyes adjusted to the bright light of the room. Although she was now used to stepping through doors into entirely different spaces, it still took her some time to process the new wonders she encountered each time.

In the case of the room they had stepped into, there were three particular wonders: the bottles of many-coloured liquids lining the walls, the yellow Williynx eyeing them suspiciously on the edge of the narrow wooden table and the rectangular, glass object occupying the centre of the table decorated by silver marks inside.

Sensing her aunt's distance was somehow linked to her dad's ongoing absence and, perhaps, her knowledge of the strange wasteland he was venturing in, Kaira thought it a good idea to continue her lessons on remedies without further ado in order to minimise the worry and concern clearly evident.

She and Guppy had already debated asking her aunt about her dad's whereabouts but realised this would not only worsen Aunt Phee's distant state but also reveal her ownership of a Follygrin - another thing she would have to explain.

It was clear to both Kaira and Guppy that Aunt Phee was carrying the burden of her brother's whereabouts to protect her niece so it was their job to do what they could to appease her anxiety.

"Don't you think it's a little cruel, keeping a Williynx locked up like this?" Kaira asked her aunt, feeling the question to be relatively uncontroversial and removed from the ongoing absence of her dad.

"Williynx are shape-shifters, Kaira. They can take the shape of any land or winged animal; the most magical and miraculous creature still in existence in our world."

"So why do they stay? Inside these rooms testing things for the Society?"

"Perhaps because their ability to sense magical properties is unrivalled. There would be no Society without the Williynx and many, many lives would have been lost if not for their ability to sniff out danger."

"So they choose to stay?" queried Guppy. "Inside the faculties, I mean ... to help the Society?"

"Yes. Society creatures have the same affinity to our world as we do; Williynx also know that the above-ground world tends to fear wondrous things, killing or caging beautiful creatures rather than seeing them as equals."

Neither Kaira nor Guppy could argue with that; animal poaching, zoos and the rapid extinction of many unique creatures was ample evidence that the above-ground world was, indeed, ignorant to wonder.

"Have you ever seen them change ... transform into other animals?" asked Kaira.

Aunt Phee nodded. "Although this isn't to be encouraged. A Williynx will most likely shape-shift when in danger so I'd advise keeping on Mivrilyn's good side."

"It would be ace to see one change, though" added Guppy still wary of the yellow-feathered creature who now moved on all fours towards the rectangular glass object on the wooden table.

"Okay, Mivrilyn is getting impatient," explained Philomeena Renn. "She's aware that I've brought you here to explain remedies and is doing her best to tolerate you both."

"Doesn't she like children?" asked Kaira.

"More that we've woken her up."

"Oh. So is she going to test the remedies for us? The Williynx in Fimiations flaps its wings and falls asleep if the magical property is dangerous or useless. It flaps its wings and stays awake if it's good news, Jacob said."

"No. Mivrilyn is here to get to know you because she's going to be keeping an eye on you."

Kaira and Guppy exchanged a puzzled look as her aunt stepped towards the wall nearest to them, running her hand along the edge of the wooden shelves. It was only when Kaira moved closer to Aunt Phee that she noticed the circular, brass contraption. It was decorated with a list of names - a large handle dominating the centre.

She watched her aunt turn the handle before stopping on the title Revenance Remedy. Aunt Phee then pushed the circular, brass contraption into the bookshelf, causing a bell to ring and a bottle of blue liquid to jolt from its shelf high above, toppling off and falling at rapid speed towards Guppy.

On Philomeena's utterance of 'Magneia', the bottle's rapid descent halted, the blue liquid swilling around inside as it hovered in mid-air. It then began to float towards Kaira's aunt who was tapping the wooden table.

Kaira watched in mild-awe as her aunt continued to tap the table, guiding the bottle of blue liquid towards her - in total control of its trajectory, to Guppy's clear relief. As the bottle rested on the wooden table next to her hand, Aunt Phee flicked the rectangular glass object on the table, causing the lid to open.

As it did so, the three, floating silver lines inside fell to the bottom. She then poured some of the blue liquid inside and gestured for Kaira and Guppy to step closer to the table: "Revenance Remedy," explained Aunt Phee as she watched the blue liquid's slow dance inside the glass container.

"No need to worry about Mivrilyn, now; she knows you don't pose a threat."

Guppy, not entirely sure this was the case, positioned herself behind Kaira.

"What is it? The thing you've poured the remedy into?" asked Kaira.

"A Nivrium."

"What's a Nivrium?"

"A water reader," interjected Guppy, still struggling with the concept of taking a back seat.

Conscious that Guppy had an insecurity about being left out or marginalised, Kaira asked her friend: "What does it do?"

"It's supposed to provide information on moods and movements in the Society, or something like that."

"That's right," concurred Aunt Phee. "The Nivrium provides an insight into the 'temperature' of the Society, let's say."

"So we read the moods and movements of the Society through remedies?" queried Kaira, already lost.

"Not quite," replied her aunt. "The Nivrium has another

ability: to read the properties of all liquid-based substances in the Society so we know if they'll provide benefit or harm."

Not entirely clear on the link between the Nivrium, remedies and the presence of the yellow Williynx, Kaira had a few other questions. "Aunt Phee, you said the Williynx ..."

At this, the creature squawked and stretched its wings in anger, causing Kaira and Guppy to step away from the table in fear.

"No need to panic, girls. It's common courtesy to address all Society members by their name."

"The Willin ... I mean, Mivrilyn is a member of the Society...?" Guppy queried.

"Of course. Creatures and humans have equal rights. As I have already stated, without creatures like the Williynx many lives would have been lost. An organisation's strength comes from recognition not division."

Mivrilyn squawked in agreement.

Kaira took a tentative step towards the table, returning to her question. "Aunt Phee, you said Mivrilyn wasn't here to test the remedies but to keep an eye on us."

"That's right."

"Why does she need to keep an eye on us?"

Philomeena Renn turned her attention from the Nivrium just as the blue liquid settled and the three silver lines inside floated from the bottom of the rectangular, glass object. Her distant expression remained, her brown eyes attentive yet not fully immersed in this exercise. "I'm going to meet your father this evening before he returns.

I didn't really want to bring this up now but it's equally insensitive of me to ignore it any longer. He has an important job in the Society, Kaira - one which demands a lot of him. One of the reasons he put off introducing you to our world was the knowledge that once you had entered, you would see less of him. We will always be here for you, but entrance to The Society for the Preservation of Magical Artefacts often comes with sacrifice..."

Kaira returned her attention to the Nivrium, watching the three silver lines rising and falling in a rhythmic motion. She assumed, based on Aunt Phee's explanation, that the three lines were 'reading' the magical properties of the Revenance Remedy inside, providing an example of how the Nivrium worked.

Guppy, keen to understand the inner workings of this new artefact, asked, "What do the three lines do inside?"

Philomeena turned away from her niece with a tense smile, studying the Nivrium. "The lines are finding the 'measure' of the remedy; what it's comprised of."

"Don't you already know if it's good or bad?"

"Of course, Guppy. This is just for purposes of demon-stration. In a few minutes, each line will settle in a position; the position they settle in determines the properties of the remedy - or any liquid, for that matter."

Kaira moved closer to her aunt, processing the news that her only other immediate family member was going to be absent from her life. "How do you read it?"

Aunt Phee placed a hand on Kaira's shoulder in a sign of reassurance and, to some degree, apology: "The first thing to look for is evenness: the more even the lines, the more stable the remedy."

"So, if they're all hovering in the middle at exactly the same height, you've got evenness?"

"Yes."

"And if they're in completely different positions - one at the bottom, one in the middle and one at the top - the remedy is unstable?" questioned Guppy.

"That's right."

"And how do you tell if the remedy is good or bad?" asked Kaira.

"By tapping the glass once, like this. Although we already know Revenance Remedy has beneficial magical properties, I'll explain how you tell this, and how you judge if the properties are useless or dangerous. First, notice how the lines now float to the bottom then towards the top of the Nivrium; this is to check for the essence of the property ... in simpler terms, the 'character' of the remedy.

If the character of the remedy is good, the three silver lines rest on the surface of the liquid - all in an even line - without stopping. If anything bad is detected, the lines will stop and begin to push at the lid, attempting to get out, before sinking to the bottom, motionless."

Kaira and Guppy watched the even motion of the lines, navigating their way through the liquid, checking its character, before resting on its surface.

"It sounds like the three lines sort of die if the liquid's bad," suggested Guppy, jumping a little as the yellow Williynx squawked and opened its wings once more.

"Mivrilyn is getting a little bored," explained Philomeena Renn. "The three lines inside the Nivrium merely react to the properties of the liquid or water. Anything a liquid with harmful properties can do, one with good properties can heal. After all, the main essence of remedies is their ability to heal."

"Revenance Remedy removes bad thoughts," stated Guppy, happy to show off her knowledge. "It stops the Melackin from going really bad."

"That's right, Guppy."

Kaira pointed to a green liquid in a jar to the left of the table. "Is that Jysyn Juice?"

Aunt Phee nodded, seemingly relieved to be discussing

remedies and not the risks her brother was taking in The Wenlands.

"And that one must be Crilliun," added Guppy, pointing to a clear liquid alongside the gap where the bottle of Revenance Remedy lived.

"I probably shouldn't ask how you know about Crilliun, Guppy," Kaira's aunt remarked.

Guppy blushed a little. "Jacob's mentioned it, I think."

Philomeena Renn let out a mild laugh before adding, "I'm sure he did. Well, you both need to learn about the important remedies, like Srynx Serum and Quintz, which is why I brought you here. You see, while I'm away, I've instructed Jacob to bring you here once a day, to learn more."

"You're letting us use your Perium to come here on our own...?" Guppy's open mouth relayed a typical gesture of excitement; she was already imagining the adventures they could have in this new part of the Society.

Philomeena Renn, knowing this expression in the young only too well, added a word of caution. "Of course, Mivrilyn will be here to guard the room and ensure you don't go wandering off. Although a few senior members of the Feleecian know, most don't and wouldn't approve if you were discovered so this is a matter of trust and discretion."

Sensing these words were directed more at herself than Kaira, Guppy quickly re-evaluated her plans of covert wanderings.

"When are you leaving?" Kaira finally asked, thinking it pointless to ignore the theme of absence developing around her.

"Early this evening," added her aunt, and for the first time today, she hugged her niece and whispered, "I'm sorry.

Farraday will be with you whilst I'm gone and your dad and I will be back before you know it."

Kaira returned the hug, suppressing the heat of tears. "I know you can't tell me anymore," she uttered, "although, one day, I hope you can so I can help."

Sitting up slightly and lightly brushing a hand over her niece's face, Aunt Phee added, "You'll have to leave the excursions to the adults for now. Can you both promise me one thing."

Each nodded earnestly.

"That you will do your best to listen to Jacob whilst he tries to teach you as much about charms as remedies as he can? And that you won't do anything to put yourselves in danger?"

Kaira and Guppy nodded again, both sensing the implication of urgency in Philomeena Renn's voice - as if the knowledge they would gain from Jacob was going to be critical in the near future.

"Thank you," concluded Kaira's aunt before brushing Mivrilyn's yellow feathers. "Time to head back to The Cendryll."

≈

THE REST of the day passed slowly with Kaira brooding on the image of her dad in the Follygrin alongside the knowledge that her aunt was now joining him in the wild terrain he was alone in.

She pondered, as she sat at the small, circular table in her aunt's quarters, how a Society so wonderful in many ways thought it honourable to allow a member to enter dangerous territory alone, and why it had to be *her* family.

Guppy's suggestion that they continue to explore the wonders of the Vaspyl had lost its allure.

Magical artefacts offered little in the way of distraction now because even with her aunt's reassurances, Kaira knew she and her dad were risking their lives for some unknown cause. She would rather be with them than experimenting with morphing steel or studying their treacherous journey with a Follygrin.

This thought dominated for the remainder of the day as Guppy, sensing her friend's need for silence rather than entertainment, chose to read the books hidden away in her Keepeasy, continuing her search to find out more about the potential existence of the Terrecet and whose hands it currently resided in.

This silent passage of time, stretching into the early evening, was interrupted by a knock at the door and the familiar sound of Jacob's voice.

"Sorry," he began, realising he had entered at a moment of contemplation. "Farraday asked me to come and get you both. There's a meeting at Tauvin Hall which Farraday needs to attend so we're all going with him."

"Where?" queried Kaira, attempting to dismiss the image of her dad journeying alone in a barren landscape.

"A Society meeting point," explained Guppy.

"Sorry, but we need to go," explained Jacob. "Everyone's heading to the tunnels and mum and Farraday are waiting."

Reference to another aspect of the Society caught Kaira's attention: "We're using the tunnels to get there...?"

"I'll explain on the way but we need to go now."

13. The Tunnels

THE TUNNELS

Kaira grabbed the new coat Aunt Phee had brought for her and tapped her pocket out of habit, forgetting that the Follygrin and Vaspyl were now safely stored inside her Keepeasy. The red coat was an Ellintz, according to Guppy, adapting to the climate for maximum comfort and protection. Although Jacob had said they were using the tunnels to get to Tauvin Hall, a cool, autumn chill still hung in the air.

They took the lift to the ground floor, Kaira noticing the crowds gathered around The Seating Station whilst others hovered by the many doors. Muted conversations hung in the building, the only recognisable figures Farraday, Smyck, Meyen Grayling and Theodore Kusp.

"Are all these people going to the meeting?" asked Kaira as they stepped out of the lift.

"Yes," replied Jacob. "Tauvin Hall holds meetings when members are restless. The whole thing with Cialene Koll and Blaze Flint has scared a lot of people; The Orium Circle have called a meeting to listen to concerns and quell fears."

At the mention of The Orium Circle, Kaira thought of

Weyen Lyell, his secret relationship with Aunt Phee and the conversation she had overheard in Helping Hand regarding the darkness rising within the Society.

"Why are we using the tunnels when we could just use Periums to get there?" questioned Guppy as they walked towards her mother, Farraday and Smyck.

"Tauvin Hall can't be accessed via Periums for security reasons. The most senior members of the Society meet there to ensure people don't just wander into important meetings."

"So we have to walk?" queried Guppy in mild disgust, as if this was a ridiculous request to make.

"Enough questions, Guppy," insisted Jacob as they reached Meyen Grayling, Farraday and Smyck.

"Long time no see, Kaira," Farraday remarked with his usual humorous smile. He was dressed in his traditional attire of black jeans, black leather jacket and brown waist-coat. Smyck offered a brief nod whilst continuing to survey the crowds.

"Stay close to us," instructed Farraday.

A Spintz charm followed Farraday's instructions, created by Meyen Grayling in order to gather the attention of the collected crowds. The Cendryll's hum eased.

"Greetings, fellow members," began Jacob and Guppy's mother in her typically detached tone. "You are all familiar with the meeting rules in Tauvin Hall: questions will be directed by The Orium Circle and hecklers will be removed instantly. I must also remind you to be on guard as rumours of attacks continue to circle.

We already have people positioned outside Tauvin Hall, monitoring movements in Society Square. In the event of any such attack, we all have our instructions and know our positions. And finally, as we all know, only restrictive and defensive charms are to be used; any member witnessed using banned magic will find themselves on Quibbs Causeway."

Meyen Grayling then turned and walked towards one of the doors situated behind The Seating Station, uttering 'Entrinias' and striding through as it opened of its own accord.

The crowds followed suit, using the same charm to enter through one of the many multi-coloured doors lining the walls. Kaira, as instructed, walked alongside Farraday and Smyck whilst trying to keep Guppy in view. She had already lost sight of Jacob who was walking alongside Theodore Kusp, his black market trading of Laudlum still very much a mystery.

Little interpretation was required to understand the threat in Meyen Grayling's concluding words, thought Kaira as she kept pace with Farraday and Smyck. She remembered Jacob mentioning Quibbs Causeway on her first day - how it sent some people mad and linked to The Velynx ... the place which stored dark artefacts: Gorrah. Reference to consequences and the possibility of attack had done nothing to appease the wave of anxiety amongst the crowd who muttered their concerns in the busy tunnels - another sight for the uninitiated.

THE TUNNELS WERE DECIDEDLY UNMAGICAL: grey-slate floors, moss-covered walls and dripping water. It was a little surprising to witness such an uninspiring structure in an otherwise fantastical place, thought Kaira as Meyen Grayling's light-blue attire vanished out of view along with Guppy's long brown hair.

She was hoping for a spectacular feature to burst through the walls or the sudden production of a charm to make this journey less mundane but the trampling echoes were all there was.

Moments later, however, something shimmered into view up ahead. The pace of the crowds eased, becoming a stroll until the lines stopped before an enormous web forming a barrier across the width of the tunnels, its many strands contracting and retracting in what Kaira guessed was a protective barrier to uninvited guests.

"What happens now?" she whispered, stepping closer to Farraday.

"We walk through without getting tangled up. You're only really in trouble if The Web of Azryllis tightens around you."

Kaira threw a panicked glance at Farraday who appeared to be deadly serious.

"Don't worry," her dad's closest friend added. "You'll walk through with me."

She watched as the queue ahead stepped towards the intricate, moving web, uttering a charm Kaira couldn't quite catch.

"What are they saying?" she asked.

"Ego vero et sincéro accedámus," Smyck replied. "It means: 'I am true and sincere'. The Web of Azryllis only allows those to pass who wish no ill. It's a form of security to protect The Orium Circle and the secrecy Tauvin Hall provides."

"I thought your penchant lost its colour when you did harm, meaning you couldn't enter the Society through Periums."

"Being up to no good and doing bad are two different things, Kaira. The penchant loses its colour only when someone has done something bad. The web senses bad intentions so pre-empts those wishing to do harm."

Kaira felt the swell of the crowd pushing them forwards, now only feet away from the enormous web, and disturbing visions of her becoming entangled and swallowed up within it made her stop.

"Move along, young lady," demanded a voice from behind, prodding her on the back.

"Take my arm," instructed Farraday as Smyck uttered the chant and stepped into the web, temporarily becoming entangled before stepping through. Just repeat after me as we step in. Remember: 'Ego vero et sincéro accedámus'."

But Kaira couldn't remember and as she was carried along by Farraday's momentum, she found herself a step away from the vast web already hosting many other members as they struggled through.

"*Now*, Kaira," ordered Farraday as he uttered the chant. "Ego vero et sincéro accedámus."

Kaira mirrored each word, terrified her pronunciation or fear would be interpreted as masking evil intentions and her body tensed in anticipation of the web tightening around her. She held onto Farraday's arm tightly as The Web of Azryllis attached itself to her arms and legs, as if it were searching her conscience, before she felt herself being pulled through and into a kaleidoscope of light beams, emanating from the stained glass-windows lining either side of the cloisters they now stood in.

Through the crowds ahead, Kaira caught a glimpse of large, wooden double-doors: their journey to Tauvin Hall had been negotiated without event.

∾

THE HALL they entered was a hexagonal chamber constructed of an open floor space and benches rising high, occupying each wing of the building. On the open floor stood a row of six empty chairs, the S.P.M.A. logo carved into each. Kaira took her seat alongside Farraday and Smyck in the east wing, each section of the chamber demarcated by the compass decorating the polished wooden floor. The sizeable audience filtered into the four wings, the hum of anticipation and concern echoing in the vast chamber which stretched to an ornate ceiling.

Kaira spotted Guppy and Jacob on the west wing, almost directly opposite. Guppy offered a reassuring wave whilst Jacob was immersed in conversation with Ivo Zucklewick sat alongside him. She continued to scan the faces filling each wing, studying Theodore Kusp's rather uneasy position in the far corner of the south wing.

The unease, Kaira believed, was due to his sense of alienation in the Society since his secret black market trading of Laudlum had been exposed: a belief reinforced by the disdainful glances from those around him.

The person occupying Kaira's attention the most, however, was Meyen Grayling. She stood proudly alongside the six chairs, a hand resting on the one closest to her: a clear symbol of her lust for power. Kaira felt a rush of anger each time she laid eyes on the woman.

How could someone so cold rise to such a lofty position in the Society? she continuously wondered. And what was at the root of her lust for power...? The answer seemed increasingly evident to Kaira: to exercise a grudge against those who had attempted to stop her disconcerting rise.

Her preoccupation with the motives of Meyen Grayling was discarded as six people - three male, three female - entered the chamber from a narrow door hidden away in the north wing. A tincture of light glimmered in the enormous stained-glass windows as the six members, led by Weyen Lyell, took their seats, causing the murmurs to fade to silence.

"The Orium Circle," whispered Farraday as Meyen Grayling took a step forward in her typically self-involved manner. "Weyen Lyell you've met before," continued her dad's closest friend, ignoring the stares of those annoyed by his introductory lesson. "The others are Baltazaar Blin, Larell Follygrin, Cynthia Grinver, Melina Guest and Ina Lyell - Weyen's sister. It's Ina you have to pay attention to: what she says goes."

Kaira nodded and studied The Orium Circle who presented a mixture of eccentricity and authority, their matching green overcoats the only uniformity distinguishing them as a collective. Their individual nuances provided a more interesting picture, from the large quartz penchant stone of Weyen Lyell's ring to the closely shaven afro hair of Ina Lyell complimented by her royal-blue outfit and silver necklace.

The other four members were less authoritative: at least from their appearance and mannerisms. Baltazaar Blin was a small, rotund figure with an eccentric beard groomed to perfection, his black whiskers giving him a feline appearance.

Cynthia Grinver's bespectacled face and tweed dress gave the impression of a librarian who catalogued knowledge of each Society member whilst Melina Guest's face was partially hidden behind a shock of erratic red hair as she scribbled away in a small notebook.

Larell Follygrin was the least animated of them all, looking decidedly disinterested in the crowd who studied each member with a mixture of curiosity and awe. After all, it wasn't everyday one was offered an audience with The Orium Circle.

"If anything's going on that we don't know about, Ina won't hide it," added Smyck just as Meyen Grayling broke the nervous anticipation:

"Good evening to you all and thank you for taking the time to attend tonight's meeting. As you are all aware, our many years of calm and relative peace has recently been interrupted by a few instances reminiscent of darker times.

The aim of tonight's meeting is to both clarify the facts and remove false rumour. By doing this, we will all be better informed of the possible reasons behind this recent activity and what we can do to keep each other safe."

As Meyen Grayling's self-indulgent parade continued, Kaira noticed that Jacob was still in discussion with Ivo Zucklewick on the opposite side of the chamber, paying no attention to his mother's self-entitled ramblings.

"Why are the current Searings being covered up?" came a shout from the south wing of the chamber, interrupting Kaira's ponderings on what Ivo Zucklewick knew. The heckler was a small, balding man in an over-sized linen suit.

"We will take questions in an orderly fashion, Elin," countered Meyen Grayling as she turned towards a figure in the front row, dressed in a red gown, a large, silver pendant resting on his large belly. This attempt at avoidance was unsuccessful, however, as the short, bald man remonstrated angrily:

"Have we really been invited here to be stage-managed or is this an open forum, as the history of Tauvin Hall dictates? If this *is* an open forum, can you explain why the recent Searings have been covered up...?"

Kaira watched as Meyen Grayling paused, a moment of uncertainty passing her otherwise expressionless face.

Nervously tapping her blonde hair, she glanced at The Orium Circle whose nodded instruction returned her attention to the furious member.

"Always has to make a scene," whispered Farraday.

Kaira glanced at him, hoping for elaboration.

"My older, slightly mad brother," he explained. "Brilliant mind; terrible temper."

Having heard no mention of a brother before, Kaira paid closer attention to the duel forming between Farraday's balding sibling and Meyen Grayling. (She was also pondering the actual name of her dad's closest friend as it couldn't possibly be Farraday Farraday). Kaira's guessing game was temporarily discarded as the polite decorum within Tauvin Hall began to slowly unravel.

"To answer your question, Elin, the recent Searings have not been covered up. They have been..."

"Lies!" yelled Farraday's brother. "Three Searings above ground in the last month and only now is *No News is Good News* fluttering with reports. It seems to have taken Cialene Koll's death for people to finally listen!"

Meyen Grayling's superior detachment was faltering as Elin Farraday's rapid-fire delivery disrupted her well-rehearsed responses. "Well, that's not quite ... that's not quite the case, Elin."

"So Cialene Koll *wasn't* murdered by the Ameedis? Isiah Renn *hasn't* been spotted on the margins of the Society and Laudlum *hasn't* been secretly sold on the black market to Melackin by one of our own...!?"

Kaira looked over at Theodore Kusp squirming in the south wing of Tauvin Hall - a flurry of disgusted looks thrown his way.

"We are here to solve these issues, Elin," continued Meyen Grayling in an increasingly uncertain tone whilst the six members of The Orium Circle studied her performance, the mild disregard in Ina Lyell's face a sign her moment in the spotlight was coming to an end.

"We want answers!" someone else shouted close to Kaira, making her jump.

"Here we go," whispered Smyck, glaring at the heckler behind who sat back down immediately.

"Where's Casper Renn!?" came another yell. This was followed by: "Why are children present!?".

The heckles became a chorus when a stout, auburn-haired lady of approximately forty dressed in an array of orange and purple stood and pointed at Guppy, saying: "Isn't *she* the one who chased Cialene through a Cympgus to Dyil's Ditch...?".

The central chamber of Tauvin Hall then descended into accusation and remonstration until the tall, imposing figure of Ina Lyell stood and mouthed something Kaira couldn't hear and no-one else was paying attention to; however , seconds after she had done so the chamber fell silent. Kaira had to blink several times to check if what she was witnessing was truly occurring.

Although Tauvin Hall had fallen silent, every member was still gesticulating furiously, hands pointing and mouths moving - yet no sound came out. To test this was truly the case, she nudged Farraday and asked him to explain what she was seeing, quickly realising that her voice had also been silenced. Guppy returned Kaira's look with a quick shrug of the shoulders.

Jacob provided a little more help, mouthing a single, silent word as overtly as he could across the distance of the opposing west wing. Kaira did her best to interpret the word, judging it to be 'Vyoxal'. It would take a few more minutes for each of the members to take their seats before sound resumed, allowing Farraday to clarify Jacob's attempts at explanation.

"The Vyoxal charm," he whispered whilst keeping his eyes on Ina Lyell. "Neutralises the voice box. There are only a handful of people who can remove the voices of a whole crowd: Ina Lyell is one of them."

"Ina likes to make statements whenever challenged," whispered Smyck as he kept his eye on the member of The Orium Circle who now held utter control of the gathering. Ina Lyell then glided to the edges of each wing, carrying the air of a long-standing queen about to render judgement on those who had displeased her.

This authoritative manner was having the desired effect for the crowd sat in silence, bodies tensed as she surveyed faces - none of which dared hold her gaze. Those positing and gesturing only moments ago were now shrinking in her presence, looking down out of deference and fear.

As Ina Lyell moved towards the east wing towards Kaira, she felt the same fear run over her, transferring her gaze to the polished wooden floor. Something told her she was being studied and when a name was called, she grimaced in shock:

"Guppy Grayling." Ina Lyell's voice echoed in the vast chamber. "The child who chased Cialene Koll to Dyil's Ditch. Your presence is required on the chamber floor."

Kaira watched Jacob tap Guppy's arm, shaking his head and remonstrating to stay put. Guppy, however, knew better than to defy a member of The Orium Circle and stood from the bench, squeezing Jacob's hand as she passed - her only noticeable gesture of concern. Meyen Grayling then moved towards her daughter like an obedient pet rather than a caring mother, ushering her down the steps towards the awaiting figure of Ina Lyell.

Guppy brushed past her mother, dismissing her feigned gesture of care and reassurance, and made her way to the chamber floor. Kaira tried to catch her friend's gaze but it was resolutely focused on each step taken towards Ina Lyell. In the vast space of Tauvin Hall and the concentrated power of The Orium Circle, Guppy looked meek and vulnerable: two things rarely associated with her.

What followed shocked every single person in the room except for the wielder of the chaos and Farraday and Smyck who stood, unmoved, throughout the panic. Kaira had spotted the silver artefact in Ina Lyell's right hand as she moved across the chamber floor; she didn't recognise it and gleaned no further knowledge from Farraday or Smyck.

A circle of solid silver punctuated with small marks was all Kaira could see - that was until Ina Lyell flicked open the lid on the silver artefact, releasing a cacophony of piercing squeals followed by a blizzard of black, flooding Tauvin Hall. Screams and crazed shouting rang around the building as Kaira felt herself being pushed and prodded as people's shock turned to horror at the sight of the Ameedis swarming high above, wild and disorientated - washed in a shroud of blood-red light.

Kaira instinctively dropped to the floor, pulling at Farraday and Smyck who remained unmoved amidst the panic.

"It's a trick," Smyck said calmly above the hysterical yells, brushing aside anyone who attempted to pass him for fear they would trample on Kaira. "Ina's using a Zombul to make a point. The Ameedis can't see or hear anyone here and only fly where she directs them.

"Look," he instructed, pointing upwards. "She's making them fly towards Tauvin Tower away from everyone and

Guppy's still standing calmly next to Ina because the trick
has been explained to her. The Ameedis pose no threat."

As Smyck's final words hollowed into the wall of noise,
Kaira got to her feet slowly, peering at Guppy behind
Farraday and Smyck who had formed a barrier to protect
her. She watched as Ina Lyell twisted the base of the
Zombul, causing the blood-red light shrouding the blinded,
disoriented Ameedis to deepen.

Smyck was right - she was controlling them with the
Zombul because, moments later, the vampiric creatures
began to attack each other as they continued to rise towards
Tauvin Tower - a rise which reversed into a rapid descent
towards the terrified crowds before each one exploded into
dust.

REMNANTS of black dust sprinkled the shell-shocked crowd
as they nervously took their seats on the dust-covered
benches. Kaira, now seated once more, shook her head in an
attempt to stop the ringing in her ears. The other members
of The Orium Circle were now standing in a line with
Guppy positioned between Ina Lyell and her brother,
Weyen Lyell.

Kaira hoped the presence of her aunt's secret partner
would offer some reassurance to Guppy. It seemed, at least
from her position relatively high up on the seventh row, that
Guppy sensed no threat from either of them. Mild coughing
was the only sound now, the black dust entering the mouths
and lungs of members, and as further particles fell across
the stained-glass windows, Ina Lyell broke the stunned
silence:

"The purpose of this meeting was to address issues and

concerns regarding troubling events above ground and within the Society Sphere. During its long history, The Orium Circle has always responded to illegal activity within the Society and the ever-shifting lands beyond.

However, when we witness heckling and accusations from those who have *never dared* step foot beyond Society Square let alone the Society Sphere, a point must be made."

Kaira watched as Farraday glared at his brother in the south wing - the heckler Ina Lyell was referring to – who was comically battling the black dust which seemed to be targeting his eyes.

"Now we have re-established order, we will address the questions posed earlier. We will then open the floor to any other concerns in the traditional way of decorum and respect. So, let's begin with the girl called into question earlier, Guppy Grayling, and the general question of the presence of children in the Society and their involvement in the recent events in Dyil's Ditch."

Kaira sat on the edge of her seat, between Farraday and Smyck, hoping that what Weyen Lyell had told them in Helping Hand after their brush with death in Dyil's Ditch was indeed true: that The Orium Circle had agreed to change the rule for under-age members entering the Society. There was, of course, no reason to believe otherwise - except for the fact that Guppy was standing amidst the six Orium members as if she were awaiting judgement.

Each member returned to their seat, and a wooden chair, distinctly less extravagant, was brought to the chamber floor for Guppy and placed alongside Ina Lyell's. Looking decidedly out-of-place and increasingly awkward, Guppy kept her gaze on her feet which swung nervously above the polished wooden floor. Her long, brown hair -

typically resting along her back - was now over her shoulders to partially shield her from the glares of disdain.

Guppy glanced up at Kaira and Jacob who both offered reassuring smiles. As the debate regarding their presence in the Society began, Guppy and Kaira unknowingly shared a thought that they had momentarily returned to the typical structures of childhood where their fates lay out of their hands.

WEYEN LYELL STOOD, brushing particles of black dust from his purple three-piece suit. Like his sister, he had a distinct way of dressing to compliment his natural authority; however, unlike Ina Lyell, his afro hair was flamboyantly large - a flamboyance completed by the large ring on his right forefinger decorated by a multi-coloured quartz stone.

Reminded of her grandfather once more as she studied Weyen Lyell's calm demeanour, Kaira thought about her aunt journeying to meet her dad in the land of wind and shadows. The Renns, it seemed, had a propensity for secrecy and bravery, willing to sacrifice almost anything to protect the Society.

Before addressing the crowd, Weyen Lyell took off his green overcoat and placed it over the back of his chair. A number of people in each wing of Tauvin Hall let out a gasp at the sight of this, an utterance reflecting that this, in some way, broke Society protocol.

It was, however, a symbolic gesture, establishing the tone for the rest of the meeting: that established laws and procedures had to be modified and, sometimes, abandoned all together in order to adapt to changing circumstances. Ina Lyell had instigated this break from tradition by using a

Zombul to release the disoriented Ameedis: an injection of fear to re-establish authority. Now her brother, Weyen Lyell, had performed a much subtler gesture in removing his green overcoat.

Rubbing the rainbow-coloured quartz stone which decorated the ring on his forefinger, Weyen Lyell began his speech, addressing each wing of Tauvin Hall in true statesman-like style.

There were no interruptions or heckles from the crowd as there had been when Meyen Grayling had tried, and miserably failed, to impress. Instead, a respectful silence held for Weyen Lyell's words: words of a man who had encountered danger in the past and, therefore, knew the warning signs.

"The situation involving the young girl sitting with us now is one which has clearly troubled many members of the Society, some of whom have repeatedly rejected the notion of lowering the age of entry. I'm also aware that there are some present tonight who believe the only reason children have been allowed entry is because of the influence Casper Renn holds over The Orium Circle ... evident in the fact, some say, that his daughter sits with us this evening."

Kaira felt herself blush as the gathered crowd seemed to turn in unison and look in her direction. Farraday gave her a gentle nudge followed by a nod which she took to mean everything was okay. Slightly reassured by this, and the fact that Guppy didn't seem alarmed in the slightest, Kaira gathered herself and returned the gaze of those who had decided to study her for an uncomfortable amount of time.

After all, she and Guppy had already been accepted as members, and it was they who had made the link between The Sign of the Symean, the supposed fragment of a Terrecet via *Menphelin's Fables* and the potential link to The

Sinister Four who had revealed something of their secret involvement before Jacob set the Quij on them.

As far as Kaira was concerned, this all suggested that they hadn't done too badly considering she had been in the Society less than a week! Thoughts, it turned out, shared by Weyen Lyell.

"So let's begin with the matter of the allowance of under-age members into the Society. As you know, The Orium Circle took the unusual decision to allow entry to certain under-age members for the time being. This was relayed to each faculty via Scribberals soon after the unfortunate incident in Dyil's Ditch. Now, to the matter of that incident and the involvement of Guppy Grayling, Miss Renn and Master Grayling. The following wasn't relayed to each faculty but will be now.

It seems that Guppy, Miss Renn and Master Grayling had spotted some suspicious behaviour in The Pancithon some days ago and, not knowing who the person involved was, decided to investigate a little further.

A combination of some creativity and persistence allowed them to discover that the person - Cialene Koll - was searching for something inside one of the books in The Pancithon: a search which became increasingly frenetic. What Cialene eventually found was a note hidden inside one of the books. A note scrawled with the message: 'The Rise of the Ameedis'."

This information garnered the expected hum from the crowd - a hum which immediately died down as Weyen Lyell raised his left hand before continuing:

"Recognising this to be a threat, the children informed our loyal members Farraday and Smyck but, whilst doing so, noticed that Cialene had created a Cympgus to exit The Pancithon in haste. Sensing she was about to carry out the dangerous trek to The Spitting Tree, the group followed her to Dyil's Ditch to rescue her; however, the Ameedis got to her first after Cialene panicked and attempted to sear Guppy."

The mutterings increased in Tauvin Hall at the shocking news of an adult member attempting to carry out a Searing on a child. Weyen Lyell's construction of heroic children coming to the rescue was working, helped by the fact that he had conveniently distorted the truth. Guppy, after all, had blindly chased Cialene Koll through the Cympgus, having no idea she was entering Dyil's Ditch which had put everyone in danger.

"So," continued Weyen Lyell, "with this information now in the public domain, it is clear that past attitudes of children being unhelpful nuisances are out-dated and unwarranted. In fact, in the case of Guppy Grayling and Kaira Renn - Master Grayling having already reached the required age of eighteen - they have each been of benefit in terms of their desire to unravel the mystery behind recent dark acts."

WITH THIS, Weyen Lyell returned to his seat and put his green overcoat back on. He then asked Guppy to stand, gesturing for her to return to her seat - the relief on Jacob's face palpable. Meyen Grayling sat behind Jacob, her dust-covered, sky-blue dress a visual representation of how her early posturing had spectacularly backfired.

Cynthia Grinver was the next to speak; a bespectacled specimen dressed in tweed. The least distinct of the six Orium members, she took to the chamber floor to remind the crowd of a number of laws and by-laws which allowed for protocols to be revised or suspended in times of crisis.

With this uninspiring moment complete, the meeting was drawn to a close by Melina Guest whose flowing red hair fell over much of her green overcoat, her constant scribblings in her notebook now revealed to her audience. As she stood from her chair and raised her hands, a touch of anxiety punctuated the crowd, preparing for another unpleasant surprise. However, this performance was altogether more fitting to the Society's magical charms and shocked only one person present.

Holding up the green notebook she had been scribbling in through the meeting, Melina Guest let it fall from her hands and watched serenely as it hung, suspended in midair, before opening and repeatedly unfolding into a seemingly endless piece of parchment paper. When the wall of paper had reached the desired size, dominating the chamber floor occupied by The Orium Circle, Melina Guest tapped one edge, causing six illustrated scenes to appear across it.

It reminded Kaira of her Follygrin although there were no letters, and this artefact required no verbal instruction to be activated. She would later learn that the artefact was called a Panorilum: a notebook which turned written descriptions into vast illustrated scenes for purposes of presentation.

As the six illustrated scenes formed, Kaira caught her breath at the sight of a landscape she had seen in her Follygrin with Guppy, and a figure much like the one in the illustration: the figure of her dad struggling against the elements in the barren landscape Guppy hadn't recognised.

"As a way of conclusion," began Melina Guest in a strangely upbeat tone, "I thought it would be an appropriate time to illustrate the challenges we face and the brilliance and bravery we have amongst us. I'm sure you all recognise the places depicted in the six scenes on the Panorilum: Dyil's Ditch, Quibbs Causeway, The Velynx, The Gilweean Gateway, The Sylent and The Wenlands.

These places represent key points in our Society and whilst some are known to be dangerous, they all play a role in deepening our understanding of our history and identity in an ever-changing world."

Melina Guest's delivery was eloquent and instructive, her flamboyant red hair and floral dress - visible beneath her green overcoat - providing a less detached presence.

"Weyen mentioned Casper Renn and the implied influence he has over The Orium Circle. If Casper holds an influence, it is based on his undeniable bravery and continued sacrifice to protect us from threats known and unknown. Even now, as we speak, he ventures in The Wenlands to seek protection for us: a place few present this evening would dare venture to.

Philomeena is on her own journey to garner further information on the fragment which has led to the recent violence, and Quibbs Causeway remains problematic as we continue to study the forces making access to The Velynx increasingly dangerous."

Kaira was only interested in the illustration she had studied earlier in her Follygrin, burning with frustration that she had only found out now her dad was in danger - a frustration which grew when she caught Guppy's guilty expression on the opposite wing. Guppy *had* recognised the landscape her dad was in.

The rest of the meeting passed her by in a blur of emotion and preoccupation, her only desire to be back in her temporary bedroom in Aunt Phee's quarters; there she could use the Follygrin to understand more about the danger The Wenlands posed to her dad. For now, at least, with those closest to her keeping secrets, she needed to rely on herself.

Farraday's nudge was the sign the meeting was over, and the crowds spilled back out of Tauvin Hall and into the tunnels towards The Web of Azryllis. Kaira negotiated the barrier of protection with greater ease this time, remembering the chant to prove she was true and sincere "Ego vero et sincéro accedámus".

She strode ahead, shrugging off Farraday's request to slow down and ignoring Guppy's calls from some distance behind. She was sick of being kept in the dark, secrets and manoeuvres repeatedly weaved around her as if she were somehow incapable of dealing with complexity. Now her best friend was keeping things from her, and as much as she loved the magic and majesty of a society she had begun to think of as home, all she wanted now was to be left alone. No more secrets or surprises - just peace and quiet to formulate a plan...

14. Follygrins & Floating Floors

FOLLYGRINS & FLOATING FLOORS

Aunt Phee's quarters were locked when Kaira arrived, a problem easily overcome with the use of the Entrinias charm. She had taken the lift with Farraday and Smyck to the fourth floor, watching as Guppy, Jacob and their mother returned to The Cendryll. In her fit of frustration, Kaira kept her eyes on the colourful array of Quij following the momentum of the lift to stop herself looking down and catching Guppy's gaze - a decision she regretted the moment she found herself alone in her aunt's rooms.

The quarters were cool and shrouded in darkness apart from the light spilling out from the bedroom: the room she'd been sharing with Guppy. Only Churchill was present now, her beloved cat curled up on Guppy's bed which only served to reinforce her friend's absence. A flicker of guilt rose in Kaira as she recalled ignoring Guppy's calls on their return from Tauvin Hall.

Why was she being so hard on her friend? Guppy was obviously trying to protect her from more worry and now she was back in familiar territory: alone and disconnected from everything. Guppy and Jacob were her only two friends in the Society, she reminded herself - friends who had been loyal and kind.

She lay on her bed, hoping to hear the door to Aunt Phee's quarters open followed by Guppy's voice. A sadness rose in her when it didn't. Her best friend had taken offence which meant, for now at least, she only had anger and regret for company.

As TWILIGHT FELL over The Cendryll, Kaira felt a tightening in her stomach as the realisation dawned that she may have damaged her friendship with Guppy. She'd had enough distance to realise she had over-reacted. Guppy knew her dad was travelling in The Wenlands. It was obvious, in retrospect, that her best friend was trying to protect her.

Kaira was also aware that no-one told the truth all the time - sometimes obstruction and misdirection were necessary tricks to stop people from getting hurt. Kaira's dad and aunt had often used this tactic whenever she asked them difficult questions, so why had she been so hard on Guppy?

Also, how would this sudden fall out affect the daily trips to the Feleecian via the smallest, wonkiest door in Aunt Phee's quarters? Jacob was supposed to take them each day to improve their limited knowledge of remedies, Kaira sensing that they would be using them sooner rather than later.

Would Jacob be influenced by Guppy's anger at being ignored or would he retain his gentle loyalty to both of them? Why hadn't she just been more *mature* and spoken to her friend about it...?

The gradual realisation that her aunt's quarters may

encompass her temporary, lonely existence only made the knot in her stomach tighten. Yes, there were wonders awaiting her behind the two doors Aunt Phee had shown them earlier. There were the numerous rows of small, square boxes lining the walls in one of these rooms, each with a brass number-plate and key hole. They might be unlockable with the Entrinias charm but what would she be looking for?

Anyway, this seemed unlikely as she remembered the key her aunt had taken out of her bag. Also, there were over two hundred boxes to search through - two of which had delivered presents to herself and Guppy - but even the presents lacked their lustre now.

Kaira then thought of the window at the far end of the room reflecting the goings on in each faculty - like the one she had seen in Cribbe & Corrow when choosing her penchant. The window might be entertaining, at least, mused Kaira. Maybe she could kill some time by studying the images although even this had its limitations.

Guppy would probably know how to manipulate the window but Guppy *wasn't here* and thinking up adventures and exploits on your own wasn't the same; it was merely an exercise in managing loneliness and boredom.

There was, of course, the smallest door which led to The Feleecian, the tapping of the silver candle-holder above the fireplace providing entry. Kaira remembered how the door rattled and scraped as it opened to reveal a room bursting with light, colour and a sweet smell reminiscent of strawberries. Now, going there alone might take her mind off things.

There was, of course, the minor issue of the room being guarded by Mivrilyn, the bright-yellow Williynx who had been tasked to keep an eye on them while her aunt was away. Kaira would probably be ejected with a loud squawk the moment Mivrilyn saw she hadn't been escorted by Jacob as per Aunt Phee's instructions.

For now, it seemed, there was no opportunity to push the circular, brass contraption on the side of the bookshelf in the remedies room, causing a bell to ring and the remedy-bottle of choice jolting from its shelf, toppling off at rapid speed towards you. Kaira tapped for Churchill to join her for comfort. As her cat jumped into her lap, she closed her eyes but sleep eluded her.

The ongoing thoughts of a life confined to a small, lonely space on the fourth floor of The Cendryll magnified a sense of abandonment not helped by the darkness which tinted her sadness. She knew she had to swallow her pride and apologise to Guppy but was also fearful that her friend would reject the apology. Luckily, Kaira had the perfect artefact to assess the current state of their friendship: her Follygrin.

Encouraged by a sense of hope, she whispered 'Come-uppance' and drew the Follygrin out of her Keepeasy, momentarily debating whether it was better to start with her dad or Guppy. Her concern was greater for her dad yet her preoccupying thought was the mistake she had made with her best friend.

What would Guppy do? ruminated Kaira, tapping the circular, leather-bound artefact thoughtfully. Guppy would work on impulse as she always did, reacting first and thinking later. If Jacob was wandering The Wenlands, risking his safety to protect the Society, Guppy would unquestionably track her brother's movements whilst formulating a plan to help. Her bravery, after all, knew no bounds.

Kaira's dilemma continued for a few more moments until she decided to follow the path her best friend would take, flicking open the brass clasp on the Follygrin and rubbing her forefinger over the letter A. She watched the ink bleed into the now-familiar phrase: Ask and You Will Find...

"Casper Renn," she uttered, inhaling deeply as the pages of the magical artefact flicked to the letter 'C', the elegant letter fading, replaced by an intricate illustration of a familiar place. The familiarity, however, caused shock and alarm in Kaira for the image forming in the Follygrin was not of The Wenlands but of Dyil's Ditch ... her eyes darting to the lone figure of her dad negotiating the mudlands and fog whilst a swarm of black insects descended from above...

She dropped the Follygrin onto the bed, momentarily frozen in fear. She had to find someone to help her! The Cendryll lay silent in this twilight hour but she would shout to wake it if she had to! She picked up the Follygrin again and quickly located Farraday and Smyck only to find them in Society Square, heading towards The Blind Horsemen.

With panic rising in her and the terrifying image of the Ameedis descending towards her dad, Kaira uttered "Guppy Grayling" and watched as the Follygrin flicked to the letter G which faded into an illustration of Meyen Grayling standing over her daughter, pointing and yelling with Jacob between them. Each illustration only served to reinforce the obvious to Kaira: help could not be garnered in the time it would take for the Ameedis to attack her dad. She was on her own.

She stood from the bed, pushed the Follygrin into the Keepeasy within her jeans' pocket and whispered 'Cympgus', watching a tiny ball of light appear from one of the penchant stones on her bracelet. 'Whereabouts' was the second utterance, this command making the ball of light morph into numerous shapes until it adopted a circular form just big enough for Kaira to step through.

Grabbing the red coat Aunt Phee had given her yesterday and kicking off her shoes for black boots, she stepped through the Cympgus and into the darkness leading towards her dad, Dyil's Ditch and the returning terror of the Ameedis...

The smell swarmed Kaira again ... the inhumane stench which seemed to worsen in reaction to human presence. Her black boots squelched as they sank into the mud, the familiar feeling of being pulled down and losing her balance - a sign No Man's Land was beginning where one wrong step could be her last.

Remembering Farraday's immediate use of a protective charm when they entered to rescue Guppy, Kaira made the same arcing motion with her arms, whispering 'Velinis' and watched as the fog around her turned a pale green. With the increased sense of security provided by the Velinis charm, she uttered 'Comeuppance' and took the Vaspyl out of her jeans' pocket; this was quickly followed by her activation of the Spintz charm in an attempt to penetrate the curtain of fog.

To her surprise, the light fountain attached itself to the Vaspyl as if it had read her need for a source of light. The light source provided by the Vaspyl and Spintz charm allowed her to distinguish the outline of one of the two solid paths separating her from certain death in No Man's Land beyond.

Kaira found her footing and walked on, anticipating an explosion of sound as an army of small, vampiric creatures attacked only to be repelled by the Velinis charm. No attack came, however, and she continued the walk along the narrow path leading to The Spitting Tree. She could not afford to lose her balance or over-react at the sight of the Ameedis.

Still, there was no sign of her dad and, more worryingly, no screeching sound signifying an imminent attack from the Ameedis. As she walked on, keeping an eye on the dense fog above her and the narrow footpath below, the silhouetted shapes of the screaming buildings came into view, crashing and rising through the mud: an army of moving monsters howling towards the fire-orange sky.

This violent orchestra was accompanied by the cracking sounds of lightning from The Spitting Tree - where dark bargains were made: a collective chorus of doom. The attack happened a split second after her dad came into view: swift and silent, surrounding Kaira in a blizzard of black impossible to prepare for or retaliate to.

The green haze of the Velinis charm was the only protection from the dark monsters surrounding her now, their features remaining indistinct amidst the fog.

These were different creatures, though ... bigger than the Ameedis ... stronger, crouched and crippled, hissing at each movement she attempted. Kaira tried once more to move towards the black creatures inches above her dad's shoulders but the army of shadows immediately closed in on her, forcing her to retreat or fall to her death.

It was only when she had no option but to await her fate that she crouched within the protective bubble of the Velinis charm and closed her eyes. She placed her hands over her ears in the hope that this, along with the cracking lightning of The Spitting Tree, would drown out her dad's screams of pain. Tears finally fell as her fate was revealed in the hissing tones of the creature closest to her:

"You must return, Miss Renn," it instructed calmly to her utter shock.

It was only as the creature crept closer on all fours that Kaira saw the terrible scars over its face and body. It was clothed in black rags, the hollows of its face a symbol of sadness and pain.

The army of creatures continued to surround her, carrying the same sadness in their thin, hollow faces.

"My dad's going to get hurt," Kaira whispered through her tears which quickly became sobs as she realised how utterly helpless she was.

"Not so, Miss Renn," the creature replied. "Your father has our protection."

Kaira held the creature's gaze, certain this couldn't be true. If they were protecting her dad why were they blocking her way? The answer came as if her thoughts had been read:

"Your father journeyed to The Wenlands, our home, to request help. We have accompanied him here to meet someone who poses a great danger. The figures you see flying above your father are for his protection ... our race ... sky urchins. You must return, Miss Renn, before the creatures of this soulless place sense your presence, putting us all in danger. We will provide safe passage for you both."

On the utterance of these words, the crouched, scar-ravaged creatures formed two lines and parted the fog with their hands, creating what Kaira could only imagine was a Cympgus.

She looked again at the creature facing her beyond the protection of the Velinis charm as it silenced the hissing of its sky-urchin army:

"I can only leave if you promise my dad won't get hurt," she said, mildly surprising herself as she clearly had no authority or power here.

The creature held out a gnawed hand, offering its three fingers: "You have my word, Miss Renn, and the word of our people. Sky urchins never dishonour those who have shown loyalty; your father has risked his life for our kind many times."

Kaira studied the deformed hand, knowing she would have to break the Velinis charm to accept it. She thought of Guppy's bravery, the knowledge that her presence here endangered her father and looked again at the sadness and pain in the face of the sky urchin inches from her. Whispering 'Undilum', she broke the Velinis charm and took the hand of the sky urchin - the green haze of the charm fading into the fog.

"Thank you," she said, conscious of the Dyil's Slime covering her hands and the scarred-covered bodies of the sky urchins.

"Time to leave, Miss Renn."

Kaira nodded, accepting this battle was for others and that her father was, indeed, safe. "Can I ask your name?"

"Ivirin," replied the sky urchin now kneeling in a position of allegiance. "I am the guide for tonight's expedition." He then nodded to the space in the fog the other sky urchins had maintained. "Now we must ask you to leave to ensure safe passage for us all."

Kaira nodded again and walked along the narrow path in her red coat, using the Vaspyl and Spintz charm to light her way until she reached the parting in the fog. She raised her hand to the sky-urchin army in a gesture of a debt which could not be repaid and stepped through the fog into darkness, the crashing sounds of the screaming buildings fading into silence.

SHE APPEARED out of the Cympgus on the ground floor of The Cendryll, the shin of her right leg banging into The Seating Station. The sky urchins evidently knew her current location or assumed she knew how Cympgus' worked, the traveller simply imagining their place of choice. The large, star-filled skylight provided enough illumination for Kaira to determine she was alone in the dark expanse of The Cendryll.

She sat in the central bay of The Seating Station, abandoning the idea of using the Vaspyl and Spintz charm to illuminate the darkness she sat within. The possibility of a Society member appearing through one of the many doors or atop the spiral staircase remained. The Seating Station also provided an ideal hiding place should anyone appear.

Her thoughts returned to her dad, and the familiar instruction of 'Comeuppance' caused the Follygrin to appear in the pocket of her jeans. Kaira unclasped the Follygrin and rubbed her forefinger over the 'A', waiting for the words 'Ask and You Will Find' to appear before whispering, 'Casper Renn'.

The pages flicked to the letter 'C' and the intricate illustration which appeared had traces of familiarity. The limited light in The Cendryll made it difficult to identify precisely what was happening in Dyil's Ditch, and she scolded herself again for her childish reaction to Guppy.

If her friend was here now, she would have produced a vial of Crilliun to illuminate their vision, the purple hue bright enough to study the illustration in more detail. For now, however, the darkness was her only company, offering both protection from observation and an obstacle to greater understanding.

What she could see in the Follygrin's ever-evolving illustration was an army of sky urchins hovering inches above her father, the ragged, black creatures forming a wall stretching on either side of him, fading in-and-out of the rising fog which enveloped the base of The Spitting Tree.

From the stationary position her dad and his protectors had adopted, Kaira could only assume that the meeting had begun: a meeting with the mysterious figure representing a danger to the society: Erent Koll, Kaira assumed.

If only she could *see* who her dad was talking to! However, this was impossible through the wall of protection provided by the sky urchins and the blanket of fog that continued to rise higher out of the bowels of Dyil's Ditch. Whoever it was, the stillness surrounding the meeting reassured Kaira that no battle was to about to begin - negotiation being her dad's weapon of choice.

The echo of footsteps near the top of the spiral staircase made her drop to her knees behind The Seating Station. She closed the Follygrin and shoved it into the pocket of her jeans, whispering 'Keepeasy' as she did so.

Who was roaming The Cendryll in the early hours of the morning? Kaira wondered as she remained out of view. Laying on her stomach, she peered into the darkness to catch the unmistakable outline of Meyen Grayling standing at the top of the spiral staircase. Despite the lack of light, the uniform of light blue and cropped blonde hair could be made out under the star-filled skylight.

Kaira's suspicions grew as Guppy and Jacob's mother remained stationary as if she were purveying any possible witnesses to her secret midnight movements. She then turned away and ascended the spiral staircase, the echo of her heels growing fainter.

Once she was out of sight, Kaira got to her feet and brushed the dust off her jeans and coat. She couldn't shake the feeling that Meyen Grayling was heading somewhere other than her quarters ... to somewhere secretive and inaccessible in the daytime ... and for the second time in the space of an hour, she abandoned reason and followed.

As she ascended the spiral staircase in the darkness, Kaira became conscious of how slippery the soles of her black boots were: Dyil's Slime. Falling down with a loud bang wouldn't help her covert movements, she realised as she tentatively climbed each step.

She paused each time Meyen Grayling came into view above, finally reaching The Floating Floor and finding refuge behind a pillar to her right. Already shrouded in darkness and slightly set back from the wall, the pillar provided an ideal hiding position.

Kaira studied Guppy and Jacob's mother standing halfway along the magical floor, looking down at the illusory water surrounding her feet. Meyen Grayling then began to mutter something - inaudible to Kaira despite her best efforts to listen in - the illusory water bubbling and rippling.

Kaira kept low, peering out a little further as she tried to understand the meaning of this strange ritual, before recoiling in shock as Meyen Grayling vanished through The Floating Floor!

She pushed her back against the pillar, wrapping her arms around her legs before peering out to confirm what she had just witnessed. Sure enough, Guppy and Jacob's mother had disappeared through the floor which had become still again, the illusory water presenting Kaira with her reflection: its secrets contained for now.

She sat for a few more seconds before getting to her feet and standing on the edge of The Floating Floor. If she was going to find out what lay beneath, she needed to fall through herself or get back to Aunt Phee's quarters where she would have adequate light to use her Follygrin.

The first option was far more exciting yet also impractical for the purpose of spying on Meyen Grayling's secret midnight manoeuvres. Crossing The Floating Floor and returning to Aunt Phee's quarters was the better option because she could quickly locate the woman she most disliked in the Society.

Bracing herself for her own sudden drop, Kaira pushed her feet through the illusory water and began the crossing, treading lightly whilst holding onto the handrail to her left. In twenty-two steps, she was safely across and running towards the familiar door of her aunt's quarters.

She ushered Churchill onto her lap before opening the Follygrin, rubbing her forefinger across the letter 'A'. As soon as the familiar instruction of Ask and You Will Find appeared, she stated, "Meyen Grayling", watching as the pages flicked to the letter 'M'. The ink slowly faded, reforming into an intricate illustration of a cluttered maze of shelves which ran in every direction, each containing numerous, glass boxes which seemed to be bolted down.

Kaira rubbed a forefinger along the glass, bevelled edge of the Follygrin to rotate the picture, tracking Meyen Grayling's movements in the secret room beneath The Floating Floor. She peered closer as Guppy and Jacob's mother paused by a particular shelf, placing her hand on one of the many glass boxes attached to the shelving. The box rattled at her touch and a sinister smile touched her lips.

The callous gesture confirmed Kaira's suspicions about Guppy and Jacob's mother: she would do anything to gain power in the Society. As the wings of sleep finally brushed her eyes, she deduced that the secret room below The Floating Floor must be The Phiadal - the mythical room where all bovies were stored - and the container enticing Meyen Grayling probably held the artefact which had ignited a flurry of violence and deaths: the fragment of the Terrecet.

15. Sinister Secrets

15

SINISTER SECRETS

Kaira rose early the next morning, discovering that she was still alone in her aunt's quarters. Neither her dad, aunt nor Guppy had returned and the cloud of silence hanging in the rooms was reminiscent of the loneliness she felt in her bedroom at 12 Spyndall Street. She searched through the rucksack Farraday had brought from her house and pulled out some green corduroys and a grey, woollen jumper.

Autumn had settled in, evident in the dampness and morning chill in the bedroom along with windows dressed in condensation. As much as Kaira loved the seasons, she wasn't a fan of the cold and was happy when she discovered her favourite scarf at the bottom of the rucksack: a present from her dad.

She washed, dressed and left her hair to dry, eager to get to Quandary Corner in the hope Guppy would be waiting for her. There was no reason why her best friend would want to talk to her after Kaira's behaviour yesterday but she had to tell Guppy about what she had witnessed last night.

She took the lift to the ground floor, judging that this

would allow her to gauge Guppy's mood before she reached her friend; the lift's position behind The Seating Station provided the occupier with a panoramic view of all aspects of the ground floor.

Kaira stepped into the empty lift and descended towards the ground floor, glancing at the A-Z buttons which could take her to numerous places beyond The Cendryll. For now, though, her only focus was making up with her best friend and sharing last night's adventures - not even the Quij were a distraction this morning.

She studied the large S.P.M.A. crest carved into the wooden floor of the lift as it made its slow descent, and a flicker of joy rose in her when she saw Guppy sat in Quandary Corner. Guppy was turning the Vaspyl over in her hands, possibly contemplating her friend's dismissive attitude on their return from last night's meeting in Tauvin Hall.

Kaira shook this thought away. She needed to go over and apologise, explain the reason for her over-reaction then direct the conversation towards last night's discoveries. After all, Guppy loved a bit of intrigue and mystery.

"Hi," said Kaira as she reached her friend.

Guppy offered the briefest of smiles whilst continuing to flick the Vaspyl into the air, transforming a spoon into handcuffs with the flick of a wrist.

"I'm sorry about last night. You know, walking off like that."

"No problem," came Guppy's curt reply.

It clearly *was* a problem but not one big enough to build into argument or accusation.

"I know you were just trying to protect me," added Kaira, trying to remove Guppy's cold detachment she associated more with her mother.

"Of course I was. Do you think I'd upset you *on purpose*?"

Recognising that Guppy felt equally hurt, Kaira elaborated on the reasons for her reaction: "I'm just missing my dad, and when my aunt said she had to leave for a while, it felt like..."

"... It felt like you had no-one and pretending I didn't know where your dad was didn't help. I get it," declared Guppy as she patted for Kaira to sit alongside her. "I knew you'd find out sooner or later, but I thought you'd had enough bad news."

Kaira sat alongside her friend: "Thanks for trying to protect me."

"Thanks for coming to my rescue in Dyil's Ditch," quipped Guppy, allowing a smile to animate her face. "Oh, and just so you know, I wanted to come back to your aunt's quarters after the meeting but being singled out by The Orium Circle went down pretty badly with my mum."

"Yes, I could tell," replied Kaira, understanding that reference to the Follygrin would inevitably lead to her mother's suspicious movements last night.

"You used the Follygrin to check where I was," stated Guppy, familiar now with the artefact Kaira used to locate people for reassurance or surveillance.

"I also used it to check on my dad and almost bumped into your mum when I got back."

Kaira had Guppy's full attention now.

Whispering 'Keepeasy', Guppy placed the Vaspyl in her jeans and said, "Back from where...?"

"Where my dad is now ... or was last night."

Guppy's eyes widened as the full weight of Kaira's statement sunk in: "*No way*, Kaira! You went to The Wenlands...!? You could have been killed!"

Kaira put a finger to her lips to gesture a need for quiet,

concerned that Society elders over-hearing further illegal exploits of underage members wouldn't help their long-term future.

"No, not The Wenlands. My dad wasn't there when I looked again."

Guppy waited, her legs jigging up and down in anticipation.

"My dad was in Dyil's Ditch when I used the Follygrin to check last night. As soon as Melina Guest used the Panorilum to show him wandering in The Wenlands and mentioned him risking his life, I had to check if he was okay. When I checked, though, he was walking towards The Spitting Tree in Dyil's Ditch."

"*What*!?"

The Cendryll elders glanced over this time, their annoyance clear.

"Sorry," offered Guppy before finally gauging the appropriate volume for such a conversation. The Worble charm, although ideal for such situations, was deemed utterly offensive in the presence of Society members. "You went to *Dyil's Ditch*?" she whispered. "On *your own*?"

Kaira began to study something by her left leg as she continued - a way of masking the secret conversation: "The Follygrin showed my dad battling the fog in Dyil's Ditch, alone again, with an army of black creatures descending towards him."

Guppy instinctively grabbed her friend's arm, shocked at what she had been told. "The Ameedis *attacked your dad*...?"

Kaira shook her head calmly, her lack of upset a clear sign her dad hadn't been attacked. "I checked Farraday and Smyck's location but they were in Society Square near The Blind Horsemen. You were being shouted at by your mum with Jacob trying to calm her down.

I thought my dad was about to be attacked and everyone else was asleep, so I used a Cympgus to find him. I didn't think; it just happened. Anyway, I used a Velinis charm to protect myself as soon as I got to Dyil's Ditch and, before I knew it, I was surrounded by what I thought were Ameedis but the creatures swarming towards my dad were sky urchins."

Guppy was completely lost for words.

"The leader of the sky urchins, Ivirin, said they were providing protection for my dad and that he was meeting someone who posed a great threat to the Society. My dad had risked his life to protect their kind, he said, which is why they had flown from The Wenlands to help. One group of sky urchins surrounded me whilst another, bigger group stayed with my dad, flying just above him as he neared The Spitting Tree.

They explained that my presence in Dyil's Ditch was putting everyone in danger, that my dad would be safe and insisted I return. They made a Cympgus by parting the fog and I ended up back here. Well, not literally here ... by The Seating Station which is where it gets more interesting, but we need Jacob for the next bit..."

"Why?" asked Guppy although a part of her already knew.

Unfortunately, Jacob was already at work cataloguing creative charms on the third floor so Kaira's revelation about the vanishing act through The Floating Floor would have to wait. Guppy and patience, however, rarely went hand-in-hand.

"If it's about my mum and you're not going to tell me without Jacob, we need to go and find him otherwise I think my head's going to explode."

Smiling at Guppy's gift for the dramatic, they considered

the option of going directly to Jacob's place of work, quickly discarding the idea for an alternative plan: "What if I tell you something amazing while we wait? Jacob needs to take us back to the Feleecian to learn more about remedies so he'll have to appear at some point."

Guppy ruminated over this proposal; it was clear from the way in which Kaira was skirting the issue that the information was about her mum. Her friend didn't have to say it: her entire manner and deflection was enough to confirm this to be the case.

Although Guppy wasn't upset or even surprised to hear that her mother was sneaking around at night, she still wanted to know the extent of her involvement and the danger she may have put them in. She had long abandoned hope that her mother would prioritise her children over her lust for power; however this sudden turn of events was still saddening for a woman whose gifts were secondary to her utter disregard for others.

THEY AGREED to wait for Jacob in Philomeena Renn's quarters, enacting a Worble charm to ensure their conversation was secret and indecipherable to external ears.

"Okay," Kaira began. "So, I arrived back here through the Cympgus the sky urchins had created for me and sat at The Seating Station. I thought sitting there would make it easy to hide if someone turned up. It was gone midnight but the stars were out, filling the skylight, so I knew I'd still be visible to anyone wandering around."

Guppy, already knowing who had been wandering around, urged Kaira to continue.

"I used the Follygrin to check on my dad which is when I saw your mum..."

Guppy jigged her legs, impatiently awaiting the revelation Kaira had promised.

"She appeared at the top of the spiral staircase minutes after I got back," continued Kaira. "I got the feeling she was checking no-one was around. I hid, obviously."

"And then?"

"And then she turned around and walked up the staircase?"

Guppy pulled a disgruntled face. "*That's it...*? That's the revelation?"

"No. Once she was out of sight, I got up from my hiding place and followed her. Something told me she wasn't going back to her quarters on the fifth floor ... that she had come from there and was going somewhere else."

"Where did she go?"

"To The Floating Floor. I hid behind a pillar and listened as she muttered something: a kind of chant."

"Did you catch what she was saying?"

Kaira shook her head. "It was some sort of command."

"For what?"

"For access to what's hidden below. Guppy, moments later, your mum vanished through The Floating Floor..."

Guppy, temporarily lost for words, drummed her fingers on the table occupying the central space of Philomeena Renn's quarters. "And you're not going to tell me the rest until Jacob gets here...?"

∾

LUCKILY FOR GUPPY, Jacob appeared not long after and was brought up-to-date with Kaira's moment of madness in Dyil's Ditch last night.

"*Sky urchins*? In *Dyil's Ditch*?" he repeatedly uttered, his shock almost comical to Kaira.

Once over the shock of Kaira befriending a sky urchin in one of the most dangerous places in the Society, Jacob was ready to hear what secret lay below The Floating Floor. With the three sat at the small, circular table and the Worble charm still in place, Jacob began with a question:

"You definitely saw our mum vanish through The Floating Floor?"

Kaira nodded.

"So the charm you heard grants access," Jacob added, more to himself than the others. "We need to know what's hidden underneath before we rush to judgement about what she's up to."

"She's up-to-no-good," offered Guppy. "That's what she's up to. Sneaking around at night and leaving us on our own."

"It's The Phiadal," stated Kaira. "That's what's below The Floating Floor."

This final revelation refocused Guppy and Jacob with the latter saying,

"What makes you say that?"

"I ran back here and used the Follygrin to check."

"And what did you see?" asked Guppy.

"A room with shelves running in every direction ... like a maze, with glass boxes bolted to the shelves. Inside each glass box was another box – made of metal, I think"

"Okay, slow down, Kaira," instructed Jacob. "You say you think it was The Phiadal ... a place hardly anyone in the Society knows the whereabouts of? There are hundreds of rooms throughout the Society in each faculty and building: it could have been anywhere."

"Except for the fact that your mum was particularly interested in one box," countered Kaira. "It was at waist height, in the furthest corner of the room. When she went to touch the box, the metal casing inside the glass rattled until she moved her hand away."

"The Terrecet fragment," interjected Guppy.

Jacob stood up from the table and walked over to the kitchen counter, the cabinets behind stretching as far as the eye could see. "The description of the room might be The Phiadal but it's a leap to the Terrecet fragment, Guppy.

Bovies are kept in The Phiadal until their complex properties are fully understood for everyone's safety. That's the main reason its location is kept secret from most people. Lots of bovies react to touch. Also, who's to say mum didn't use a charm when she touched the box."

"It's the Terrecet fragment," insisted Guppy again. "Why else would she be sneaking around on her own at night?"

"So you're willing to believe our mother would hide one of the most dangerous artefacts for her own benefit?"

"Yes," replied Guppy matter-of-factly.

"Why is she going there to check on it?" queried Kaira. "That's the part I don't get. She was always going to run the risk of being seen."

"Because the Terrecet's power seduces people," replied Jacob. "Remember the legend we read in *Memphelin's Fables*? If it is what we think, we need to tell someone and transport it to The Velynx as soon as possible. Who in their right mind would hide one of the most powerful Gorrah artefacts in The Cendryll?"

"Someone who is planning to use it against the Society," stated Guppy.

"So now you think she's evil and on a path of destruction? We each have reasons to dislike our mother, Guppy, but that's stretching things a bit, even for you."

Guppy stood and circled the table: "I think she'd do anything for power."

"But you don't think she would hurt people for it?" asked Kaira, herself finding it hard to believe that Meyen Grayling was entirely bad. "Blaze Flint, I mean, and Cialene Koll."

Jacob shook his head: "Remember that penchants lose their colour once an act of Gorrah is committed, Kaira. You also lose the ability to access Periums so it wasn't our mother who attacked them."

"But she could have ordered the attack or asked The Sinister Four to use their well-known methods as Implementers to locate the artefact," suggested Guppy.

"You really won't let this go, will you?" countered Jacob in mild annoyance at his sister's implication.

"I think she's selfish and obsessed with being above others. You might have a better view of her, Jacob but yesterday is a perfect example of my point ... shouting and yelling at me because Weyen Lyell praised my courage in Tauvin Hall. She was behaving like a child because the attention wasn't on her, desperate to impress The Orium Circle but instead embarrassing herself when she got shouted down."

"Okay, so what do we do now?" interjected Kaira, attempting to halt another sibling spat.

"Well, if you're right, Kaira, our mother will go there again soon ... unable to ignore the pull of the fragment."

"Do you think she'll go tonight?"

Jacob nodded: "Yes. Until it's moved, she won't be able to resist."

"So we follow her," stated Guppy. "We follow her tonight."

THE PLAN WAS SIMPLE: Jacob would follow his normal evening routine of visiting Ivo Zucklewick, leaving Guppy to be the model child - a joke which passed her by - heading to bed without fuss. Jacob wouldn't actually go to Zucklewick's but to Philomeena Renn's quarters where he and Kaira would use the Follygrin.

As soon as Meyen Grayling headed to The Floating Floor, they would use the Scribberal to let Guppy know the coast was clear. Once she had received word via her mother's Scribberal, Guppy would sneak out and down the steps to the fourth floor, staying hidden on the bottom step and doing her very best to decipher the charm used to vanish through the magical floor. Assuming this all went to plan, phase two would then be enacted...

The following evening, Jacob would create a distraction to cause worry and concern in his mother, referring to the work he and Ivo were doing in Zucklewick's each evening. He would imply their investigations offered clues to those who had retrieved the Terrecet fragment (or what was believed to be the fragment) from Blaze Flint.

If Guppy's assumptions were right about their mother's involvement in dark matters, she would panic and contact her partners in crime via a Scribberal or, better yet, go with Jacob to Zucklewick's to find out how much he and Ivo actually knew.

Of course, Jacob had no actual intention of revealing how much he and Ivo had discovered but felt confident he could present an authentic picture of interest in recent events without raising suspicion. Meanwhile, with their mother otherwise engaged, Guppy and Kaira would attempt to access The Phiadal via The Floating Floor. Despite Jacob's earlier doubts regarding his mother's involvement in dark matters, it was hard to argue with Guppy's logical deductions:

"Let's just say that Kaira is right, for now, and that the place she saw in the Follygrin is The Phiadal and the fragment mum's interested in really is part of a Terrecet.

Someone with power and influence in The Cendryll helped to hide it there because we know, until three days ago, it was in the possession of Cialene Koll who sold it on the black market as soon as she knew the danger it posed. Kaira overheard Weyen Lyell telling her aunt this at Helping Hand after the Ameedis tried to attack us in Dyil's Ditch.

Then we overheard Sylan Ryll and Aneesha Khan discuss their involvement when we went to The Pancithon the other night to look for a link between the Sign of the Symean and the Terrecet. Aneesha was trying to reassure Sylan that they hadn't 'left a trail' whilst he was concerned that 'the mess with Cialene had started rumours' and 'why those three had to turn up', obviously meaning us."

Guppy paused, checking to see if Kaira and Jacob were following her train of thought: they weren't.

"So the 'trail' they were referring to was their trail of movements."

"Which is …?" queried Jacob.

"Tracking down Blaze Flint for the fragment of the Terrecet and bringing it here."

"What, and just dropping it into mum's hands when they arrived?" Jacob countered dismissively, still struggling to accept the possibility that his mother could sink as low as

The Sinister Four; the group who had attacked him on his first day in the Society.

"But if your penchant loses its colour and you can't access Periums, how would they have brought it here, if they attacked Blaze Flint to get the fragment?" asked Kaira.

Guppy continued: "So Sylan Ryll was worried that the 'mess' with Cialene had started rumours."

Jacob nodded, following his sister's reasoning: "So if they were involved in Cialene's death in some way, maybe scaring her to reveal how she'd got her hands on the fragment, they'd be worried about being implicated. That would explain why they were angry with us snooping around in The Pancithon, using the Blindman's Watch to track what Cialene was doing."

"She did come out of one of the reading rooms before she escaped to Dyil's Ditch," added Kaira, also seeing a potential connection. "She looked like she'd been there all night; she was wearing the same clothes and her makeup was all messed up."

"Under the guard of The Sinister Four, maybe," Jacob conjectured.

"Probably keeping a close eye on her until they found out more about the fragment," added Guppy.

"And if she'd told them who she'd sold it to, they could easily have used their powers as Implementers to retrieve it on behalf of the Society."

"Which still doesn't explain how the fragment is in The Phiadal now, assuming it was The Sinister Four who retrieved it from Blaze Flint," declared Kaira, sensing there was a part of the jigsaw she was missing. "A Voxum Vexa curse was used on Blaze Flint so the person or people who used the curse wouldn't be able to use Periums anymore."

"But what if The Sinister Four retrieved the fragment

but didn't curse him?" suggested Guppy. "They'd be too clever to leave such an obvious trail and, also, wouldn't just throw away their Implementer status at someone else's bidding."

"But then Blaze Flint would remember them taking it."

"Not if they threatened to transport him to Dyil's Ditch," countered Guppy.

"Or used a Removilis charm," suggested Jacob, "then he would either choose not to remember or genuinely have no memory of it."

"Well, it all makes sense," stated Kaira after a brief pause, "except for one thing: Cialene sold the fragment to Alice Aradel."

"Who sold it to Blaze Flint," continued Guppy. "The Sinister Four only had to find Alice Aradel in The Blind Horsemen, or another black market location, and ask about the fragment."

"And Blaze Flint lives alone in the middle of nowhere which would have made it easy to pay a visit without being seen," added Jacob.

"So if we're saying The Sinister Four brought the fragment here, we need to check when they last visited," declared Kaira. "Blaze Flint was attacked three days ago so if they've been here in that time period, we've got a strong case for both being up to no good."

"I'll check with Theodore," Jacob replied. "They try to intimidate him whenever they turn up, reminding him of the consequences of another mistake. For now, though, we need to follow your aunt's instructions and go to the remedies room in The Feleecian.

There's obviously a reason she wants you to learn about remedies as quickly as possible. Also, any change of routine might arouse suspicion if we're being watched."

Kaira and Guppy agreed, and the plan was set to follow Meyen Grayling to The Floating Floor when night-time fell.

THE DAY SEEMED TO DRAG, mainly taken up with unsuccessful attempts to learn more about remedies in The Feleecian. The room's unique host, the yellow Williynx named Mivrilyn, displayed the same impatience and suspicion expressed on their first visit and each mistake was greeted with an ear-piercing squawk.

Aunt Phee had made it look so easy, thought Kaira, as they first attempted to navigate the powder-filled bottles from the tall shelves only for the first three to fall and smash on the floor. Covered in purple, green and red powder, and with Mivrilyn's ear-piercing squawks ringing in their ears, Jacob took the decision to abandon remedies and return to the peace and quiet of The Cendryll.

The resounding image each left with was the sight of Mivrilyn's enormous, yellow wings flapping as she floated above each broken bottle, squawks turning to birdsong as the powders rose from the floor and into a perfect circle, spinning as the shattered pieces of glass reconnected. With each bottle returned to its original state, the powders had found their homes again.

NIGHT-TIME FINALLY FELL and the plan was enacted, Jacob leaving his mother's quarters on the fifth floor, taking the lift as he always did but only to the floor below, knocking and entering Philomeena Renn's quarters where Kaira awaited.

Guppy went to bed at the normal time in order to stick to the plan.

With the Follygrin open on the fourth floor and the Scribberals within reach in both rooms, the only thing to do was wait for Meyen Grayling to descend the stairs towards The Floating Floor. Jacob placed the Scribberal on the small, circular table whilst Kaira continued to study the illustration in the Follygrin, saying "Now" to Jacob the moment Meyen Grayling began her journey.

Guppy, standing over the Scribberal, opened the silver artefact the moment it rattled, worried the noise would send her mother back inside. Waiting a few moments to check this wasn't the case, she quickly took a vial of Crilliun out of her Keepeasy, blinking until the familiar purple hue illuminated her surroundings.

She knew she only had a few seconds to get down to The Floating Floor before her mother vanished out of sight so crept out of the room and descended the narrow, spiral staircase. Thankfully, she caught sight of her mother in the reflection of The Floating Floor, the illusory water allowing her to stay hidden behind the pillar at the bottom of the steps.

As Kaira had described, Guppy's mother stood halfway along The Floating Floor, muttering a charm which she strained to hear. Moving her head outwards a little so her right ear was away from the pillar, Guppy caught the chant on the second incantation:

"I understand what is below and, with your help, desire to know."

The chant was repeated, and just as Kaira had described, Guppy's mother vanished through The Floating Floor.

As soon as the illusory water had settled, Guppy ran

through it and burst into Philomeena Renn's quarters, locking the door before sitting down to study the Follygrin.

She was desperate to see the picture Kaira had described - of a place as mythical as the Symean. It took very little time for Jacob and Guppy to agree that Kaira had, indeed, found the location of The Phiadal.

"A brilliant stroke of luck, Kaira," commended Jacob as they all studied the moving illustration.

"There are only rumours and hearsay regarding The Phiadal's actual structure but this fits the picture, particularly the way it's hidden in plain sight: a place no-one would imagine it to be.

Also, the maze of boxes bolted to the shelves makes sense because until their magical properties are discovered, bovies are unstable."

"It's *got* to be the Terrecet fragment," declared Guppy, her nose almost touching the Follygrin as she watched her mother stroke the glass-encased box once more, disgusted that she could express affection for an artefact but not her children. "And after the way she treated Theodore when they brought him in ... just for selling Laudlum on the black market."

"So I distract her tomorrow night and you two use the chant to have a look around," Jacob clarified. "As great as the Follygrin is, we need to know for sure before we tell someone we trust."

"Who *do* we trust with Kaira's dad and aunt gone?" Guppy asked, sitting up and looking away from the illustration.

The question was left unanswered, although the following morning would bring unexpected help - and relief.

16. A Sudden Return

A SUDDEN RETURN

Kaira woke to a tapping sound and a muted voice from behind the bedroom door. Unable to identify the sound, she placed her feet in her slippers and crept towards the keyhole of the door, peering down to peek through.

The door opened and she looked up at the imposing figure of her father, standing as calmly as always with his arms open. She didn't hesitate to run into them, hugging her dad tightly and not wanting to let go.

"You're back," she muttered before releasing him.

"Yes, I am," her dad replied with a quiet laugh.

They crossed the landing to her dad's quarters after Kaira had thrown on her green cords and grey jumper, the Quij fluttering closer to the bannister as a way of celebrating Casper Renn's return. Groups were already making their way up-and-down the spiral staircase as crowds formed below on the ground floor of The Cendryll. Kaira threw a gaze towards The Floating Floor, itching to fall through to The Phiadal: a plan thwarted by her dad's return.

"Is Aunt Phee with you?" she asked as they entered her

father's quarters, noticing Farraday on the battered sofa under the window, Churchill curled up on his lap.

"We're meeting her later on."

"Later today?"

"Yes. A little distance away."

"Away?"

"Don't worry. We're going together?"

"Okay. Where?"

"Slow down, Kaira," advised Farraday from the sofa as he stroked Churchill's chin, something her cat never allowed Kaira to do. "Give your dad a chance to catch his breath. Anyway, where's my hello?"

"Sorry." Kaira offered Farraday a sarcastic wave - a game they played once she'd outgrown hugs for everyone except her dad and aunt.

Farraday returned the comical wave and pushed his heavy figure off the sofa, moving towards the Parasil perched on the dining table containing Jysyn Juice.

"It's been a long night," he declared, filling his glass before falling back onto the sofa.

Kaira, of course, knew he and Smyck had been wandering Society Square near The Blind Horsemen, checking on those up-to-no-good which made her think of someone else who was up-to-no-good, wondering when she should tell her dad about Meyen Grayling.

"So, what have you been up to?" her father enquired, his prying eyes studying her. "Learning lots, I hear."

Choosing her words carefully, Kaira said: "Jacob's taught me a lot about charms and Aunt Phee's introduced me to remedies."

"Through the crooked door?" quipped Farraday, clearly referring to the small, wobbly door her aunt used to access The Feleecian.

"Yes."

"So, you've met Mivrilyn then?" continued Farraday from his sunken position on the sofa under the window. "Charming, isn't she?"

Kaira was careful not to mention last night's trip to Dyil's Ditch or Meyen Grayling's vanishing act. She knew she had to tell her dad about the latter event although when would be a decision she, Guppy and Jacob needed to agree on.

She loved her father dearly but also found it hard to predict his reactions to things and, given the current tensions in the Society and the fact he had just risked his life to protect it, she doubted his response towards Meyen Grayling's suspicious behaviour would be sympathetic.

"It sounds like you've been busy," her dad concluded before giving her another quick hug. "You'll need to pack some things to bring with you; Farraday says he brought you a rucksack from home?"

Kaira nodded, still struggling with her father's role of saviour in the Society and the fact he was leaving again - although this time with his daughter for company.

Guppy and Jacob arrived soon after hearing the news of Casper Renn's return. They were unfortunately accompanied by their mother who didn't seem to share Kaira's joy and relief. If anything, she seemed uneasy in his presence as if her secret, midnight visits were not so secret after all. It could also be the fact that she, like Kaira, found Casper Renn hard to read.

Whatever the reason, she chose to hover in the doorway rather than follow her children inside, declining Farraday's offer of Jysyn Juice before interrupting the happy occasion with Society business: a surprise to no-one.

"You asked for me, Casper?" she queried.

"Are you sure you won't join us in a small celebration, Meyen?" offered Kaira's dad in reference to the Jysyn Juice on the dining-room table.

Her stubborn position in the doorway provided a definitive answer.

"Very well," he continued. "I need you to oversee things for a few more days: other reaches of the Society call. I realise I have burdened you with ..."

"Of course," interrupted Meyen Grayling flatly. "I'm sure Jacob and Guppy will be happy to keep Kaira company while you're away."

"Kaira is coming along this time."

Guppy paused in her attempt to sneak some Jysyn Juice in a tea cup, accidentally knocking the delicate china on the wooden surface in response to this news.

Jacob, mildly amused by his sister's erratic impulses, risked a proposal:

"If I can be of help, Mr. Renn." He could see the fury in his mother's eyes, throwing a contemptuous glance her way in response.

"Well, if The Cendryll can do without you for a few days, Jacob, and your mother agrees, your presence would be appreciated."

Guppy banged the china teacup on the table again - this time intentionally - unable to hide her feelings of rejection. Wasn't *she* Kaira's best friend? Why did adults always believe age somehow made people more capable?

A pause hung over the room as Meyen Grayling darted looks at each of them, suspicion mixed with an understanding that, like in Tauvin Hall, her authority here was not absolute. Should she contest Casper Renn's offer, her son would surely argue, undermining her authority further. There was only one appropriate response:

"Why don't you take Guppy with you as well; I'm sure Kaira would enjoy her company."

Guppy banged the cup on the table in triumph before quickly feigning sadness, fearing her mother would change her mind.

"Well, that settles it," declared Meyen Grayling. "I will distribute roles accordingly and inform the senior members of your extended hiatus."

Kaira's dad chose to ignore the bitter tone, choosing to raise a glass to Guppy and Jacob in a subtle gesture of validation: "Welcome aboard," he stated with a brief smile, watching as their mother turned and stormed out.

"Well," said Farraday as he heaved his tired frame off the sofa once more, "that went down well."

Guppy and Kaira suppressed a laugh while Farraday walked over to close the green double doors.

"Pack lightly," Kaira's dad said once the doors were closed. "Enough for a few days."

"Where are we going?" asked Guppy, realising quickly that Kaira's dad, very much like herself, worked to his own rules and rhythms.

"All will be explained in due time. Pack lightly and quickly. We leave on the hour."

Kaira, still bemused by the Society's ongoing reliance on her father, wondered if she should ask for some Jysyn Juice to ignite her bravery.

"We'll sneak a cup in once we've packed," whispered Guppy, nodding towards the Parasil, and they headed off to their respective rooms to get ready.

THE JOURNEY out of The Cendryll was very similar to Kaira's initial one in - except, this time, the Perium used wasn't in Cribbe & Corrow but the kitchen door in her dad's quarters. With luggage in tow and the main doors to the rooms locked, the group congregated by the door as Casper Renn pulled the brass doorknob with the S. P. M. A. logo engraved onto it and began turning.

The familiar dizziness returned as the door grew larger followed by words in gold lettering. Kaira recognised more places now - *Feleecian, Orium, Pancithon, Quibbs Causeway, Tauvin Hall.*

The doorknob clunked as it was pushed back in and they stepped through ... into another room furnished with nothing but another door at the end of a corridor. Farraday waved away Guppy's questions regarding the empty room, his expression suggesting this wasn't relevant to their journey. The location the second door took them to *did* need explaining or, more to the point, explaining again.

Once through the second door, they stood on the pavement of a street which led nowhere, made up of nothing but walls. Kaira exchanged a glance with Guppy who responded with a blank look. Jacob was studying the walls as if there were some beauty hidden within them. They stood, waiting, until Guppy could bare it no longer:

"Sorry, what exactly are we doing here? Waiting for a bus?"

Casper Renn looked to the morning sky, immune to Guppy's comment, whilst Farraday stroked the stubble on his weary face.

"Do we just wait?" queried Kaira in an attempt to manage Guppy's impatience.

"Yes," came Farraday's curt reply.

"For what?" added Guppy.

"Patience may benefit you on this trip," Casper Renn replied, his face still turned to the sky.

Guppy's answer finally appeared - a streak of yellow circling in the sky above.

"Mivrilyn?" uttered Jacob in complete shock.

The bright, yellow Williynx swooped and circled above until one of its yellow feathers floated down towards them, landing on the pavement opposite.

Farraday held Guppy back as she attempted to step towards the yellow feather. A shake of his head was enough for Guppy to understand that there was purpose to this seemingly random act: a purpose which soon became clear. Seconds after the feather landed on the pavement, its colour drained onto the concrete - a line forming around the pavement's edge until it looked like it was lit by fairy lights.

"It's *moving*," Jacob said, pointing as the pavement retreated into the faceless wall, revealing concrete steps below.

With the pavement now an apparition, Casper Renn and Farraday stepped towards the wide, concrete steps leading downwards to a hidden world: a new wonder within The Society for the Preservation of Magical Artefacts.

KAIRA, Guppy and Jacob followed, peering down in an attempt to decipher what lay ahead. It took some time for this to be revealed as they continued to descend, Kaira's legs beginning to ache as she studied the featureless walls on either side. The concrete steps finally ended where a body of water began: a stream formed of two separate parts.

Kaira spotted two boats, fitted with oars, chained to wooden pillars and studied the arc of the parallel streams, leading outwards under a tunnel. A large, glass door stood behind the wooden pillars with a lantern hanging above it.

The door was the main decoration to the tower they now stood in front of, narrow windows running in line with the glass door, each lit from within. Casper Renn led the way inside with Farraday gesturing for the others to follow, the sound of water lapping against the concrete offering a welcome tranquillity.

17. Water People

WATER PEOPLE

The interior of the building was distinctly more comforting than the concrete steps which led towards it. Long sofas and large rugs decorated each room and the walls were lined with elegantly patterned wallpaper - patterns which changed every few minutes, leaving Kaira to briefly wonder if anything within the Society was devoid of magic.

The rear of the building was also in stark contrast to the concrete frontage, rolling hills viewed through the window encompassing the entire south wall. The stairwell was located in the south-west corner, arcing up the four floors of the tower, revealing six bedrooms and three bathrooms along with a single room in the eaves and what looked like a meeting room on the second floor.

Philomeena Renn was found sitting at a second-floor window - a bed, chair and bedside table the only other decoration in the room. Kaira's aunt stood at the sight of her niece, embracing her as she entered the room. Guppy occupied the doorway as a mark of respect for the moment of reconnection, realising that this briefest of separations had still affected her friend.

"No need to stand on ceremony," Philomeena Renn stated warmly to Guppy.

Guppy entered a little awkwardly, conscious that she and her brother were encroaching on a family who had already suffered a number of losses: Kaira's mum and her grandfather, Isiah Renn, who was no longer accepted.

"Are you hungry?"

Kaira and Guppy exchanged a glance: they were starving.

LUNCH WAS cold ham with new potatoes and salad - simple but much appreciated after their descent down seemingly endless steps. Conversation began over dinner which led to clarification and revelation.

"Is this your house?" Guppy asked Philomeena Renn, judging this to be neutral ground.

"Of sorts," replied Kaira's aunt as she filled their plates. "I stay in different places depending on circumstances. This is my favourite one, though: it feels the most like home."

"I think it's lovely," added Guppy, working hard on the manners she sometimes misplaced.

"Thank you."

"Are we staying here while we're away?" Kaira asked her dad who shook his head lightly.

"We head off later."

"Today? Where to?"

"To a place with answers we currently lack."

"About what's happening?" queried Jacob.

"Yes," replied Casper Renn, never a man to waste words.

"What answers don't we have?" asked Guppy in a blunt tone.

"Guppy," interjected Jacob.

Casper Renn raised a hand: "It's okay. I've brought you all along for a number of reasons: to protect my daughter and to benefit from your collective gifts."

Kaira frowned: "Gifts?"

"Abilities," her dad continued. "Some magical, some intellectual and others instinctive. We are closer to understanding recent events because of your desire and ability to help - the main reason The Orium Circle has lifted the age restriction on entrance to the Society."

"I can't wait to help," added Guppy as she gobbled a big mouthful of ham to everyone's amusement.

"Is it a dangerous place?" asked Kaira yet to acquire Guppy's fearlessness.

"No," replied Aunt Phee. "The place we are going to presents no danger."

"Allies, not enemies," added Farraday as he matched Guppy, stuffing a chunk of ham into his mouth.

Jacob looked out at the clouds hanging over the rolling hills, before saying, "I didn't realise Mivrilyn left the Feleecian. I thought of her as more of a guard."

Farraday stuffed the last three potatoes in his mouth before explaining: "A Williynx has many talents, Jacob, one of which is their feathers which hold unique access to a number of Society buildings."

"You mean only a Williynx can do what Mivrilyn did?" asked Kaira. "The feather, I mean, and how it made the pavement disappear?"

"Yes," came her aunt's reply, "which is one of the reasons I wanted you to spend time in the Feleecian learning remedies. By doing so, you would also learn about the powers a Williynx possesses."

"Ace," declared Guppy as she tried to match Farraday by stuffing three potatoes in her mouth at once, without success.

"Are we allowed to know the name of the place we're going to?" questioned Jacob, his manners a little more polished than his sister's.

"Gilweean," replied Philomeena Renn before reaching under the table and producing the rectangular, glass arte-fact they had first seen in the Feleecian: a Nivrium. "The tunnel the stream leads out to is known as The Gilweean Gateway."

The sight of the water reader seemed to put Guppy off her food as she, Kaira and Jacob studied the three, silver lines, rising and falling in a rhythmic motion before reaching the surface, attempting to escape the glass encasement.

"Do you remember what this means, Kaira?"

"It means whatever's inside is dangerous."

"What's inside?" asked Guppy ever impatiently.

"Water," replied Philomeena Renn. "The water which surrounds the Society Sphere. The Nivrium is regularly used to assess the temperature of the society."

"By temperature, we mean 'goings on'," added Farraday. "Whose behaving and who isn't."

The collected group watched as the three, silver lines slowly fell to the bottom, lifeless.

"Is the Renn rub an actual thing?" Jacob asked, entirely out-of-the blue.

"The Renn *what*?" queried Guppy, increasingly surprised at how much her brother knew.

"Yes," confirmed Casper Renn, placing his knife and fork

onto the empty plate. "Each family in the Society is said to have a unique gift. The Renns are water people: able to read the properties of water."

"So it *is* true," continued Jacob. "The Renns can interpret water to read the mood of the whole Society?"

"Yes," added Kaira's aunt.

"I thought we used a Nivrium to read water and the 'temperature' in the Society," queried Guppy.

"Yes," replied Aunt Phee, "but it's limited to identifying stability, neutrality or danger. It doesn't have the power to specify what that danger is."

"And the Renns do?"

"To an extent," Kaira's dad replied. "Hence, the Renn rub. Our family has a long history of heightened intuition specifically linked to water."

"So, if you're hiding something, you'll get found out," quipped Farraday, causing a flicker of anxiety in Kaira.

Did her dad already know about her trip to Dyil's Ditch last night? The sky urchins would have told him, wouldn't they? He was probably just waiting for the right time to react. But here she was, about to journey to a place called Gilweean, so how angry could he be?

"Okay," stated Casper Renn, standing from the table. "Time to depart."

"Already?" questioned Guppy as she eyed the left-over potatoes being removed.

"This way," instructed Farraday, turning back towards the glass door they had entered through. "Don't forget your bags and wrap up; the temperature falls pretty fast once we head out."

'Heading out' could only mean the boats, concluded Kaira as she grabbed her rucksack and pushed her hand inside, searching for her favourite scarf.

THE BOATS ROCKED on the water, the chains securing them to the wooden pillars clinking as they moved with the quiet tide. Kaira and Guppy stood alongside one of the boats whilst her dad removed the chain. A few feet away, on the other side of the stream, Aunt Phee and Jacob watched Farraday carry out the same action on the second boat.

Kaira looked back at the concrete steps they had descended, appearing beneath a faceless street less than an hour ago, and wondered if she was ready for another quest to a new part of the Society Sphere.

Guppy was her normal fearless self, throwing her bag into the boat and stepping in, politely declining her dad's offer of help. Kaira followed her friend into the boat and wrapped her scarf a little tighter under her chin. All the lights had been turned off inside the tower, the lantern above the glass door the only remaining illumination.

"Okay?" her dad asked quietly as he sat alongside her, reaching for the wooden oars.

She nodded.

"I'm proud of you, Kaira. I didn't expect this to be your introduction to our world, and I'm sorry for that."

"I'm just glad you're back," she replied.

"It won't always be like this," her dad added before signalling the start of the journey to Farraday.

Kaira had the distinct feeling that it would be, and the journey to Gilweean began.

Link to Book 2 on Next Page

TEASER CHAPTER - BOOK 2

As Casper Renn pushed against the wooden pillar to usher them towards the Gilweean Gateway, Kaira sat alongside Guppy, watching her dad ease into position in the central bay of the boat, stroking each wooden oar through the water as if he had enacted this passage many times before.

The lone light in the tower behind them illuminated their way as the boats moved towards another magical realm. Farraday eased the oars through the water a few metres ahead, gesturing for Jacob to take the blanket on the bench in the middle of the small, wooden boat.

"Wrap up," Kaira heard Farraday say. "The temperature drops once we enter the gateway."

Kaira looked over as Jacob reached for the blanket, throwing it over his legs before offering to share it with Aunt Phee, who politely declined. Like Farraday and her dad, it seemed that Aunt Phee was conditioned to this journey, appearing calm and serene alongside an evidently nervous Jacob who was bracing himself for the impending cold.

As the small, wooden boats glided through the water, Kaira looked back at the tower they had occupied a few minutes ago. She reflected on the incredible journey she had been on from the moment she'd stepped into Cribbe & Corrow, acquired a penchant and walked through a door into a world of magic and mayhem.

It had been a fantastical adventure which had brought her friendship, tested her bravery and tried the patience of the adults she was accompanying now - and she knew the journey had only just begun.

Guppy shuffled alongside Kaira, trying to get comfortable on the single plank of wood, acting as a seating area for the two of them.

"Is it a long journey?" Guppy asked Casper Renn who steadied the right oar in the water, manoeuvring them towards the entrance of The Gilweean Gateway.

"It can seem so, particularly passing between The Gilweean Gateway and The Gilweean Ghenant."

"What's The Gilweean Ghenant?" asked Kaira, reaching for an extra layer of clothing from her rucksack.

"It's the passage of water immediately after The Gilweean Gateway: the slowest part of the journey."

"Why?" asked Guppy.

"Because the Ghenant acts as the first layer of security to The Gilweean Gateway; our boats will be inspected there to ensure our journey is one of education and not disruption."

"How long will that take?" continued Guppy to Casper Renn's evident annoyance.

"I suggest you wrap up and get some rest; there will be little time for sleep once we arrive and much to do afterwards."

Guppy attempted to continue her line of questioning before Kaira nudged her, symbolising a need for pause in enquiries. Kaira was lessoned in her dad's expressions - a man who emitted subtlety in all things, including his mannerisms and temperament.

As the two boats eased their way towards the large arch which seemed to shimmer with light, Kaira studied her dad more closely, conscious that, although his air of natural authority and outward calm remained, there was something else preoccupying him - concern, perhaps, regarding the uncertainties surrounding the Society for the Preservation of Magical Artefacts.

After all, Kaira had discovered the location of The Phiadal after returning from her journey to Dyil's Ditch where she had met the sky urchins - her dad's army of protection - as he approached a mystery figure near The Spitting Tree.

Not to mention the fact that it was Meyen Grayling, Guppy and Jacob's mum, who Kaira had seen vanish through The Floating Floor and down into the secretive room which held all bovies: artefacts with complex magical properties. The lucky discovery of The Phiadal would have been incredible enough; however, Kaira knew there was much more to Meyen Grayling's covert, night-time movements in The Cendryll.

It was what lay beneath The Floating Floor that created a combination of alarm and awe within Kaira - a dark fragment which seemed to hypnotise Meyen Grayling... a legendary artefact which people had recently been killed for ... an artefact which gave the owner the power to defeat death, beckon the creatures of the underworld and bend the will of men: the Terrecet.

Guppy continued to shuffle on the narrow, wooden bench before taking the grey blanket forced upon her by Philomeena Renn, her legs jigging up-and-down in nervous anticipation of the wonders awaiting beyond The Gilweean Gateway. The temperature noticeably cooled as they reached the large archway, the boat containing Jacob, Farraday and Philomeena Renn entering the mouth of the gateway first.

Kaira studied the oars cutting through the translucent water as they entered the large arch, preparing herself for the sudden drop in temperature. As yet, there was no familiar sense of dizziness nor the magical appearance of a new world; the only suggestion of magic at work was the lifting of the oars into each boat as the narrow stretch of water began to guide the boats under the shimmering arch.

Guppy's legs continued to jig up-and-down in expectation of a wondrous revelation until, realising there was none forthcoming, she pushed her legs under her chin. "Is this *it*?" she whispered to Kaira in typically impatient tones.

Kaira sensed there was far more to come, gesturing for Guppy to share the blanket as her breath became visible in the darkening archway. With Aunt Phee, Jacob and Farraday beginning to fade into the darkness, Kaira pulled the blanket over her, shaking off a sudden bout of drowsiness which rested more heavily on Guppy whose eyes were beginning to close. As the light continued to fade within the archway, the only illumination now the shimmering inner walls, Kaira shifted on the wooden seat as Guppy fell asleep, allowing her friend's head to rest on her shoulder.

The drowsiness increased its hold, seemingly caused by the hypnotic effect of the shimmering inner walls of The Gilweean Gateway. Kaira watched as her dad buttoned his jacket before turning towards her, smiling at the sight of Guppy's sleeping figure.

"Are you warm enough?" her dad asked before uttering 'Spintz', creating the familiar shower of light to illuminate their way. Kaira smiled at the use of the charm - a reminder of the wonders of the magical world she had recently discovered. With Guppy fast asleep, she lowered her hand into the cold water, fascinated by the way it magically transported them towards Gilweean without any guidance from the wooden oars.

"The water of Gilweean is attuned to all things," her father began in way of explanation. "In fact, every aspect of Gilweean is alive to activity, from the shimmering interior walls to what lies beneath the water."

Kaira quickly took her hand out of the water, imagining monsters which lurked beneath, although her dad's smile suggested this not to be the case.

"The Nivrium - the water reader that judges the temperature of the Society - was created in Gilweean," her dad added before placing his hand into the clear water.

Not quite ready to return her hand to the water, Kaira brought up something Jacob had said before they began their journey. "Jacob mentioned the Renns being water people."

Her dad nodded. "Some families in the Society have a notable tradition; our family are known as 'water people' because of our ability to interpret many things through the study of water."

"Doesn't a Nivrium do that?"

"To a degree, although the Nivrium tells us if the mood of the Society is stable or unstable; it doesn't specify or locate the source of peace or disruption."

Kaira overcame her nerves and returned her hand to the water, concluding that if she came from a family of water people, she should be able to sense danger.

With Guppy still asleep, and the accompanying boat cutting a silhouette ahead, Kaira judged this to be an opportune moment to discuss recent events with her dad. She wanted to ask about the purpose of the journey to Gilweean, how it was linked to the Society and why they couldn't just use a Perium to get there.

There were other questions, including her grandfather, Isiah Renn, and what had actually happened to make him go bad, along with the fact that Kaira had Koll blood. She had yet to hear of a *good* Koll, continuing to wrestle with the thought of turning bad herself and ending up a Melackin. There was also the mystery surrounding Theodore Kusp and the reasons behind his illegal selling of Laudlum.

Within the sanctuary of The Gilweean Gateway, leading to another magical sphere, Kaira prepared herself to question her dad on the dizzying events of the last few days. She was also conscious that too many questions would suggest she had made certain discoveries - discoveries she would have to explain. Yet, of all the questions Kaira wanted to ask, there was only one which would help link recent events.

"Do you think the Terrecet is real?"

She watched her dad turn slowly, a familiar frown and penetrating gaze returning; he was a combination of

Caribbean sternness and English reserve, making it difficult to read his mood.

"What do you know about the Terrecet?" he asked, removing his hand from the water.

Judging the question to be laced with suspicion, Kaira chose her words carefully. "Just what I've read in *Menphelin's Fables*. Guppy and Jacob have been working out ways for me to learn Society history, so we've been going to The Pancithon a lot."

Not entirely untrue, Kaira mused, holding her nerve under the scrutiny of her dad's gaze.

"As the fable suggests," her dad replied in a measured tone, "the Terrecet is a famous legend which many have studied and others continue to hunt."

"So, it doesn't exist?"

"Dark artefacts have always existed, Kaira, whether it's the potential existence of the Terrecet or some other threat. The principles of the Society remain the same: to learn, preserve and protect our magical history, ensuring the wonders of our world exist for generations to come."

Kaira sensed the conclusive tone in her dad's voice, recognising that he wasn't going to elaborate. One impression remained however - the look of concern on her dad's face when she raised the subject of the Terrecet. It *did* exist, Kaira concluded, and her dad knew more about it than he was letting on. For now, however, it seemed advisable to let the matter drop and enjoy the journey towards another magical sphere.

A gentle nudge from her dad woke Kaira, bringing her back to the dark archway with shimmering walls and a fountain of light created by the Spintz charm. With Guppy still resting her head on Kaira's arm, she shuffled a few inches away, causing Guppy to jolt awake, lifting the lids of her eyes rather comically in an attempt to shake off the veil of sleep.

"We're almost there," Casper Renn explained as the two boats rested side-by-side on the stretch of water.

Kaira didn't know how long she had been asleep for and wasn't entirely thankful that her dad had woken her - for they were now faced with something altogether less inviting: row-upon-row of illuminated trees, lining the stretch of water which seemed to end suddenly a few meters ahead, replaced by a curtain of darkness.

What happened next rapidly removed any remnants of drowsiness as the luminous trees began to move, causing Jacob to reach for one of the wooden oars.

"*Put that down*," ordered Farraday who, like the other adults, sat calmly inside the wooden boats as if the sight of moving trees was the most normal thing in the world! Kaira and Guppy sat close together as the trunk of each tree began to bend, arching forwards whilst the branches formed into legs - a different type of moving monster coming to life, resting on the bank of the stream.

"The Guards of Gilweean," Aunt Phee explained, noticing that Kaira and Guppy had taken out their Vaspyls - magical morphing steel which could form into any object imagined. "Gilweean's first line of defence."

"I'm sensing more attack than defence," Jacob replied nervously, keeping a hand close to the wooden oar whilst using the other to brush the long fringe out of his eyes.

Kaira, increasingly skilled at managing her fear, looked towards her dad to measure the level of threat they faced; his calm demeanour suggested there was none, although she and Guppy kept a tight hold of their Vaspyls as the strange, luminous creatures slipped into the water, heading towards the boats.

Sensing that the adults' explanation hadn't appeased the children, Casper Renn turned towards the three, young travellers.

"As we mentioned at the start of the journey, The Gilweean Ghenant is the passage of water acting as the first layer of security before entering The Gilweean Gateway. What's happening now is perfectly normal, ensuring our journey is one of education and not disruption."

"I don't think you mentioned The Guards of Gilweean are massive, weird *spiders*," countered Guppy with as much courtesy as she could muster.

"Take it easy," interjected Farraday who sat adjacent to Kaira and Guppy in the accompanying boat. "The Guards of Gilweean are just another type of Nivrium; they're water readers, checking the measure of us." Farraday moved down the boat a little, keeping his feet on both oars whilst glancing at Jacob in mild warning.

Keeping his attention on the three young passengers, he continued. "Remember the three lines in the Nivrium...? How they rise and fall, depending on what they read in the water?"

Kaira, Guppy and Jacob nodded.

"Well, The Guards of Gilweean are doing the same thing now."

"Why are they coming towards the boats?" asked Kaira, Vaspyl at the ready.

"To check the measure of us, as explained," replied Farraday matter-of-factly.

Jacob gripped the top of the boat and closed his eyes as the strange creatures neared - visions of falling into the water and being dragged to the bottom swimming his mind.

Guppy required further clarification. "So, how does it work? The Guards of Gilweean? How they check, I mean?"

"They will attach themselves to the bottom of each boat," replied Casper Renn before moving over to sit alongside Kaira. "It's perfectly safe, as our journey is expected and without questionable intentions."

"So, why is it necessary?"

"Because words and intentions are two very different things, Guppy. The Guards of Gilweean will assess if our words match our intentions."

"Like The Web of Azryllis!" added Kaira.

"That's right," replied her dad with a reassuring smile, moments before each boat began to rock slightly on the water.

"It won't take long," Aunt Phee added, radiating her usual calm which always made Kaira feel better. When Aunt Phee didn't smile, Kaira thought, *that* was the time to panic.

Unable to help himself, Farraday added, "Just think of the creatures as Nivriums with a bite."

Guppy offered Farraday a disdainful look: "That's not helping."

Yet, within minutes, the young travellers realised the purpose of Farraday's joke: to highlight the need to distinguish between genuine danger and perceived threats. As the adults had assured them, The Guards of Gilweean were harmless to those who posed no threat, and with the oars returned to the water, each boat continued its journey towards the curtain of darkness which lay ahead - where The Gilweean Gateway ended and a new, magical sphere began.

Once enveloped within the curtain of darkness, Kaira felt a familiar sensation of dizziness return, taking this to mean that they had entered a natural Perium - a portal transporting them to Gilweean. A glimmer of light was the first evidence of life beyond the darkness, followed by a sound of waves as if water were about to rush into the tunnel.

Moments later, the curtain of darkness fell away, and Kaira found herself staring out at a vast expanse of water surrounded by cliffs, decorated with a multitude of colour - colour which took the form a familiar Society creature: the Williynx.

Guppy's mouth hung open as she stared up at the sky filled with a shower of colour as hundreds of Williynx flew high above, while others joined from the surrounding cliffs.

"Wow," uttered Jacob as the Williynx circled high in the sky.

"This is *amazing*," added Guppy, her gaze caught between the circular, thatched houses on the shore and the spectacle of a group of Williynx diving towards the water. In a stunning display of transformative might and majesty, the creatures re-appeared out of the water over ten-times their original size, their squawks replaced with a battle cry.

"It's a display of welcome," explained Aunt Phee as she caught Kaira, Guppy and Jacob jolt in shock as the enormous, shape-shifting creatures climbed towards the sky once more, water dripping off their bright coats of varying colours: yellow, red, blue, green and snow white: a carousel of colour indeed.

"Shapeshifters!" Kaira cried in awe, stunned at the sheer beauty and scale of Gilweean and its majestic, winged inhabitants. She wondered if Mivrilyn had also made the journey here - the bright, yellow Williynx in Aunt Phee's quarters who had cast a spell with one of her magical feathers, causing a pavement to disappear into a wall on a faceless street, beginning their journey here.

"Welcome to Gilweean," Casper Renn added as he and Farraday raised an arm to a figure dressed in linen trousers and a white shirt, awaiting their arrival on the shore: an ageing, Caribbean man who returned the gesture of recognition.

A nudge from Guppy took Kaira's attention away from the mysterious figure waiting on the shoreline.

"Do you think we can ride them?" asked Guppy as she studied the Williynx who continued to dive into the water before re-appearing transformed - their enormous, winged bodies dominating the sky.

"*No*, Guppy," interjected Jacob who was inches away in the accompanying boat.

"I was just *asking*," replied Guppy rather sullenly.

"We're going to stay *out* of trouble here," added Jacob - a comment that made Kaira wonder what trouble they could possibly get into in a place which sat proudly in a vast, open landscape, its wonders on full display.

Gilweean was a place for temporary rest where they could learn more about the dark events circling within the Society; it wasn't the time for new discoveries and adventures - or so Kaira thought.

ALSO BY R.A. LINDO

The Rise of the Ameedis: A Fantasy Prequel

The Gilweean Gateway: Kaira Renn Book 2

The Legend of the Terrecet: Kaira Renn Book 3

The Call of The Wenlands: Kaira Renn Book 4

The Fate of The Devenant: Kaira Renn Book 5

ABOUT THE AUTHOR

I'm the author of the Kaira Renn fantasy series set in The Society for the Preservation of Magical Artefacts. The Sign of the Symean is the first book in the series. The series will consist of five volumes, spanning the magical realms of the Society and Kaira's many adventures within it as she attempts to unravel ever-deepening mysteries

If you enjoyed the book, **please consider leaving a review on Amazon.**

To receive updates and a chance to win free copies of future titles, sign up to my newsletter **here.**

Made in the USA
Coppell, TX
25 May 2021

56323656R00187